"THEY ARE
QUICK TO KILL"

"In their ignorance, they might kill the Prime Mother. We must stop at nothing to prevent that."

Marfor understood her agitation. Oomis's faith could not be shaken, but she had to reconcile it with a contradiction to the teachings of the Egg, which held that the Cosmic Spirit had designed the development of life to lead to the supremacy of the Heesh, and the Heesh alone. Research into the past had proved it. There were no other beings able to make spaceships and robots and lasers.

"We must find out what kind of creatures the aliens are, where they come from, and what they want," Marfor said. "We must be cautious, but let us assume that intelligent creatures are reasonable. They might help us in our search. If not, we can and will prevent their interference."

Marfor stood up, signaling an end to the meeting. "Further speculation is pointless. We will land and make contact."

"That will be your job," Oomis said. "I want nothing to do with monstrosities."

Other AvoNova Books by
Lee Grimes

RETRO LIVES

DINOSAUR NEXUS

LEE GRIMES

AVON BOOKS • NEW YORK

DINOSAUR NEXUS is an original publication of Avon Books. This work has never before appeared in book form. This work is a novel. Any similarity to actual persons or events is purely coincidental.

AVON BOOKS
A division of
The Hearst Corporation
1350 Avenue of the Americas
New York, New York 10019

Copyright © 1994 by Lee Grimes
Cover art by Matthew Stowicki
Published by arrangement with the author
Library of Congress Catalog Card Number: 94-94093
ISBN: 0-380-77319-8

First AvoNova Books Printing: October 1994

AVONOVA TRADEMARK REG. U.S. PAT. OFF. AND IN OTHER COUNTRIES, MARCA REGISTRADA, HECHO EN U.S.A.

Printed in the U.S.A.

RA   10   9   8   7   6   5   4   3   2   1

To Stephen, Deborah, Edward, Kenneth,
Jennifer, and Matthew

A serendipity of siblings

Chapter One

Dinosaurs running loose. Dinosaurs chasing you with jaws agape, lording it over their terrain. Scientists traveling sixty-five million years into the past expect to find them, the last of their kind, titanic herbivores and ravenous carnivores. They do not expect to find stranger creatures and an unimagined universe.

For most of its plunge through time the *Pegasus* had clung to a place in the shadow of an Earth whirling at more than three thousand revolutions per second beneath it. The computer measured 8.35 years of regression per second of ship's time, normal time, or 721,440 years per day. At that speed the majestic wheeling of the galaxies became visible. For three months the crew watched the stars slide backward in their orbits and shuttle through changing constellations against a firmament brightened by the fierce flickering of novas.

"The Big Dipper is already gone," Rusty told the rest of the crew on only their second night after launching. "It's been squeezed into a hairpin, and the stars at each end are moving farther away from the rest."

"We're lost!" Nick exclaimed, and the others laughed.

"Take a close-up to file along with your full scan," Carlos said. As geographer for the expedition, as well as meteorologist, Rusty was assigned to map the heavens during the trip before mapping the Earth when the *Pegasus* reached the end of the Cretaceous Period. The others would help, of course. Observations of the stars were secondary to the principal mission of the *Pegasus*, but they remained important. Carlos, as commander, had sworn to himself that astronomers would have no complaints.

1

"First dibs on the telescope," Allie said.

Carlos already knew that she was assertive, if not aggressive. "Go ahead," he answered. "What do you want to look at?"

"Andromeda."

He nodded with understanding. M31, the great galaxy in Andromeda, resembled the home galaxy, the Milky Way. During the trip they would all watch the spiral arms move clockwise back in time. But Andromeda, splendid as it was, was viewed almost on edge. As a colonel in the Space Corps, Carlos was the only one aboard who was required to know astronomy, and he predicted to himself that as soon as they spotted M51, the Whirlpool Galaxy, that was the one the *Pegasus* team would want to watch. Seen as if from above, M51 looked like a pinwheel.

"Hey, it's our turn," Nick said after a few minutes. Allie, rapt in the glory of the nebula she had chosen, shook herself and moved away from the telescope. Nick, deferential as a husband, waited for Meg, his wife, to precede him before he took a look. Last, before Carlos, came Dan, a large man who was careful not to intimidate others.

I must be careful not to think in stereotypes, Carlos told himself. Dan is a paleobotanist, but a man who studies the leaves and pollen of long-dead plants in quiet solitude is not necessarily meek. Their specialties reveal no more about the personalities of the others. Meg is a vertebrate paleontologist, Nick an invertebrate paleontologist, and Allie a biochemist. Individual characters and attitudes differ, but I am satisfied from what I learned about them during training that we will work together well.

The crew exercised, played games, drilled each other on their specialties, entertained each other or turned to tapes, and found time for solitary hobbies—painting, puzzles, reading, the guitar, computers. They talked until each man and woman knew the others better than parents know their children.

In the crowded quarters of the space-time ship they also gradually got on each others' nerves. From the engine room, garage, and supply room at the broad base of the ship up to the laboratories and storage space for specimens, on up to the exercise room and small hangar for the flier, up farther to the wardroom and three cabins, up to the control room and finally to the twin pods for laser cannons in the narrow cone on top, every surface was painted the same dreary gunmetal gray. A neutral color, meant to be ignored, but it was depressing. Members of the crew found that seeing the same few faces every day, unavoidably, was also depressing.

"It's like taking four other people on our honeymoon," Rusty told Carlos.

"After we're married, I'll take you on a real honeymoon to the wilderness of your choice," he promised. They had agreed that a relationship that would have lasted twice sixty-five million years, if you wanted to look at it that way, by the time they returned should be made permanent.

Dan liked to whistle, softly, almost unconsciously, but inescapably. Allie surprised him one day by saying, "If you do 'Yankee Doodle' once more, dear husband, I'll scream."

"Oh. Sorry," he answered. "Supposing I upgrade to opera." Reared in New York, he had started to learn about plants in Central Park as a boy, and his parents had seen to it that he began attending operas in his teens. Allie had heard several on his discs. "How about *Rigoletto*? Do you like 'La donna e mobile'?"

"No. The song calls women fickle, and then a woman is murdered because she's faithful to the cad who sings it."

He smiled indulgently. "Opera has spoiled a lot of great tunes with lyrics that aren't politically correct." He continued to whistle other tunes, when he wasn't thinking, but stopped whenever he caught himself at it.

Meg strained patience by repeating anecdotes. "Did I ever tell you how somebody planted a rubber bone where I was digging for Late Jurassic mammals?" Yes, and she had gone one up on the trickster by announcing a new species, *Stretchabilus counterfeitus*. An academic joke, not very amusing even the first time.

Allie insisted on telling people things for their own betterment. During bridge games she couldn't refrain from impromptu lessons. "You have to count cards in every suit, not just trumps," she told Nick. "Your two of clubs would have taken a trick."

"Sometimes when I play with you my death wish takes over."

Rusty drew unflattering caricatures of the others and taped them to the wardroom wall. Meg was a fossil reptilian skull with eyebrows and lipstick. Nick had the bulging compound eyes of a fly. Dan was a mushroom and Allie a cell splitting in two. Carlos had a video screen for a face and twisted tapes for arms and legs. Rusty showed herself disassembled into parts and spread across a map.

Someone took the drawings down and destroyed them.

None of this was serious, Carlos thought. He made sure that they all spent an hour a day on the exercise machine, to remain fit, and that they stood watches, for the sake of discipline.

And always they returned to the windows and a sense of wonder at the shifting myriad of hard bright points of light, the pulse beat of the universe itself, outside. The sky was full, not empty, and it seemed that every night more stars poured into it. When the *Pegasus* reached back twenty million years, the sun returned to the swarm of lights in the spiral arm of the Milky Way, which it had abandoned temporarily that far in the past. Distances were still measured in light-years, but space looked more crowded from within the arm.

"The sun is dragging us along in its orbit around the center of the galaxy at 220 kilometers per second," Carlos told his crew. "In sixty-five million years we'll travel about one quarter of the way around for a new perspective on billions of neighboring stars and a better look at stars on the other side."

And always they remembered that the galaxies were beacons along a highway through time that they were the first to travel so far. Jubilant when they were chosen to go, matter-of-fact or bored and touchy during the trip, they grew excited and wary as they neared their destination. Monsters would be there, brought back to hungry life from the bones and teeth in museums.

To expect more would have been unreasonable.

* * *

Carlos slowed the fusion drive at minus sixty-four million years. As a year passed every quarter of a second, a scanner caught the fireball of the impact on Earth of a gigantic chunk of cosmic debris. A computer programmed for the signal cut power to a trickle, and the ship slid against the gradient back into normal time.

Earth looked as it always did from near the moon, a jewel on velvet, a sapphire flecked with the white of clouds. On the ground the world would be strange. Dangerous. Carlos felt the thrill of an explorer about to reach a legendary goal. Rusty was grinning at him, and he returned her grin. The others looked serious, very serious, as they watched the view screen that showed what lay below them.

"We have three months before Earth gets hammered by an asteroid," Carlos said, looking at the real-time clock. "Rusty, pull her down to 300 K, put us on a polar-axis orbit to take photos for maps, and pinpoint our site." Colonel Carlos Lecompte gave orders crisply, even to Rusty.

"Coming up on one eighty," she answered in a voice as controlled as his. She fired bursts from the guidance rockets.

Her cool efficiency was one thing that he admired about her. Once he had tried but failed to think of anything he didn't admire. Only her paintings, with the wild colors and distorted perspectives that she favored, were past his understanding, but they showed both talent and practiced technique, and therefore they had to be admired. Trying to analyze her personal magic, the spell she cast over him, was like ripping a tapestry apart to look at separate threads. Her hair shone softly red in the sunlight and refused to lose its luster under fluorescents. Full lips had been divinely designed for bewitching smiles. Large blue eyes and white teeth sparkled when she laughed, or when she teased him, which she did gently, because she admired him lavishly too. He thought of the freckles on her nose as beauty accents. A sum of more than its parts, her face was altogether captivating. Her figure would draw a crowd of men on a beach like foam surrounding a surfboard. Add the attitudes they shared and her unreserved response to his devotion, and Carlos would have been desolate if a stern attention to duty had forced him to leave her behind. Fortunately he could take her on the *Pegasus* Expedition because she was fully qualified, bright, and capable.

The expedition's dinosaur expert was Meg. She watched the spiral course on the screen as the Earth rotated from west to east and the *Pegasus* circled it from north to south. Her husband, Nick, rested a hand on her shoulder.

"Hold me tight," she told him. His touch was comforting when everything below them was in the wrong place. She had seen it before, when the *Pegasus* stopped at minus 20 and minus 40 in Tertiary times to gather fresh provisions in fresh air, but this scene was the most outlandish.

"Outlandish" was exactly the word for it. A narrow sea cut North America into eastern and western parts. Europe was mostly islands. India appeared to be adrift in the ocean on its way from Africa to crunch against Asia. Australia touched Antarctica.

"I feel awfully far from home," Meg said.

"Cheer up," Nick said. "Soon you can frolic with your dinosaurs." Nick was indulgent with a wife who was hung up on bones. "That's the guy who knows all about ammonites," was the way he had first been pointed out to her across the room at a party. In the era they had reached he would search for the last ammonites, which were about to take their own leap into extinction.

"A few dinosaurs are still around," Meg agreed, mustering the enthusiasm with which she had started the trip. "I have a lot to learn that fossils can't show us. It's too bad we'll miss *Tyrannosaurus*." Most lines of dinosaurs had died out before the effects of the asteroid had finished off the survivors.

Dan, large and blond, and Allie, tall and dark, watched the screen silently. They had met on the laser range during the training course for candidates for the expedition. They had married before it had been announced that marriage increased the chance for selection. Common sense called for fully supportive pairs during nearly a year of isolation from others.

"How would you like me to be the first woman to have a baby sixty-five million years before she was born?" Allie had asked.

"Please, let's not," Dan had answered. "As our biochemist, you're our *ex officio* physician. As captain, Carlos is ship's doctor when you're out of commission. I don't think he's ever seen an umbilical cord."

Rusty identified the landing site. Someday it would be Hell Creek, Montana. Latitude and longitude had changed, but corrections could be made from sophisticated calculations of continental drift, and geologists had told the team to look for a flood plain 150 kilometers west of an inland sea. Hell Creek had been chosen because the fossil record was continuous across the K/T line, from the end of the Age of Dinosaurs in the Late Cretaceous to the beginning of the Age of Mammals in the Early Tertiary. Mammals had crossed the line and dinosaurs hadn't. Why had one happened and not the other? There were plenty of theories, which would be tested in the field by the *Pegasus* team.

"Strap in," Carlos ordered. "I'll take her down."

"There's even a creek down there," Rusty said. "The Hell Creek we know won't show up until after a lot of geological churning, but let's call this Hell Creek anyway."

"What else?"

He landed vertically on rockets in a clearing in a heavily forested plain, near the creek and a marsh. Volcanos three hundred kilometers to the southwest had been visible from the air, but from ground level no mountains or other rock formations could be seen. When the smoke and steam of landing dissipated, the team saw trees and shrubs but no animals of any kind.

"Where's the brass band?" Allie asked sardonically. "Don't they know we're lords of the universe?"

"Tell that to a cockroach," Nick answered.

"Our rockets must have started a stampede," Meg said. She was disappointed. Something gigantic should have been glaring at them.

Carlos pushed buttons to deploy the watch pods near the nose atop the ship and to swing a ramp to the ground. "The natives are around somewhere, all tooth and claw," he said.

"Our first job is to stay alive. Dan and Allie, man the pods. Toast anything that charges. The rest of you grab your guns and follow me."

He put on a radio helmet, rested a laser rifle on one arm, and walked down steps on one side of the ramp. A minute later he became the first human to set foot on Late Cretaceous soil. He felt like a boy exploring new surroundings, thrilled by his adventure but feeling uneasy. Grass had not yet evolved, not even crabgrass. He didn't recognize the plants hugging the ground in scattered clumps. For that matter, he wasn't sure about the trees. Ferns grew near them. Dan would have to tell the rest of them what the plants were.

Gloomy with dense undergrowth, the forest brooded silently. No breeze whispered through the branches of the trees. It was as if the forest resented the arrival of strangers who didn't belong there and waited for them to make a mistake. Dead vegetation decaying in the wetness left by rains gave off a mildly disagreeable smell.

"All right, the official foot has been planted," Carlos said. Standing parade-ground straight, he filled his chest with a deep breath and lifted his chin to gaze boldly around, as if daring the dinosaurs to come out of hiding. Until they did, he would defy the strangeness and the silence with routines learned from military service. Start with the captain's log, which was brief and dull for the months of their journey. Star charts had been kept separately. Just possibly they might someday help a time traveler navigate. Meanwhile astronomers would love them. Now, however, he could begin to log substantive entries about work on the expedition's tasks. He spoke into his microphone. "For the record, it's 10:47 A.M., March 18, the year Minus 64,724,119, on the future site of Hell Creek, Montana. The *Pegasus* Expedition has begun to explore the area." Cutting off the recording, he said, "Let's take a stroll before getting down to business."

"Hail the conquering hero," Rusty said impishly.

Carlos suspected that she was laughing at him and frowned. "What brought that on?"

"You should see yourself strutting. Shoulders back, jaw lifted, every word in ringing tones. You should have a steel breastplate and a flag to plant. Never mind me, Carlos. You have a right to be proud. I'm proud of you."

"Just so my head doesn't grow top-heavy, is that it?"

"That's never been a problem. I think you can take a fantastic triumph in stride."

"We'll find out when we, not I, have the triumph." He turned to Nick and Meg, who had listened to the exchange as if looking for psychological nuggets. "Now let's have that stroll."

Most of the trees near the ship were conifers, including ancestral pine trees with small cones. Two trees had shaggy bark, like sycamores. There were shrubs with leaves like magnolia. Carlos recognized cycads, which looked like giant pineapples standing on the ground with fernlike fronds of leaves sprouting from their tops. Palmettos grew near the creek. He couldn't guess what plants low to the ground might be. Flowering plants had evolved, but all he could see was green. It was too early in the spring for flowers, he supposed, although it was warm. Rusty reported the temperature at 26 degrees C, 78.8 F.

"Aha!" Nick exulted as he bent and snatched a brown oval insect from a magnolia. "A beetle. Our first specimen."

They saw no other animal life before returning to the *Pegasus*. Like sailors given a taste of shore leave, Dan and Allie were allowed to take their turn going for a short walk near the ship to satisfy their eagerness to get out of its confines and tread solid ground. "Something gone so long before we were born might disappear at any moment," Allie said. Dan led her on a race twice around the ship, a contest they had been unable to enjoy while aboard.

"Those were magnolias you saw, all right," Dan told Carlos. "They should have a few scattered flowers later in the spring, but the large white blossoms that we know haven't evolved yet."

All hands were put to work after lunch inspecting the heat shield and patching thin spots with quick-hardening ceramic paste. Carlos couldn't imagine a threat back here that lasers couldn't overcome, unless it was a natural disaster like an earthquake or a volcano, but he liked to be ready for the unexpected. He wanted to be able to lift off on sudden notice.

Damage was minor, repairs quickly made. Carlos extended a shelf, with the flier resting on it, and brought the truck and the maximum robot down a ramp. He sent Meg, who could identify any animals she saw, and Nick on an aerial survey. Reconnoiter the territory. The next priority was their water supply.

The max could bulldoze trees out of the way if necessary. It carried a large water tank on this trip and would follow the men to the creek to fill the tank. Water to drink, water to rehydrate food, water to be split into oxygen, to mix into new oxidizer for rocket fuel and to breathe in space, and into hydrogen for the fusion drive. Audiovisual equipment would handle communications with the ship.

"I'll drive the truck," he told Dan. "You ride shotgun and tell me if you see any plants we can eat."

"There won't be much. There were no fruits, nuts, or berries in the Late Cretaceous. No grains, either. Our fresh food will be fish, and maybe filet of dinosaur."

Meg's voice came over the speaker on the truck. "Got 'em! Three triceratopses two kilometers east of the ship. How wonderful! They're browsing through low shrubbery like twenty-five-foot mowing machines. Lovely long horns. I'll put it on your screen. Carlos, can I take one home?"

"Maybe if you find a baby one. You know the limits of our pens."

Carlos drove to the creek and ordered the max to take on water. As it was programmed to do, the robot moved to the edge of the creek on its treads, extended a hose that was protected by a sieve at its inlet, dropped the inlet just below the surface of the stream, and started the pump.

Dan stood at a laser mounted on the truck and peered successively in all directions. "Look at the trees across the creek!" he said suddenly. "The branches are moving."

Lifting a camcorder from a bracket that held it near the steering wheel, Carlos aimed it at the branches. "I'll record the scene and transmit to ship's memory. Meg, monitor us and tell us what we've got."

A creature the size of a small rat leaped from a branch of one tree to a branch of the next. Carlos and Dan wouldn't have seen it if it hadn't been in motion. A much larger creature, about a meter long, leaped after it and chased it higher on the tree. The first one came to the end of a branch from which there was no escape. It turned and bared its teeth. The larger one moved close, reached out swiftly with long arms, and sank claws into its prey. As the small one struggled violently, the branch swayed and broke. Both animals fell six meters to the ground.

Shaken by the fall, probably injured, the predator moved weakly, but its claws kept their grip. They ripped the body of the victim, which died gushing blood. The hunter bit into a leg.

And it screeched as something twice its size raced on two long legs from cover in the trees, leaped on it, and slashed gaping wounds in its sides with claws like sickles.

Meg's voice came over. "Watch out for that thing. It's a dromaeosaur, fairly small for dinosaurs, but it's as vicious as two wildcats crossed with a shark. It has sharp curved claws on all fingers and toes, and two toes with four-inch claws that could rip rhinoceros hide to shreds."

Carlos refrained from reminding her that he knew about dromaeosaurs. Everyone in the team had studied all that was known about the creatures they might encounter back here. Fossil bones of dromaeosaurs had been found in southern Canada, not at Hell Creek, but experts had been right in guessing that it could have ranged this far. They hadn't guessed that it had dull red splotches on gray sides.

The dromaeosaur heard the noise of the speaker. It looked at Carlos and Dan. Whether it saw them as rivals for its catch or as better prey, or whether it reacted to an instinct to kill, it charged toward them. Dan reacted as quickly. His tightly focused laser beam burned through the dinosaur's chest into its heart before it reached its own side of the stream. It fell, screaming hoarsely, and died.

Counting on Dan to handle his laser as well in action as he had in training, Carlos had continued to shoot the

scene. Dan appeared to be a mild man, but he had been a
wrestler in college, and wrestling requires quick reactions
and spurts of aggressiveness. It hadn't been necessary for
Carlos to drop the camcorder and grab his own gun. Now
that the excitement was over and he was no longer in danger, he realized how big a risk he had run and how much
he had taken for granted.

"Nice shooting," he told Dan. "Keep me covered while
I collect some specimens." He attached the camcorder to
a mount and activated it for automatic recording. A wide-
angle lens tracked him and showed what was around him
as he waded across the creek.

The dromaeosaur was two meters long from nose to tail,
the height of a tall man, but it wasn't as heavy. Carlos slung
it over his shoulder, ignoring an unpleasant odor, to bring
it back. Since wounds cauterized by a laser don't bleed,
he got no blood on his jacket or pants. When he returned
for the other two creatures, which had died bloodily, he
wrapped them in plastic sheets.

The small one was hairy, a mammal. The one that had
killed it surprised him so much that he radioed to Meg.
"Come back to the ship. We need you."

Later, in the lab, Meg had only a glance for the
dromaeosaur. "The hairy one is *Purgatorius*, the earliest
known primate," she said. "It's an important discovery,
because it's known only from fossil teeth. But this other
one! Incredible!"

Dan had seen it and was now stationed before screens
in a watch pod. The others, standing around a table in the
lab, knew what she meant.

Building to a climax, Meg described the creature slowly, methodically. "Ninety-eight centimeters tall. Very long
slim legs. Three long toes in front and a short one high
up in back. All have claws. Long thin arms. Three fingers, all with claws, on each hand. Narrow tail, moderately long neck, rounded skull, large eyes set forward. It
looks like a stenonychosaur but those are twice as big.
There's been speculation that some small dinosaurs might
have climbed trees with their claws, but not about what
makes this thing unique. Sensational! It's covered with

down. There are no stiff feathers. They're all small and soft."

"Is it trying to become a bird?" Nick asked.

"I doubt it. That's been done. This thing found a way to insulate its body. It's a natural adaptation. Feathers are essentially frayed scales." Meg shook her head and looked around at the others. "I think we have an entirely new class of animals here, one that died out so soon after it appeared that it left no record."

"Why won't it survive the cold spell that's coming?" Rusty asked.

"Who knows? Maybe we're lucky it didn't. With no dinosaurs to fear, this thing and others like it could clean up on the little mammals of the Early Tertiary. There might never have been an Age of Mammals. And we might never have been able to boast about being the lords of creation."

Marfor Endos Limfor Astelis and so forth for twenty-five names, all of which she had memorized by the age of five, stared at the planet below her from the bulging rim of her ship. Good, but racing back through time was the easy part. She watched daylight spread across a green-brown continent divided by a narrow blue-green sea. As soon as she found one small animal hidden in the forests down there she could go home to glory. Maybe.

How stubbornly would one small animal surrounded by dinosaurs hide? If she found it, Senior Matron Marfor of the Hall of Ancients would become a grand matron. She might even be the first of her egg line to join the Council of the Matriarchy. Maybe. Oomis would try to steal the credit.

"A perfect crossing," said Nim, her attendant male, loudly, for everyone to hear him. He stood close behind her. As he often did, he had sensed her mood, satisfaction and hope marred by foreboding. He had tried to encourage her with praise that should have come from Oomis.

"Give thanks to the Spirit of the Egg," Marfor answered. Inwardly she gave credit to the ship's computer, but Oomis was listening, and Oomis was a senior matron from the Hall of Guardians. Formidable in size and strength, inflexible on faith and doctrine, Oomis had the power to take command to enforce orthodoxy. She was probably waiting for her chance. Running a long finger across the medallions dangling from her Necklace of Twelves, Marfor added, "May the search for the Prime Mother go as well."

"In the name of the Egg," Oomis said piously. She fingered her necklace.

Marfor heard Nim strangle a giggle. Too many males gave only lip service to worship of the Egg. At home some males had dared to become openly rebellious.

"In the name of the Egg," Lippor chimed in, touching her necklace too. Lippor was a junior matron in the Hall of Transportation, an engineer who had mastered travel in space and time. She taught me every detail about this ship and learned eagerly from me about the past, Marfor thought, but she is unsure of herself and afraid of Oomis.

Haban, Oomis's attendant male, quickly recited the formula of piety. So did Nim, who knew when it was foolish to cause offense. Oomis stared pointedly at Dorkin, Lippor's attendant male, and fingered the whip that she always carried in her belt. "In the name of the Egg," Dorkin said with perfunctory acquiescence to due form. Oomis would not hesitate to slash through his crest with her whip.

At least I know where to hunt for the Prime Mother, thanks to the fossil of a male Ishinol, Marfor thought. A complete skeleton stretched out as if asleep, every bone in place. If I hadn't chipped it out of the rocks myself, I wouldn't believe it. Usually fossil bones are strewn every which way, and some of them are missing. Let's pray for another miracle.

A poota, bright blue with orange spots on its breast, launched itself from its stand and glided to a perch on Marfor's shoulder. That was supposed to be a good omen. This time it wasn't.

"Senior Marfor," the voice of a tech in the scanning room said, "there is a large unidentified object in our landing area."

Marfor felt a faint chill as she came alert to the unexpected. "Lens it."

On her duplicate of the scanning screen she saw what looked like a cone with a rounded top. Impossible! Here in this far distant past, so many millions of years before the dawn of intelligence, was an artifact, manufactured, not natural.

"Report data," she ordered, controlling the tension she felt at an encounter that should have been impossible and might be dangerous.

"The object is nearly beneath us. Sensors detect radar, and residual heat, as if from rockets cooling from a ship that has just landed. Sacred Egg! Forgive my outburst, senior, but it is very near our designated site."

"That's not a Heesh ship," Nim said. Ripples of excitement passed along the feathers of his crest.

"No," Lippor agreed. "Its design is strange. But where could it be from?"

"Not Planet Four," Marfor said. "It never had intelligent life. The stars? The Heesh have investigated only the nearest stars but have found no life on the planets around them. I cannot believe in a coincidence that would bring a ship all the way from any star to arrive at precisely this time and place."

Lippor's attendant male, Dorkin, said thoughtfully, "If two ships from different times and places of origin had the same destination, their simultaneous arrival would not be the coincidence it seemed."

"Which leaves the question of why they chose to arrive exactly when and where the Ishinol arose," Marfor said. Dorkin's perceptive comment surprised her. He was a guide in the Makinen Game Preserve before Lippor became infatuated with him during a hunting trip and brought him home with her, Marfor thought; he says so little that nobody knows what he is thinking. All they notice is his handsome crest and the scar on his face.

"These strangers threaten the search!" exclaimed Haban, attendant male to Oomis. "Fly the ship right over them! Melt them with our rockets!"

He acts like the stereotype of a male, emotional, tempestuous, Marfor thought. To listen to him is to be reminded of all that he hasn't considered. How fortunate I am that I found Nim, who uses his mind. Everything Haban says appears designed to please Oomis. Subject to her whims, he has the most reason to fear her.

Marfor ignored Haban and made an announcement over the intercom. "Attention all personnel. We have encountered a ship of unknown origin. Presumably it carries intelligent life. Identifying them will be of prime importance to the Matriarchy. We will maintain stationary orbit and observe them, then land and make contact."

"Are you forgetting the priority of our search?" Oomis asked.

"Certainly not." Any other answer would bring an immediate confrontation with Oomis. Nor would Marfor forget her mission, a personal dream, the climax of her career, an opportunity that she would not have won without the skillful intrigues of female relatives. Nevertheless she felt that the discovery of alien intelligence was more important than finding an extinct ancestor alive. Let priorities shift silently. "We must identify a possible obstacle to the search."

What if they are hostile? she asked herself. Nothing in my career has prepared me for this. All of my work has been with creatures long dead. I am a paleontologist, a bone finder, an expert on the animals from which we are descended, not a warrior. None of us is, although Oomis knows police methods. I am a peaceful student of vertebrate evolution. I have never had to face anything more dangerous than wild animals, and that was only during my single hunt. I was well briefed on that and well equipped. We have lasers, and we came prepared to drive off dinosaurs, to kill them if necessary, but we have had no preparation for combat.

At home my daughter's first female egg is ready to hatch. Whatever happens to me, the egg line will be unbroken.

Triceratopses, those huge horned dinosaurs, showed up near the *Pegasus* next morning. Allie and Dan had taken the max to the creek. They would ride on it while it cleared away debris it had left on the trail that it had opened the previous day. Then Dan would collect plants in and near the creek. There should be horsetails in quiet water.

Allison Steele, the molecular biologist, felt that she would be making better use of her time in the lab, where she had taken cells from the strange new creature for study. If Carlos had had to send her out with anybody, she was glad it was with Dan.

Allie had written a textbook about the geometry of antibodies. A tall brunette, she had gone through college on a basketball scholarship. Her husband, Daniel Lundgren, had the size, strength, and stamina of a heavyweight wrestler, which he had been. A man who studies fossilized pollen needs patience, which he possessed, and equanimity, which he used to soothe Allie when she became caustic. Dan was levelheaded, so calm that he seemed phlegmatic, but he was alert and moved quickly when necessary.

"It's absurd for a woman to take her husband's name just because she marries him," Allie had told him.

"I'm glad you don't think it's absurd to get married," he had answered.

While Dan and Allie rode the max, Meg and Nick were busy in the lab. Meg began to dissect the strange, down-covered creature to describe its anatomy while Nick looked for parasites like fleas and worms. Rusty made photographs and drawings. Carlos, who had a hunch that the creature was as significant as anything they would find, wanted to get his own hands on the lab work, but somebody had to stay on watch in a pod near the top of the ship. He elected himself.

"I keep imagining nasty critters hiding in wait for us," Allie told Dan. "I will keep my finger on the trigger." Dan was the proven expert at shooting dinosaurs, but she had scored well as a marksman on the laser training range.

"Maybe you'll bag a trophy," Dan said. He concentrated on the work of the max, which gathered leaves and branches on its bulldozer blade and tossed them aside. Two jointed metal arms with rakes for hands helped gather the debris.

Allie held on to her seat as the max uprooted the stump of a tree it had knocked over yesterday. The trail would never be as smooth as an interstate but it would be better than many country roads. She relaxed and chided herself for feeling that the forest was hostile.

Tropical rain forests at home were more dense with foliage, but this one was gloomy enough to seem menacing. No birds called from the trees; no small animals rustled in the underbrush or peered at her from branches. The tiny mammals of this age and small early lizards must be near, but they concealed their presence. The silence was eerie. Allie was glad of Dan's company although he didn't say much, and of the mechanical growling of the max as it worked.

"We have a problem," Dan said as they reached the creek. He halted the max and pushed a button to throw it into defensive mode. The bulldozer blade rose just off the ground, and heavy sharp claws replaced the rakes at the ends of the steel arms.

Two triceratopses were dipping their beaks rhythmically, past their nostrils and the short horns above them, into the stream to gulp water. Twice the size of rhinoceroses, gray and scaly, they were more than twice as formidable, six tons of solid muscle with two long horns near the eyes and a shield that started near the horns and curved backward over the neck. Each time a head came out of the water it turned from side to side to look around. Protecting the broad expanse of back and sides required detection of a predator in time to whirl and face it. A triceratops was vulnerable when drinking.

"They'll spot us soon," Allie said. "Let's get out of here."

"Right. I think the max could stand up to a charge, and its claws might dig into them and toss them aside, but why take a chance?"

"I would be too close to the action to watch in comfort," Allie said.

Dan pushed a button, and the max turned opposite treads in opposite directions to turn around. Allie swiveled the heavy laser on its mount to keep it trained on the dinosaurs. Attracted by the noise or the motion, they looked up.

"They see us, and they look surly," Allie said. "I don't think they like to be interrupted. Here they come! Get moving."

Both triceratopses splashed across the stream with heads lifted and charged. The max roared away at forty kilometers an hour, its top speed, but couldn't outdistance them.

"They'll chase us right up the ramp into the ship," Dan said. "Better burn them."

The trail had been cleared but was still bumpy. Allie managed to keep the laser more or less focused on one of the dinosaurs and sent an arrow of energy at it. The beast screamed as the fringe behind its head caught the beam and a smoking hole appeared. It slowed down, but the other one kept coming. Allie swept the laser across it. It was holding its horns high until it could ram them into this strange challenger for its territory, and the beam swept beneath its head and across its legs. It collapsed, screaming, on the ground, unable to move.

"Put it out of its misery," Dan said.

"Move around to one side of it," Allie answered. "We should try not to damage the head."

She kept her eyes open for the first triceratops as Dan maneuvered the max off the trail, but it had disappeared. As dispassionately as a surgeon performing an unpleasant but necessary operation, she burned a hole into the second one's side to the heart and killed it.

"Good," Dan said as he stared at the lifeless hulk. "I'll have the max throw chains around it and drag it back to the ship."

"Carlos," Allie called on the radio, "do you know what I've always wanted?"

"No champagne for breakfast!" he came back at her.

"I want to mount the head of a triceratops over my bed."

"You'll have to do the taxidermy. That's after you get the triceratops."

"I have one. Dan and I are dragging it in behind the max. You should have been listening in on us." Allie told what had happened.

"We should all listen continuously on the common channel," Carlos said. "Meg, do you read us?"

"With great interest, over the speaker in the lab. If you have a triceratops, there's a lot in the head for me to look at. What its brain amounts to, of course, and things like the attachment of muscles to the shield fringe." Meg didn't have to look around the lab before adding, "There's no room for the carcass in here. Dump it outside the ship, and I'll cut off the head with a power saw."

"Put it away from the ship, at the edge of the clearing," Carlos ordered. "What we don't bring inside will draw every meat eater from here to the sea."

All three matrons, all three attendant males, and two technician males, leaving only one of the latter on watch, gathered in the wardroom of the Heesh ship as it held its position far above the ground. A technician projected telescopic photographs on a large screen.

"This is the alien ship on the ground," he began. "The narrow rim above the base of the cone and the rocket level may contain video, radar, and other devices. There are two projections near the apex, in a good position to be mounts for weapons, and operational openings on the sides. A flier took off from this shelf. This is the flier. Here are two aliens on a truck, followed by a large robot."

He glanced at Marfor for approval. He wants to supplant Nim as my attendant male, she thought. Nim was too lucky a find to be discarded, and I've grown too fond of him. "Show the killing," she ordered.

The technician ran a tape. It showed the truck and a massive robot at the creek, then a flurry of action as a two-legged dinosaur the size of a Heesh charged out of the trees toward the creek and was cut down by a laser. An alien carried the dinosaur to the truck and retrieved two objects in wrappings that hid their identity.

"The aliens are about our size, but hats hide their faces from above," Nim said. "I want to know what they look like."

So do we all, Marfor thought.

"They are quick to kill," Oomis said. "In their ignorance they might kill the Prime Mother. We must stop at nothing to prevent that." She clutched the central pendant on her Necklace of Twelves tightly. "Who are these aliens? What are they doing here?"

Marfor understood her agitation. Oomis's faith could not be shaken, but she had to reconcile it with a contradiction to the teachings of the Egg, which held that the Cosmic Spirit had designed the development of life to lead to the supremacy of the Heesh, and the Heesh alone. Research into the past had proved it. There was no other intelligent life. There were no other beings able to make spaceships and robots and lasers.

"We must find out what kind of creatures the aliens are, where they come from, and what they want," Marfor said. "They killed that small dinosaur because it threatened them, not out of malevolence. Why did they take it back to their ship? For food or to study it? Obviously they do not belong in this time or place, so the most likely reason for their coming here would be scientific. We must be cautious, but let us assume that intelligent creatures are reasonable. They might help us in our search. If not, we can and will prevent their interference."

Marfor stood up, signaling an end to the meeting. "Further speculation is pointless. We will land and make contact."

"That will be your job," Oomis said. "I want nothing to do with monstrosities."

Nick and Meg took the flier to a point over the inland sea a kilometer from shore. So often the fieldwork in their specialties had kept them apart that they enjoyed the chance to work together. Married since their first year as graduate students at the University of Colorado, in a state rich in fossils, both had dug up their share, although of very different kinds. He teased her about her fondness for "great galumphing brainless dinosaurs," and she asked what was so special about small and brainless trilobites and crinoids and ammonites that couldn't even galumph.

Hovering close to the water, Nick lowered a cable that held an underwater scope, lights, and a suction trap. If his luck was good, he would catch an ammonite. He would learn about the life of these mollusks with spiral shells, which had existed for nearly 450 million years before dying out like the dinosaurs at the K/T line. At least he would retrieve plankton, most kinds of which had also died.

Meg yawned. She had stayed up late. After a multilevel internal scan of the carcass of the down-covered creature, she had given blood and tissue samples to Allie for analysis. She had opened the heart and found, with only mild surprise, that it had four chambers. It would deliver oxygen-rich blood to the brain. Sawing off a section of the skull, she had determined that the brain was relatively large for a primitive creature, but smooth, with a large occipital lobe and small cerebral hemisphere.

With much more to do today, she had been interrupted by the return of Allie and Dan with the triceratops. She had had to go out and photograph the thing up, down, and sideways, with the max hoisting it for views from underneath. Rusty was sketching it. Meg had had the max pull the neck shield forward so that she could start the saw behind the head to cut it off. The head was awkward to handle because of its size and the jutting spikes of the horns, but the ship's elevator got it to the lab. After it had been deposited in a cooler for attention later, she had resumed work on the brand-new creature. She would have examined the structure of the teeth this morning and traced the blood vessels from the heart and lungs, but Nick needed help. He was impatient to collect an ammonite. Everyone was impatient. Dan had gone back out in the truck with Allie.

While flying at little more than treetop level from land to sea, Meg had seen birds like oystercatchers where gentle waves lapped the beach. Maybe they could net one on the way back to the ship. *Archaeopteryx*, the earliest known bird, much like a small dinosaur but with feathers, had lived more than sixty-five million years earlier than the time that the *Pegasus* had reached. Because few birds had been fossilized, very little was known about their evolution since then. Birds, like mammals, had crossed the K/T line of extinctions and were part of the *Pegasus* Expedition's study. Meg would describe the anatomy of any they found and pass tissues along to Allie for analysis of cells and chromosomes.

Lowering the flier to stay on autopilot three meters above the sea, Nick dropped his trap assembly into the water, turned on its light, and watched the video screen to see what might appear. Meg had brought a rod and reel. She baited the hook with a small chunk of triceratops and let it fall.

"I feel like a kid again," she said.

"It's hard to believe this isn't the Caribbean," said Nick.

"I wouldn't know. I never fished the Caribbean. I went after mountain trout. With grasshoppers. I got a lot of their brown juice on my fingers baiting the hook."

"They spit on you to show what they thought of you. Grasshoppers have feelings too, you know."

Meg looked at him and laughed. He was staring at the screen but had a smile on his lips.

"I spent a lot of time on beaches as a kid," he said. "I liked to dig creatures out of the sand, mainly clams, and once off the Oregon coast I got geoducks." He pronounced the name of the long-necked clams properly as "gooeyducks," like any experienced beachcomber. "But the little crustaceans that curled up like sow bugs when I dug them out of shallow, wet sand made me more curious. Hold it. Something big is swimming around the trap. Hey!"

Something had seized the trap assembly underwater, and the cable was unreeling. Nick tightened the clutch on the cable and eased the flier upward. A gigantic fish came out of the water with its teeth locked around the trap, writhed in the air, and let go and splashed back into the water.

"A wolf fish," Meg said. "Almost five meters long."

"With an appetite to match, I'm sure. The beach is hereby closed to swimmers. What does it eat?"

"Possibly sturgeon. They've been around for a long time. Primitive herring and salmon exist now too. Garpike, bowfin, sharks. The seas are full of fishes. I want to catch some."

"Agreed. Meanwhile I think I'll try another spot. Your wolf fish could like big mollusks like ammonites, too, and they would scatter."

A shadow skimming across the water made Meg look up. She grabbed Nick's arm and pointed while she broadcast a warning. "Carlos! Everybody! There's another ship, flying low and headed toward the *Pegasus*. I hate to say this, but I swear it looks like a flying saucer."

"Follow it, but don't go close," Carlos answered. A ship of strange shape and unknown origin could present a danger much greater than dinosaurs. "If it flies past us, take a bearing or see where it lands, if you can. Keep in touch." Now he had to assemble the rest of his crew in relative safety and prepare defenses. "Dan, bring Allie and the truck in." They would have heard Meg's startling report too. "Rusty and I are manning the pods just in case."

Each pod contained a laser cannon designed to fry a herd of charging triceratopses at two kilometers. How much good they would do in a battle against a ship with modern armament was unknown.

Senior Matron Marfor felt her ship settle solidly on its twelve landing pistons. She had a section of the hull rolled back above the upper deck and ordered a technician to raise the tower and man it. Junior Matron Lippor and her attendant male took the flier up and hovered above the ship for aerial observation.

Marfor had watched the alien flier follow her ship at a distance as Lippor guided it slowly to the place determined by careful calculation, hovered, and landed. The alien ship was no more than an hour's walk away, on the other side of a creek. Lippor reported that its flier had returned to a shelf extending from the hull and that there was no sign of activity.

They know we are here, and they have not reacted, Marfor thought. Am I naive to think it is a good sign that they haven't attacked?

Oomis is in a foul mood, pacing angrily and fingering her whip. Without knowing anything about them, she feels that the existence of the aliens is an outrage, a personal insult by creatures who challenge her beliefs. Lippor knows that we face an emergency, but she is cautious and offers no opinions.

Marfor turned to her attendant male, standing beside her. "Nim, consider my reasoning. We came here to find proof of the doctrine of the Prime Mother. We know that the proof, the Prime Mother herself, is here to be found. The aliens cannot have the same reason for coming. If any other intelligent race had descended from the Prime Mother, we would know about it."

"Could they be searching for a different ancestor?"

"There is no evidence for it. Intelligence develops over millions of years and can be traced by measuring brain cases. The Hanishan led only to us, the Heesh."

"So we are left with aliens of unknown origin and motives."

"Yes," Marfor agreed. "Whatever their origin, the most plausible reason for their coming to this savage world would be to find out something. They did not pursue us here. I believe they are making a scientific investigation."

"It seems most likely."

"If that is their nature, they are a race worth knowing," Marfor said. "They present an opportunity."

"One with consequences we can't guess," Nim observed.

"That is a chance we have to take. There will be consequences for them, too."

Nim brushed a hand over his crest thoughtfully. "They must have as many questions about us as we have about them."

"We must start asking them." Marfor straightened in her chair. "I will take the initiative."

Leaving Dan on watch but linked to the others by phone, Carlos assembled the rest of the crew in the control room. They were solemn, tense but subdued. No panic, he was glad to see. They would react to a totally unexpected and possibly dangerous confrontation, one far outside their experience, as professionals, analyzing it to determine what should be done. He thought he knew that already, but he wanted their input so that the decision would be unanimous and they would act as a team. They should follow his orders without secret reservations.

A preference for facts over fancy had helped Carlos Lecompte become the youngest colonel in the Space Corps. He didn't believe in flying saucers. They didn't exist, never had existed, and never would exist. Nevertheless, Meg's pictures from the flier had shown a big one descending a few kilometers away, riding down on rockets, not on some mysterious antigravity drive. In one way, at least, it was more advanced than the *Pegasus*. It had slowed down as it slanted to a landing, then settled smoothly to the ground, trusting to the precarious balance of its rockets only in the last moments.

"We've all seen the strange ship or pictures of it," Carlos began. "The questions are: where did it come from, who is aboard, what do they want, and how will they react to us?"

"I've always wanted to meet some little green men, but not much," Allie said.

"I think we can forget the myths about flying saucers," Carlos responded. "The saucer shape is a good one if you want to whirl to maintain artificial gravity while in flight, and it's easier to walk around a circle than to climb up and down to get anywhere."

"They could be a lot worse than little green men," Nick said. He had been reading science fiction since boyhood and would never forget one story about a war against giant insects with mandibles that could cut a man in half. "How about something slimy, with lots of tentacles?"

"Let's not start out scared," Carlos cautioned him. "They could also be a lot like us."

"They didn't come from the Earth we know," Rusty said. "That's a start, but it doesn't help much."

Dan added his thoughts from his watch pod. "If they were humans from our future, I think they would have paid us an immediate visit. They must be from another planet, one from near another star. Which doesn't tell us anything about them or why they are here. The only thing we can be sure of is that they are intelligent. Otherwise we have insufficient data to speculate."

"Except that their mission is probably scientific, like ours," Carlos said.

But if they were hostile? He reviewed his knowledge of his own background and those of his crew to judge their ability to meet a threat.

The son of a French-Canadian father from Montreal

and a Mexican mother from Guadalajara who had met in Washington as junior diplomats from their respective countries, Carlos had been born in the United States and raised in a grab bag of nations. He had learned the basics of diplomacy from his parents. Citizenship counted when he applied to the Space Academy. So did his background, not his aptitude for languages but his adaptability, his love of the rugged life of camping and climbing mountains, his respect for the techniques of survival, and his high grades in math and sciences. In his seven years at the Academy he had received a thorough background in liberal arts as well as engineering, astrophysics, computers, weapons, and tactics.

His first trip into space had been a milk run for cadets to Moon Base. When he was commissioned he was put on satellite patrol. In a troubled world, someone was always trying to sneak a platform for nuclear missiles or antisatellite weaponry into space to have an ace up his sleeve if war came. All space vehicles had to be inspected by a United Nations team before launching and registered for orbital tracking, but illegal devices could be concealed or disguised. They might be dropped off by a space factory or even a ship carrying passengers on one of the popular cruises to the moon. The patrol cleared space of worn-out junk and inspected everything else. If a satellite or vehicle wasn't receiving and broadcasting signals, if it was larger than necessary for its announced use, or if it was unidentified, it was destroyed by beams of subatomic particles. Those were no good in an atmosphere but worked fine in space. Seconds after Carlos locked onto a target it was gone.

He took command of a squadron during the most improbable of all wars, the Space War, in which contending fleets fought like gladiators for hostile alliances that maintained an uneasy peace on land and sea and in the air. His squadron confused an enemy squadron with decoys and destroyed it. By the time the war died down, inconclusively, time travel had been discovered.

As the universe expanded, time stretched into the future.

The future did not exist except as a concept, the direction of continuous creation of the present. But the past, already created, remained in existence. By escaping the standard progression of time and reversing direction, one could travel into the past. A time traveler carried his built-in clock of normal time with him and returned later than when he had started. He could not simultaneously occupy a given period of normal time with two versions of himself. Those who had tried it had not returned.

Time travel had to take place off Earth because a ship easing back into normal time would push against anything already there, and if what was there was massive, the collision would destroy the ship. The Space Corps got the job. Carlos was assigned to the Time Project to lead the *Pegasus* Expedition. He recognized a chance to embellish his career or shatter it. He had to take a team farther than anyone had traveled into the past and return safely, and he had to coordinate the team's research to produce results that would justify the enormous cost.

"Isn't there a danger of changing the present by changing the past, maybe by something as innocuous as stepping on an ant?" Carlos had asked.

"Yes and no," an instructor had answered. "Mathematicians have worked out the probabilities very carefully. We can't let somebody go back and assassinate Hitler to prevent World War II and the Holocaust, for example. Those horrors might occur anyway, and the ancestors of people alive today might never meet and marry. But there is great inertia to time, and many changes would be absorbed without significant effect. The loss of a few ants among the billions would make no difference, or a few fishes among many of the same kind."

Nevertheless, to remove the temptation to change history, the time drive on a ship was locked to prevent emergence into normal time less than two million years before launching. Explorers were taught what animals they would encounter were about to become extinct and could be killed without interrupting a line of descent that would lead to the present. Exotic diets resulted. Scientists looking for the origin of hominids in the Lower Oligocene of North Africa dined on steak from a rhinoceros-like *Arsinoitherium*. It was tough.

Carlos had to learn much more about the distant past than he had known. He got to know scientific experts who had been lured by the excitement of a trip to the Late Cretaceous and were training in survival techniques, and he had much to say about who joined his team.

Almost immediately he knew he wanted Rusty. She was Deirdre Rourke. When they met, in the lounge at Time Base, she asked, "Carlos Lecompte? Where did you get a combination of Spanish and French names?" Others had always accepted the unusual combination without asking about it. He liked unabashed curiosity. Rusty freed her thoughts like birds hatched in her mind and fluttering to escape. She was also good at her work. One afternoon she looked at the sky and said, "Buckets of rain will start falling about 9." The first drops fell at 8:55. His admiration of her ability led him to see more and more of her until he was totally captivated by her good humor, love of fun, thoughtfulness, and, of course, her looks.

Allison Steele was a woman of strong feelings. Since she was sardonic, not sarcastic, when she disagreed with others, they got along with her. If she ruffled any feathers, her husband, Daniel Lundgren, smoothed them with his general good humor.

Nick and Meg Ingraham were on leave from the junior faculty at the University of Colorado. Carlos had watched them work hard on a training trip in the jungles of Yucatán, and he had seen them face hardship cheerfully.

They all respect each other and they agree that every scrap of knowledge is important because no theory is worth more than the facts that support it, Carlos thought. We get on well. Now we face something brand new in human existence, intelligent aliens. What good will their expert knowledge be if we also face hostility? They know how to use lasers, but I am the only person aboard trained in combat. I hope that intelligent beings will not be arbitrarily bloodthirsty.

When he confided this hope to Rusty, she answered, "Humans are intelligent but they can be bloodthirsty without good reason. I think we have an opportunity that was never offered to humanity before, but we have to approach it cautiously."

"The aliens know we are here," Carlos said to his crew. "That must be why they landed near us. We will keep four-hour watches around the clock, but until we have evidence to the contrary, I think we should assume that they are friendly. We have to take the chance. We will go on tip-toe because we are entering a dark room. There has never been a contact with an alien civilization before. We can't guess what will come of it, but we don't want to mess it up."

The others agreed, with some trepidation but on the whole eagerly. Traveling back through time had been an adventure, but although they had gone farther than anyone before, they had not been the first. They had known, or thought they had known, what to expect. A meeting with aliens was brand-new and completely different. This adventure was unprecedented.

"Maybe we can sell them some aluminum siding," Allie said. She saw from several frowns that this was no time for wisecracks.

Dan put his arm around her and said, "It's a scary situation, but it has the greatest possibilities since our early ancestors discovered fire."

"We will sit tight to show them that we are not hostile but to draw them out," Carlos said. "Let them make the first move."

Chapter Two

Carlos sent Meg up in the flier to scan the forest on both sides of the creek between the two ships. Anything from the alien ship would come through the forest if it came toward the *Pegasus* by land. Radar would pick up anything that flew. He didn't have to wait long.

"Here they come," Meg reported. She transmitted pictures of a wheeled vehicle moving slowly as it picked its way through trees. Call it a pickup truck. It carried two beings the size of humans. Something the height of a man but strangely formed, with multiple appendages and a mechanical look about it, followed them. Probably a robot.

"Come back and take a position on the north side of our clearing, fifty meters up," Carlos ordered. "Be ready to fire on command. If they send a flier, be ready to engage it. Our cannons will back you up."

And please don't get shot down, he added silently.

He posted Nick in a truck, with a laser mounted on it, behind trees on the other side of the clearing. Dan and Allie were in the ship's pods. His limited defenses ready, Carlos waited. He hoped that they wouldn't have to fight. Meg was in the greatest danger because she was in the most exposed position. He would hate to lose Meg. He would hate to lose any of them.

Watching a screen, he saw the wheeled vehicle emerge from the trees and stop at the edge of the clearing, sixty meters away. He stepped up the magnification of his scope, glanced at the beings on the truck with surprise at their appearance, and studied the robot for signs of danger. It resembled a spider because it had eight legs and a round head with many eyes, but it also had eight arms and a thick tubular body. No weapons were visible. This thing might not need any.

As strange as the robot was, the creatures on the truck were more unreal. They could pass for humans at a distance but looked wildly different through the scope. Both of them wore short-sleeved turtleneck shirts, pants, and boots that came to the knee. Their heads and faces, like their forearms, were bare and brown and looked fuzzy. One creature was a head shorter than the other and had a high crest like a ridge of feathers, mostly red but yellow at the tips. But these things weren't birds. They had arms, not wings, and jaws, not beaks. The jaws protruded below large eyes and small nostril slits in broad faces. There were no eyebrows or lashes. Carlos could see no ears, which might be concealed behind fuzz on the heads. Ugly, he thought, caricatures, apelike because of their jaws, manlike because of prominent foreheads.

What in the name of all that lived could they be? Where had they come from?

Moving swiftly and with precision, wasting no motion, the robot used arms like cables made of many joints to take from the truck a load that it unfolded into a long table. It placed several pieces of equipment on it. One box with a glass front was evidently a viewing screen. After putting a chair on each side of the table, the robot withdrew to the fringe of trees and stood motionless.

Only then did the two creatures leave a seat in the vehicle. With lean bodies and sinewy arms and legs, they moved with the easy grace of greyhounds. The larger one put a pad of paper and two pens on the table and sat in the chair facing the *Pegasus*. It had three long fingers, not five, Carlos saw, and one of them worked like a thumb. Something like a blue feather duster with orange spots and bright eyes rested on its shoulder. The smaller creature, the one with a crest, stood beside its companion. Evidently fuzzy head was boss. It wore a necklace with a large gold medallion dangling from its center and twelve small silver medallions on each side. A symbol of rank? And what was the feather duster?

"They want to open communications," he announced to his team. "They assume that we are watching and someone will come from the ship to make personal contact. The second chair is for me. I think I'll pin on my eagles. They are brave, for they must know that they are under our guns. They carry no weapons, so I will carry none. They are civilized, and they count on us to be civilized too. There are two of them, so you're invited to the party too, Rusty."

"I would go into world-class sulks if you didn't take me," she answered. "I feel like it's a Halloween party and I should wear a mask. Don't they look frightful!"

"They may have won beauty contests at home. Anyway, this will be all business." He hesitated before making a minor decision. "We'll walk. I'll have the max pick up a communications combo and follow me to set up our side of the table. I don't expect trouble, but stay alert, everybody. Dan, leave your pod and come to the control room to watch us and help with the computer if I need anything. Allie, tape all this from your pod for recording in the computer. I will transmit close-ups and the audio."

The larger creature stood up when the humans approached. It placed one three-fingered hand across the other, palms up, and said something unintelligible. Carlos imitated the gesture and said, "Welcome." It's looking at my five-fingered hands, he thought as its eyes glanced down. The backs of its hands, its forearms, and its head are covered with down, just like that primitive wonder we have in the lab.

Both of them sat down, and Rusty stood beside Carlos. "Marfor," the creature said, pointing to itself. It pointed to its companion and said, "Nim."

Introductions first. For an unprecedented, unbelievable, encounter, one sought the stability of familiar forms. How else should one begin? Carlos named himself and Rusty.

A picture appeared on the alien screen. It showed a group of the creatures, large and small, apparently adults and juveniles. Some of both had crests and the larger ones among those that lacked crests wore necklaces. "Heesh." the creature said.

The respect that Carlos had felt for the alien because of its bravery grew as he realized the careful thought it had given to the problem of communication. He spoke to the ship. "Dan, dig up a picture of a crowd watching a launch and cast it on my monitor." Pointing to the picture, then to himself and Rusty, he said, "Humans."

A voice came from a box on the table, surprising him. "Carlos, Rusty: Humans. Marfor, Nim: Heesh."

"They're learning our language," he said for the record. "We'll learn theirs too. Crests and necklaces are probably different sexes. Let's take off our hats, Rusty."

His own hair was short and black, graying at the temples, possibly of interest to the Heesh but probably unimpressive. Rusty's hair, a soft shining red flowing to the base of her neck, might get a rise out of them.

"Eh-h-h," Nim breathed, and stepped forward. He glanced at Marfor, who granted approval with a syllable, and walked around the table to Rusty. Holding one hand toward her hair, he waited until she nodded and said "Yes," and then he fingered it gently. When she reached out her hand, he let her run it along his crest.

"The feathers are thick and flexible," she reported. "They don't have stiff shafts."

Carlos pointed at the feather duster and asked, "What is that?"

"Ork!" Marfor croaked in brief laughter. "Poota," she stated, and touched it with her finger. It launched itself into the air, flew around her head with aerial somersaults like a tumbler pigeon, and returned.

Carlos saw that it had small jaws, not a beak. "They like pets, and they must have a sense of humor to like one that performs that stunt. Good."

Allie's cynical voice came from a speaker. "Maybe it cleans lice from her fuzz."

"Allie!" he exclaimed. "That was unforgivable."

Marfor drew a large egg on a piece of paper. She held the paper against her belly and tapped it, then pushed the paper toward Nim and crossed out the egg.

"It's a female!" Rusty exclaimed. "She lays eggs! Nim is a male."

Carlos drew a large egg, crossed it out, drew a very small egg with an arrow from it to a baby in fetal position, enclosed the fetus in an oval, and pointed to Rusty. "Rusty is a human female." He crossed out the picture and pointed at himself. "I am a human male."

Marfor sat up straight, folded her hands on the table, and looked from Carlos to Rusty as if in disbelief. Her eyes, already large, widened. Nim bent forward and exploded in sound, "Ork, ork, ork!" until Marfor said harshly, "Kee!" Nim fell silent.

"I think he was laughing," Carlos said. "Why?"

"He thinks it's a wonderful joke that a male can be bigger than a female and be in command," Rusty answered. "Personally, I think it's ridiculous."

"No insubordination until we tie the knot, please. You have to wait another sixty-five million years."

Marfor crumpled the two pieces of paper and threw them aside. After pointing to the sun, she drew a circle on a fresh sheet, then nine planets in dotted orbits around it. Touching the third planet with her pen, she stamped on the ground and said, "Naneg." Her voice was a baritone, and the articulation was distinct.

"Earth," Carlos answered. "We are here on Earth."

Quickly Marfor drew a small cartoon of the human ship off to one side of her diagram of the solar system. She drew a line from the ship toward Mars and ended the line with a symbol like a "w," then a line toward outer space, also ending in a "w." She handed the paper to Carlos.

He guessed that the "w" was a question mark. "This is the big one. Where do we come from?" He drew a line from the ship to the third planet. Then he drew a picture of the Heesh ship, a thick saucer with a bulging top, attached a line with a "w," and handed the paper back to her.

She shook her head and crossed out the line he had drawn from the *Pegasus* to Earth. It was interesting that both Heesh and humans used the same gesture for "no."

"She doesn't think I understand," Carlos said. "She thinks I'm only telling her where we are now. Dan, give me a shot of Earth from space in our own time, close enough to see the continents of the Western Hemisphere."

When the picture appeared he said, "Earth. Humans."

Staring at him, the Heesh commander muttered something. A picture of the Earth also appeared on her screen, but it was turning. She halted the image at the Western Hemisphere and said, "Naneg. Heesh."

"Rusty, you're the geographer," Carlos said. "Study the two screens. Can you see any difference?"

She examined the pictures and shook her head. "None. They're from our own time, or very close. I don't believe it."

The impossibility of two such different races coming from the same future Earth without previous knowledge of each other had struck Marfor too. She folded her hands together and stared at the humans as if not knowing what to say.

Are we mistaken about the time? Carlos wondered. He drew a stroke with his pen and said "One." Touching the circle that represented Earth on the diagram, he traced a complete orbit with his finger and said, "One year." As rapidly as possible, on another sheet of paper, he wrote and named the figures for the decimal system from 1 to 100, then "$10 \times 100 = 1,000$," "$1,000 \times 1,000 = 1,000,000$," and finally "$65 \times 1,000,000$." He pointed to the picture on his screen and said, "Earth in sixty-five million years." Raising a hand in the gesture for "Wait," he wrote down the exact figure, 64,724,119. Let this creature know that his instruments were precise.

Marfor gave an order. A printout appeared from one of her boxes. It carried the Heesh numbering system beside the human equivalents. Carlos saw at once that the Heesh used a duodecimal system, to base 12, not 10. While he had been drawing numbers, they had had a computer reading them, matching them to their own, and adding a human character set to its memory. A nice trick. He watched, feeling a chill, as Marfor drew a small cartoon of the Heesh ship next to the top number, drew a line from it to the last number, and added the ship again.

"Did you notice their last number?" Rusty asked.

"I saw it," Carlos said unhappily. Next to a string of Heesh symbols was the number 64,724,119.

They claim to be from our time and place, he thought. Turning reality topsy-turvy makes me dizzy. If their Naneg is our Earth, I would rather be told that they came from a distant future that does not yet exist for me. How can their target as well as their origin be the same as ours?

Rising to her feet, Marfor slipped off of one downy wrist what was obviously a watch, which showed a grid of six rows of four dots inside an oval of smaller dots. A dot in the grid and one in the oval glowed red. It was a 24-hour timepiece, one of many anomalies of measurement among humans but natural to a race that counted with a base of 12. She laid it on the table.

Carlos laid his own wristwatch beside hers. She examined the marks around the dial and said "Twelve," the first human word she had used.

"Twelve hours," Carlos said, "or twelve and twelve."

Marfor spoke, and her talking box translated. "We here two hours." She and Nim left in their truck. The spidery robot followed them, leaving the equipment on the table unattended, as if in a gesture of trust.

Senior Matron Marfor, Senior Matron Oomis, and Junior Matron Lippor argued while their attendant males served them lunch. "Disgusting creatures!" Oomis raged. "How dare they pretend to come from our time and place? What can we expect but lies from things so ugly? They spring from the Spirit of Evil! They are here to destroy our mission."

"It does indeed appear to deny reality to have both Heesh and humans come from the same time and place," Marfor said calmly. "Nevertheless, I don't think they're lying. They stated their origin before we did."

"They cannot be in any egg line from our revered Prime Mother," Lippor said.

Count on Lippor to state the obvious in a way that would please Oomis without antagonizing Marfor. Marfor answered her with contempt. "Of course not. They are mammals. They have hair and they give birth to live young. Mammals exist in this ancient time we have reached, but they are small and furtive, like the pests in our fields and forests at home. They are very little like humans."

Nim volunteered a comment. "Their hair is soft and pleasant to the touch." Oomis muttered angrily, and Marfor gestured to Nim to remain silent.

"The Prime Mother, all honor to her, shared little of our likeness," Lippor said cautiously. "Could humans have evolved from such insignificant creatures as the mammals here?"

"From them or something like them, and they could have changed more than we did in sixty-five million years, but they could not have evolved while we evolved," Marfor answered.

"They are freaks," Oomis grumbled. "They are unnatural monstrosities. They have no right to exist. We can expect nothing but treachery from them. We should wipe them out."

"From their ship and their clumsy robot and their communications devices I would guess that their technology is not as advanced as ours," Marfor said, "but we have seen that they would not risk the age of dinosaurs without weapons. And consider this. If by some means they defeated us in combat and destroyed us, our egg lines at home would remain intact. Wiping them out would be equally useless."

"Except to protect our mission," Oomis said.

Marfor controlled her impatience. "This afternoon I will send techs out to start the search. I will inquire into the ancestry of the humans."

Allie reported continuous transmissions between the Heesh devices on the conference table and the Heesh ship. The computer that was learning English was apparently on the ship. "I don't trust them," Allie said. "They're too clever and they're gaining an advantage over us."

"They'll be talking to us fluently soon," Carlos conceded. "I'll instruct our computer to create a translation program. It has the memory and can match equivalencies. The tricky part will be analyzing grammar."

"I'd rather talk to an alligator. These Heesh are ugly, as frightful as devils dragging sinners down to hell, like what you see in a stone carving on a medieval cathedral. The way they stare with those big eyes is creepy."

"But they want to communicate, which is more than you could say for an alligator," Dan said quietly. "I think that's promising."

"They make me nervous," Nick said. "They look like something out of the lab of a mad scientist who lost control of his experiment. I wonder if we look like food to them."

Nick was back among the fantasies of his boyhood, Carlos thought. "They didn't come at us with butcher knives," he answered. "They may wonder about our diet too, and you have to remember that we eat everything from snails to rattlesnake meat. I prefer to think that their race and ours can work together."

"Maybe I'm a little bit afraid of them, but I'm rhapsodic at finding creatures so new," Meg said. "They will add volumes to what we know about biology. The best part is that I get first crack at describing them."

"I'll draw the illustrations," Rusty said. She laughed. "I'll make them look cute."

Allie snorted. "Cute as cobras."

"Why are you so sure they threaten us?" Rusty asked.

"No race ever reached the top without a gift for killing off other species. They'll see us as rivals and fair game."

For the afternoon session Carlos borrowed from Allie a kit to take blood samples. Since he, like Marfor, had decided that it was urgent to explore the lineage of two races whose mutual existence appeared to be contradictory, he had Meg, the vertebrate paleontologist, join him instead of Rusty.

"I'll watch the screen and paint them," Rusty promised. "You'll have a million photos of what the Heesh look like, but it would take a director picking camera angles to catch the mood, and he might miss the inner essence, the significance, of what's going on."

When Rusty talked about art, she left Carlos behind. He could recognize that she painted well, using a light pen with different settings for different colors, on treated plastic. The computer scanned and recorded the painting before

Rusty wiped the plastic clean for a fresh surface. So much was mechanical. Her theory seemed to be that her art was meant to reveal herself through the transmutation of what she observed in the crucible of her soul. An artist buried a treasure of impressions for a perceptive observer to interpret. Sometimes Carlos succeeded. He remained dazzled by her when he failed. You never could tell; she might be a genius.

"Don't hesitate to express yourself," he told her.

When she drew maps of Earth in the Late Cretaceous, he knew, she would decorate dull masses of land with illustrations of dinosaurs, as early cartographers had embellished expanses of ocean with monsters. She had added giraffes and zebras and lions to a map of Africa, tigers and pandas to a map of Asia. Original maps drawn by Rusty Rourke were collectors' items.

Marfor opened the afternoon session by having her printer unreel a series of pictures to portray the evolution of vertebrates. A fish, with eggs, in the water; an amphibian, with a tadpole form emerging from an egg in the water and changing to a form that climbed onto land; and a reptile, with an egg on the land. Here Marfor glanced at Carlos to see whether he understood the sequence. He nodded, named the pictures, and drew arrows from one to the next. Marfor gave the Heesh words. In each case she also pointed to an egg and said "Oon."

"Egg," Carlos answered. Humans didn't put eggs in such pictures. Why did Marfor make such a big deal out of eggs?

More pictures showed the proliferation of reptiles into different orders. Meg named each one. As new orders arose over time, Marfor crossed out those that became extinct. Before she crossed out the thecodonts she showed them branching into flying reptiles, crocodiles, and dinosaurs. Each picture had an egg beside it. At the same time that the dinosaurs appeared Marfor showed a small hairy creature, with an egg, branching from the vanishing therapsids.

"Mammal," Meg said. "That's right," she told Carlos. "The first mammals had eggs, like a platypus."

Marfor's pictures continued with the well-known large dinosaurs, but she emphasized coelurosaurids, small and two-legged. She showed birds branching from them. When her line of coelurosaurids reached the Late Cretaceous, she paused at *Stenonychosaurus*, slim and fast, with a relatively large brain and with large eyes placed for stereoscopic vision. Then came a picture that looked like a stenonychosaur but was only half as big. It had small downy feathers, which she indicated with many quick short strokes of her pen.

"Ishinol," she said.

Carlos realized that the strange creature in his ship's lab was an Ishinol. He glanced at Meg and shook his head slightly, warning her not to reveal that she had it. "Display a picture of a fossil stenonychosaur," she told her computer.

A drawing of a skull and skeleton appeared on her printer. Meg pointed to the picture that Marfor had shown, and Marfor nodded. Then Meg drew a "w," the Heesh question mark, beside the picture of the Ishinol.

Marfor produced a picture of a fossil still in its rock matrix. It was not a typical fossil, a jumble of bones, but was laid out from head to tail as if it had been carefully buried.

Carlos gestured with his hands and said, "More."

First Marfor crossed out pictures of creatures that would become extinct in the Late Cretaceous, like *Triceratops* and *Stenonychosaurus*. Carlos and Meg watched, incredulous, as more pictures showed post-Cretaceous evolution. Descendants of the Ishinol spread in many forms, large and small, herbivores and carnivores. Mammals with and without eggs continued, but the marsupials soon died out. There were no kangaroos in the Heesh world. Other mammals remained small. And one line from the Ishinol led to the Heesh.

"They're dinosaurs," Carlos said softly.

"No more than birds are," Meg answered, "and they aren't birds. Now it's our turn."

Dan beamed pictures of evolution since the K/T Line as humans knew it. Reptiles and birds continued but mammals took over the land and entered the sea. One line, the primates, led to humans.

Meg saw the feathers of Nim's crest twitch.

If they couldn't explain each other's existence, they could at least find out more about each other. Carlos took out his blood sampling kit, rolled up a sleeve, and drew two cubic centimeters of blood from a vein. He expelled the blood from the syringe into a vial, which he put on the table in front of Marfor, and offered her another syringe. She gave it to Nim, as if a test made upon a female would be demeaning. He took a sample of blood from a vein high on a downy arm. It was red.

Allie's voice came from the speaker. "Good. I'll get the hemoglobin chains from that and find some cells with chromosomes to analyze. Some nifty microorganisms may be splashing around there too."

Carlos and Marfor traded sets of pictures. Marfor stood up, but before she left, a flier brought another Heesh female, who was introduced as Lippor, and a large male identified as Dorkin. Lippor showed a picture and named the objects in it. Language lessons, too routine for Marfor, Carlos thought. He called Dan to take his place for an exchange of vocabularies. This was a task for a patient man. Besides, he wanted the Heesh to see Dan's size and his blond hair.

By suppertime the Heesh were speaking English, through their computer and its translation program, with facility.

"Why did the Prime Mother survive the coming meteorite in our history but not in theirs?" Marfor asked her computer.

"The question contains a contradiction of fact. My logic nets do not accept contradictions of fact," the computer answered. Sometimes the computer was hard to deal with. If it could not answer a question, it sounded insulted that it had been asked.

Nim looked thoughtful. "If they kill the Prime Mother while they are here, we will never evolve."

"Can anything that might happen prevent us from existing? I don't think so, for we exist."

"But so do they, and they shouldn't. I have been think-ing of speculation about time tracks. They are supposed to be exclusive. An event that leads to one future should pre-vent alternatives from existing. They should not be equally probable. I don't see how it could happen."

"Keep thinking, Nim." Marfor squinted at him fondly. Since finding Nim she had never regretted the loss of her first attendant male, the father of her daughter. "Your brains are one of the things I like."

A technician arrived, with Oomis so close behind him that she could have been following him. He reported that he had examined the sample of human blood under a micro-scope. "It looks like ours, with the same kinds of cells, but it clumps with ours, so it's a type we don't have."

"Is that all you can learn from it?"

"Yes, Senior. I found no parasites."

"Save what's left of the blood. That will be all."

Nim watched him leave and asked, "Could the exchange of blood have been a ceremony?"

"No," Marfor answered. "He accepted your blood instead of mine. I suspect that they have some means of learning more from it than we do."

"You're wasting time," Oomis said scornfully. "These humans are vile, miserable creatures. I know more than I want to know about them without contaminating myself with their blood. You sent out a party to hunt the Prime Mother. I'll go spur them on."

Marfor watched Oomis leave and said, "I hope we find the Prime Mother, but not too soon. I want to learn as much as possible about the humans before we go home. Oomis sees them only as ugly creatures that throw her tight little world into chaos. She doesn't recognize the opportunity we have."

"Their hemoglobin is very similar to ours," Allie report-ed, "but many of the nucleotide sequences in the chromo-somes of a leucocyte bear no resemblance to ours at all. Theirs are closer to those of the Ishinol in our lab and fairly close to those of the dromaeosaur that Dan killed, but they have hundreds of different genes."

"Like I said, they're dinosaurs," Carlos commented.

Meg shook her head. "It's just that mammals split off from reptiles millions of years before they did."

"They also have a lymphotropic virus we don't have, but they bind it and aren't harmed," Allie said. "I'll synthesize antibodies in case we catch it. I feel contaminated just looking at the blood of those creatures."

"But we have to deal with them. We still can't account for them, and we don't know why they're here." Carlos took a deep breath. "I'm going to open them up. Meg, you've gone far enough with your dissection of the Ishinol. Put it back together as best you can and sew up the skin. Rig the fabricator to make a plastic box and lid, and put the carcass in the box. I'm going to give the Heesh a present."

"No-o-o!" Meg wailed. "I need more time! This is the most important specimen that science has ever looked at. Its value is incalculable. Think of all we can learn from it."

"You've learned the big things already. It's more important to learn about the Heesh."

Rusty moved slowly to the window to look at the sky. She had made sketches for a painting to show the meeting of Heesh and humans, but she hadn't found symbols to convey the unutterable strangeness of the encounter. The stars formed the same constellations tonight as they had last night. Rusty felt that they should be arranged differently after so much had happened. How many other incredible events had the stars observed with equanimity? They wheeled in their courses like the hands of a clock, and she had watched them change as the *Pegasus* moved backward in time. Now they were stable again, moving slowly and imperceptibly, measuring a resumption of normal chronology. It seemed to Rusty that they symbolized a new beginning.

The box rested on the ground, unexplained, as Carlos and Marfor faced each other across the table again. The Heesh commander laid her necklace on the table. Could she make this alien, a male at that, understand? She spoke through her translator.

"This is my Necklace of Twelves. Every Heesh female wears one. It commemorates twenty-four of our ancestors. We revere our ancestors, and we try to uphold the honor of our egg lines."

The gold medallion in the center of the necklace and the twelve silver medallions on both sides were all ovals, and all bore symbols. Marfor touched the nearest medallion on the right. "This represents my mother. She is senior aide to a member of the Matriarchy, our governing body." And I needed her influence to get this job, Marfor thought. She touched the next one. "My grandmother. She was governor of Mars colony."

"You had two grandmothers," Carlos remarked.

"But only one was in my egg line." Marfor's finger went down the medallions for twelve generations, and in each case she recited a distinction. Moving to those on the left, she said, "Many generations are skipped in this group, which is chosen by a female's grandmother, but this one, nearest the center, is always present. She lived twelve times twelve generations ago. Mine was named Siflik. She was a guardian of records."

One hundred forty-four generations, Carlos thought with astonishment. If you figured thirty years per generation, Marfor could trace her ancestry for more than four thousand years. Human genealogies weren't in the same league. Did she kowtow to all of these ancestors? What an oppressive weight of obligation!

Marfor draped the necklace over her three-fingered hand so that the gold medallion rested on her palm and the side chains dangled. "The gold emblem represents our Prime Mother, who was only a necessary postulate until recently. She had to exist as the first of our class of down-covered vertebrates, the Hanishan. We venerate her because she was the source of our egg lines. Without her, we would not exist. Our studies of the past have had one goal, to find her. Over the past two hundred years we have mined many rocks in the search, and we have filled our Hall of Ancients with the fossils of extinct Hanishan that descended from her. Some were our ancestors, step by step through many changes. Finally we have discovered the bones of her species, in this time and place. The Prime Mother was an Ishinol. We came here to find her alive."

"Senior Marfor found the Ishinol fossil herself," Nim interjected with obvious pride. Marfor did not change expression.

Thank God the one we killed was not the Prime Mother, Carlos thought. Meg had told him it was a male. "What will you do with her if you find her alive?"

"We will capture her but not harm her. We will study her to learn about her and then release her. We will add a new chapter about her to the beginning of our sacred texts, and we will place a statue of her in our Grand Hall of the Egg for our ceremonies."

Carlos decided that it was time for his surprise, but he had to prepare for the moment. "You may know that an asteroid is about to strike Earth and devastate it," he said. "We came here to study the survivals and extinctions. If we see your Prime Mother we will tell you. I hope you find her soon. She lives in constant danger."

He caused a tape of the encounter near the creek to appear on his screen. As the rat-sized creature jumped from tree to tree he froze the frame and said, "Something like this was our ancestor." *Purgatorius* may not have been in the direct line but was close. When the tape showed a larger creature leaping in pursuit, he froze that frame.

"Ishinol!" Marfor exclaimed.

The tape continued with the fall from the tree, the Ishinol starting to eat the mammal, and the dromaeosaur racing from the trees to kill it. Dan's laser killed the dromaeosaur. Carlos was shown bringing the three animals to the truck.

Sorry, Meg, Carlos thought. He lifted the box to the table. "This should be yours," he said, and took off the lid.

Marfor jerked forward to examine the carcass, which lay face up. "It is male," she said. She put her necklace around her neck. "We will dissect it for study and bury the bones."

She said something that was not translated, and her robot scurried to the table on its eight legs. Each of its arms, or tentacles, ended in three thin cables like fingers.

"This robot is strong and has many uses, but it was designed to seize the Prime Mother in a gentle grip," Marfor said. "It will carry this Ishinol for us." The robot picked up the box. Marfor stood up to leave. "Thank you. We will monitor the frequency you use and call you if there is reason for it."

Nim cut open the chest of the male Ishinol as Marfor watched. "They got this far in their dissection," he said. "The heart has been opened and the blood vessels near it traced. There's hardly any blood left. And see how they sewed up the skin? That was to make it presentable for us. It still shows rips from the claws of the dromaeosaur as well as incision lines. They took samples of different tissues. This line of stitches shows where they went in to open the skull and examine the brain."

"It's strange, but I don't feel outraged," Marfor mused. "I wouldn't tell anyone but you, but it's hard to revere a Prime Mother who was like this primitive animal. Fossil bones are so much simpler and cleaner. They become abstractions. I must remind myself that it's what they stand for, the body that can be reconstructed and the manner of living that can be inferred, that counts."

"Bones are facts. Perhaps the Matriarchy should have been content with the Egg as a symbol. Perhaps, in reconciling the discovery of fossils with our doctrines, they tried too hard to find scientific support for questions of faith."

"You are daringly frank today," Marfor said. "Go on."

"You know what the League of Males is saying at home. Females became dominant because they were bigger and stronger and faster and could fight better against dangerous Hanishan long ago during our years of savagery. Modern weapons let males fight just as well, except in hand-to-hand combat, and their brains are just as good."

Nim had begun to talk quietly in an exchange of confidences, but his voice grew heated. "Males still tend the females' eggs but they have become scholars and teachers. They do much of the technical work, like my tasks with computers, as well as the jobs that females think are beneath them. Attendant males routinely perform confidential missions of great importance. They want equal rank."

"You sound like a member of the League."

"No. If I had to guess about who might be aboard from the League of Males, I'd look at Lippor's male, Dorkin. He keeps his thoughts to himself. I am content to be your male. My only regret is that you will not rise as high as your talents merit."

"What!" Marfor was taken aback. "How can you say that! What will stop me?"

"High offices are awarded in deals made by members of the most aristocratic egg lines. The Matriarchy has very nearly become hereditary. Supreme Matriarch Tellima is good at her job, but the twelve matriarchs voted her into office for two reasons. She headed the Hall of Finance, one of the three or four most powerful halls. Just as important, her ancestral line is full of matriarchs. Your Necklace of Twelves is a record of distinguished service, but there is not a single matriarch among your forebears. Oomis has two in hers."

"Oomis!" Marfor exclaimed with contempt. "She's nothing but a zealot."

"Which is exactly what the Matriarchy wants when it faces dissension by males. Who, I should add, have many supporters among low-ranking females. Females without distinction cannot have their choice of males. Some of them do routine work side by side with males in offices or use their strength working harder than males on farms or fishing boats. They are embarrassed by the nonentities they have to show on their Necklaces of Twelves. How does the cult of the Egg help them? Their chief claim to superiority is the official ban on allowing females to do the most demeaning work, like trapping rodents."

Nim gestured toward the body on the dissecting table. "What will all the Heesh who have no status or its rewards think when the matrons parade around a golden statue of something like that, ringing their bells and inhaling incense?"

Marfor didn't want to face the question. "I've never seen you so upset," she said.

"I suppose it's the humans. Finding them pushes us to the edge of a cliff, and a fog of paradox hides what lies below."

Chapter Three

Vertebrate paleontology, Marfor's specialty, requires a knowledge of geology to know where to look for fossils and a knowledge of anatomy to reconstruct a creature from its bones and teeth. She had camped out in barren country, hiked across desolate terrain, and climbed up and down hills and mountains in search of telltale bits of bone exposed by erosion from rocks. Sometimes the upper part of a complete bone would appear; sometimes only a sliver would reveal itself. Patiently, often roasted by a blazing sun, she would hammer and chisel away fragments of rock and use a small pick and a brush for delicate work until she had as much of a fossil as remained. If she was lucky when she worked around and beneath what she had found, she would turn up more bones from the same animal. She would map their position in the formation that contained them, to date them, and because she might want to return to explore the site further. Then she would wrap the fossils for safe transport and take them back to her lab. There she would work painstakingly to free a fossil from its remaining matrix and would figure out what it was and where it fitted into the great parade of evolution.

Hardships in the field were minor, no more than discomfort. In good condition, Marfor could carry a pack wherever the terrain was too rough for a truck. She took a little food and a day's supply of water. Upper and lower eyelids closed to a slit to shield large eyes that were sensitive to bright light, and she wore dark glasses. Protected by a broad hat and lightweight clothing, she avoided the worst of the sun by starting work early in the morning and ending early in the afternoon. The nights were worse, for it stayed too hot inside her tent for her to sleep well despite her weariness.

Work in the laboratory was never tedious because she was absorbed in it. She lived for the triumph of discovery and the reward of knowing that she had filled gaps in the history of life on Naneg. And yet she felt a growing discomfort, a gnawing of ambivalence about the doctrine of the Prime Mother.

Beginning two hundred years ago the Hall of Rites had accepted the evidence for evolution as proof of the wondrous power of the Cosmic Egg. Sixty-five million years ago the Egg had caused the appearance of a class of down-covered animals, the Hanishan, and these had led to the Heesh. Since there had to be a first Hanishan, there had to be a Prime Mother. She was named an Ishinol, and strenuous efforts were made to find her remains. But Marfor could not understand why the appearance of this primitive animal was more important than that of her immediate ancestors, which were stenonychosaurs, or their ancestors as far back as one could look.

As she gained experience Marfor led teams to do fieldwork on four continents. Planning the logistics came easily to her. Eventually she was appointed chief of the Department of Hanishan in the Hall of Ancients. After she found an Ishinol, she was named a senior matron. Her pride in the discovery weighed more heavily than her doubts about its sacred nature. When time travel was discovered, her position and expert knowledge made her the natural choice to lead the Heesh expedition to find the Prime Mother alive.

She did not doubt that the Ishinol was the most important species of the distant past. Now she had the unprecedented chance to learn its anatomy without depending on comparisons with animals from her own time. She worked in the lab with Nim, totally absorbed, dissecting the male Ishinol and designing a plastic replica of its body.

"Let Nim do it," Oomis said to her. "You are stealing time from the search."

"Nim is capable but he doesn't have my training," Marfor answered. "This is our only chance to learn what an Ishinol

is like inside its skin. We cannot cut into the Prime Mother
when we find her."

"Cut into her!" Oomis was horrified. "All right. Maybe
what you are doing has some importance."

Marfor did not believe that Oomis would make a concession without seeing an advantage. Probably she thought
that if Marfor was buried in a laboratory, she would have
no chance to find the Prime Mother herself. Lippor was
leading search teams, but Oomis would believe that her
own skill at hunting, proved in hunts for wild Hanishan
on Naneg, made her likelier to succeed. Lippor's male
had guided hunters but he had never tracked an Ishinol,
and Oomis would dismiss him as merely a male.

Trophies of the hunt adorned Oomis's house. She had
the one that was prized above all others, the crested head
and the pelt of a male samdak. She had tracked it herself,
without a guide, Marfor knew, and had felled it with one
shot before it had seen her. Marfor might lead the present
expedition, but whoever found the Prime Mother would
win the highest honor.

Late in the afternoon Oomis had found a team searching
fruitlessly near the tree in which the humans had watched
the male Ishinol kill its prey and be killed in turn. No
one knew how far the Ishinol ranged, or how often a male
and female came together. The two sexes might avoid
each other except for mating, as those of many species
did. Nevertheless, they would share a territory, and the
Prime Mother should be fairly near. She would hunt small
mammals and probably small reptiles, she would avoid
dromaeosaurs, and she might stay near water.

At dawn, for many animals sought water at dawn, Oomis
took Haban with her in the truck to the creek and drove
to the site of the male Ishinol's death. Probably the Prime
Mother had been near him at the time. Since he was dead,
she might well have roamed elsewhere, but this was as
good a place to search as any. The large eyes that the
Heesh had inherited from the Ishinol, millions of years
later, implied that these ancestors hunted in dim light.

Both Oomis and Haban carried guns loaded with

tranquilizer darts as well as their lasers. Their truck carried a box trap large enough for an Ishinol but too small for a dromaeosaur to enter it.

Every time she looked toward it, Oomis felt resentment at seeing the rounded cone of the human ship. Fortunately no humans were in sight. Oomis detested them because of their appearance, mocking the Heesh, and because their very existence eroded the doctrines that she defended so implacably. She sensed, without understanding, that their discovery would bring wretched changes to her world. Far better if they could be eliminated and forgotten.

"I see movement," Haban said. "Something's in those ferns."

Small bright eyes stared through the fronds. "It's a mammal," Oomis said. "They crawl all over this place. Put a dart into it. The Prime Mother eats those things. We'll leave it in the trap for her in case we don't run across her."

Haban aimed carefully, shot the mammal with a dart, and walked to the ferns to retrieve it. It was no longer than his hand. He pushed it through the swinging door of the trap, which he placed at the foot of a tree, and they left the truck to resume the hunt on foot. They moved stealthily, avoiding noise, and examined the branches of the trees as well as hiding places on the ground. A small lizard with a long tail skittered behind a tree when it saw them. Dragonflies skimmed the air near the creek. Other forms of animal life remained successfully in concealment.

Toward noon, tired, Oomis gave up and returned with Haban to the truck. If there was an Ishinol in the area, it had hidden too well for them to find it. "We'll check the trap tomorrow, and if the Prime Mother isn't in it, we'll move it to another location," Oomis said.

As they drove away, she saw a gray bulk, rounded and bigger than her truck, enter the clearing that held the human ship. A triceratops. What a magnificent animal, perfectly adapted to this age, its jaws formed into a beak for chopping plants, its weight, which would be devastating in a charge, its three formidable horns, a short one over the nose and two long ones over the eyes, and its broad protective fringe of bone behind the head.

It trotted curiously toward the human ship. A laser beam from a watch pod immediately seared the ground in front of it, driving it back with heat and the smoke from scorched plants. It screeched and galloped into the forest. They keep good watch on that ship, Oomis thought. May they rot for eternity! Could they handle several triceratopses charging at dusk? That's an idea. How could it be managed?

"Drive the truck behind that triceratops," Oomis told Haban. "Not too close."

She didn't explain. A male didn't deserve explanations.

The truck lurched over rough ground, maneuvering between trees, until it was behind the dinosaur, which had forgotten its alarm and was moving at a slow walk. Oomis set her laser at low power and fired at the ground on its left. It veered to the right and continued to move ahead. A shot on its right made it turn left. Finally Oomis scorched its rump, and it screeched and charged straight ahead. Before it stopped to look around it had battered down four trees.

"You can herd them!" Haban exclaimed with admiration. "That looks like fun. Can I try it?"

"No, you fool," she answered. "If I can control them, I can herd them to the human ship with lasers and make them charge it at dusk, when it will be hard to see and stop them. If they get to the rocket nozzles, they will smash them. The humans won't know we were involved, and they will be at our mercy."

Haban wondered if she were crazy, but he said, "What a clever plan! You should tell the others." Maybe they would stop her.

Oomis took him by both arms, near the shoulders, and lifted him off his seat and turned him so that his frightened face stared directly into hers. "If you say one word," she roared at him, "I will break every bone in your body."

Satisfied that Haban had been cowed into silence, Oomis indulged in a fantasy. She pictured herself riding on a triceratops as a demonstration of her power on a mount worthy of her. Reluctantly she abandoned the idea. These beasts had tiny brains. They were too stupid to be tamed.

*   *   *

Although their time had been far from wasted, their research had been interrupted. Members of the *Pegasus* team began a systematic collection of specimens and a study of Late Cretaceous ecology. Letting the Heesh have the area near their own ship to themselves, they caught only glimpses of them.

Rusty stood watches and helped the others on the team, but she had time on her hands. A geographer is much more than a surveyor on a grand scale. She had traveled on land and sea, in air and space, to maintain the accuracy of maps in the face of those small changes in its configuration that Earth made continuously like a living creature. Latitude, longitude, and variations in magnetic attraction were only the beginning. From mountain ranges to continental shelves, she was involved in geology. A good map shows the type of vegetation, and a text on geography should tell what crops and minerals are produced, so she learned botany and mineralogy. What are the temperature gradients? Where are the ice packs, the ocean currents? What are the prevailing winds? Such questions led her into meteorology. Population densities? Political boundaries? A geographer should be able to tell someone all about an unfamiliar area. Rusty was an expert on maps, but they were maps of all kinds. More than any one else on the *Pegasus* team, she was a generalist.

Her instruments told her all she needed to know about the atmosphere and weather locally in the time they had reached. To learn what it was like elsewhere, she would have to travel around this half-forgotten world. There would be no time for that before the *Pegasus* returned home. She had made maps of what she had seen when the ship had traced its spiral around Earth before landing, and she would have to be satisfied with those.

What she could do was study Heesh language and culture. She started with the pictures and tapes traded to the humans.

"We're missing a bet," she said to the others. "I know you all have once-in-a-lifetime opportunities to work on your specialties, but aren't the Heesh more important? We act like we're avoiding them, as if we were little kids scared by other kids in goblin masks on Halloween."

"We don't have to be afraid of them if we keep our guard up," Carlos said. "I think I might enjoy having a beer with Marfor some time, even if her face does look like a bad dream."

"I like Nim. He's a quiet little cockatoo, with that crest of his, but he shows his feelings and I think he's clever. I'd like to find out more from him about the subordination of males in Heesh society. The tapes hint at a lot of things without giving details. Finding the Heesh is bigger, more important, than discovering America. We are looking at a complete world nobody ever thought of. I hope Nick finds a live ammonite, but we already know a lot about ammonites. This may be the only chance anyone will ever have to talk to the Heesh."

"Don't bet your pension on it," Carlos said. "If we stumbled over them once, it could happen again. I've been thinking about the theory that time tracks are mutually exclusive. That's obviously haywire, but I haven't figured out why, or what to do about it. Our coming together here, and only here, suggests that this period is the nexus for two time tracks, one for the Heesh and one for us. Could the very fact of our meeting have caused such a split?"

"Aren't you reasoning in a circle?" Rusty asked. "We met the Heesh because we're on separate time tracks. We're on separate tracks because we met the Heesh. That doesn't make sense to me."

"Here's another speculation: our ships are locked into their time tracks. The horse goes back to its own barn. If we launch and return through time, we will get back to Earth, not Naneg. The Heesh ship will get back to Naneg. How do we make contact except right here and now?"

"There must be some way to cross between tracks."

"That's not necessarily true but it's probable, for there must be a single geometry to space-time no matter how many lines are drawn through different dimensions," Carlos said. "We have to rethink the nature of time. Maybe there are circles in it like a snake biting its tail. Start with the normal time everybody knows as a one-dimensional line. We traveled backward by reversing direction on that line. The Heesh evolved on a separate line, which may be parallel to ours or may go off at an angle. In either case we have a second dimension, and time becomes a plane. How does one turn onto their line instead of ours?"

"Maybe time has three or more dimensions, like space, and you could rise above the plane from one line and drop back to a different one."

Carlos nodded at her with approval. "I like that idea, if we can figure out how it is done. Here's another thought. If two time lines are set up, do they affect the entire universe? Or is the effect local, restricted to the solar system perhaps. Could you have alternative time tracks around inhabited planets elsewhere? All local in their effect?"

"You're losing me with that one. I hope you can figure it out."

"Any minute now," Carlos said, grinning. "Meanwhile you can call the Heesh on the transmitter and trade chitchat."

"Can I trade pictures as well as talk?"

"Sure," Carlos said, but he frowned. "Better skip our technology until we are certain that they're friendly. It's too soon to put all our cards on the table."

Rusty opened an audiovisual dialogue with the Heesh and discovered one who wanted more information about humans. The computerized voice belonged to a Heesh named Dorkin, who had a typical broad jaw but could be distinguished from Nim by a taller crest and a scar on his cheek. He identified himself as attendant male to Junior Matron Lippor. Rusty knew that Meg and Dan had seen the two of them together.

"What does an attendant male do?" she asked.

"He follows orders. He does what his female tells him to do." Even with a computer speaking for him, Dorkin sounded resentful.

"Are you her slave?" Rusty asked in astonishment.

"No. It's a legal relationship, and I could end it by filing notice of separation at the Hall of Records. So could she. The difference is that she would still have a good job, and I wouldn't. Being an attendant is the best job a male can have. If he can help his female rise in rank, he gains influence. He gets to do interesting work, like mine as a machinist, and he lives in comfort. Often the two of them build a strong personal relationship, and he becomes the father of her eggs. A female may have that possibility in mind when she invites a male to attend her."

So the relationship could be affectionate. Rusty tried to compress into one question all that she wanted to know about courtship among the Heesh. "How did you and Lippor meet?"

"I was a guide for females who came to hunt several kinds of wild Hanishan in the Makinen Game Preserve. Lippor came on her first hunt and wanted a samdak, a dangerous beast admired for its crest, which is bright red, and its pelt, which has red-and-black stripes. We hunt with bullets because lasers would make it too easy. Lippor was tireless and cheerful when we had rough going through the jungle. When a samdak charged, she stood her ground and fired. But Lippor is not a good shot, and she missed. I stepped in front of her and fired. I hit it, but it was very close, and before it died it clawed my face. I was only doing my job, but Lippor admired me for saving her."

Carlos would do the same for me, Rusty thought, but not just because he was doing his job. She suspected that Dorkin had welcomed a chance to make himself look good to Lippor.

"Has your experience helped you to hunt the Prime Mother?"

"No. I see tracks and droppings on the ground and claw marks on the trees but I don't know what made them."

Dorkin had questions too. Being a wife could be rewarding but it was not the best job a woman could have, Rusty told him. He was fascinated by the rise of a physically weaker sex to equal status.

"The League of Males is trying to bring that about at home but is not having much success. Change comes very slowly on Naneg. The matriarchs call stability a benefit, which they credit to the wisdom of the Cosmic Egg."

"I get the impression of a static society," Rusty said. "Does that offend you?"

"No. You are correct, although the sciences are bringing changes."

"I think I will transmit a picture I painted." Rusty's paintings had ranged in style from impressionistic to surrealistic, with several of the latter to capture her feelings about the fragmentation of reality that the *Pegasus* team had encountered. Carlos would puzzle over the latter and ask her to explain each element in a scene. The painting she sent to Dorkin was more of a cartoon, symbolic of a feeling that had been growing within her about the Heesh. It showed a Heesh female sitting on top of an egg, which was on wheels and was larger than she was. Three males with bright red crests leaned forward to drag the egg along by chains around their waists. Without prompting him, she waited for Dorkin's reaction.

"I will save this in my file," was all he said.

I offended him, she thought. But then why would he save it?

One day Meg and Nick took the flier and spotted a green-and-black duck-billed hadrosaur raising its head twenty feet to feed on leaves of a tall palmetto.

"I need it, and I'll have to get as much as possible of it inside the ship," she said. "You know what happened to the triceratops we left outside."

That night a pack of three slim two-legged stenonychosaurs had descended on the carcass for a feast. When the couple on watch reported what was happening, Carlos had ordered floodlights on the scene and had led the rest of the crew outside with lasers. A stenonychosaur had deadly teeth and claws and would resist becoming a specimen. It might also prefer live prey. The team had been too slow. The scavengers had scattered at the lights and had vanished swiftly into hiding. Speed was their specialty. Much of the bulky triceratops remained, but the heart and liver, which Meg particularly wanted, had been consumed. She had tried to console herself with the thought that she could be certain now that stenonychosaurs were in the area. In time she would bag one.

Triceratopses were all over the place, but this hadrosaur, six kilometers from the ship, was the only one they had seen. Meg suspected that the tall plant eaters were easy prey for dromaeosaurs. Too bad, she thought as she killed it, but it would die anyway when the meteorite struck. She dropped a radio beacon and called Carlos to ask him to send the max on automatics to home in on the signal, pick up the three-ton creature, and return it to the *Pegasus* for dissection and chromosomal analysis.

She sighed and said to Nick, "I forgot when I was biting my nails to be taken on this expedition that I would have to carve up elephant-sized critters and drag them into the lab piece by piece. You don't have to worry about anything bigger than an ammonite." Quickly she added, "I hope you find one."

"I will," he answered equably. "Plenty of them are still around. If you want something small, help the Heesh find the Prime Mother."

"They would name me to the Sacred Order of Grand Matrons."

A bit later she reported to Carlos, "I see Marfor and Nim and their mechanical spider near the creek. They have our box with the Ishinol's bones."

The others listened as she described the burial of the bones. The robot used spade and scoop attachments to dig a pit two meters down into clay. It lowered Nim and the box into the pit, and Nim laid the skeleton out carefully. After pulling out him and the box, the robot filled the pit, and they left.

"If Marfor had found her Eve, I think we would have heard about it," Meg said at lunch. "Meanwhile she treats Adam with respect. Why did she bury him with such care?"

Rusty had an answer. "I think she's planning ahead in a big way. Marfor was planting the bones she will find in sixty-five million years, the fossil that will tell her where to look for the Prime Mother."

"What a strange loop in time!" Allie exclaimed. "It sounds like cheating."

"What's this talk about Adam and Eve?" Nick asked. "The Ishinol isn't the same race as the Heesh any more than *Purgatorius* is the same race we are."

"The Ishinol were ancestors," Meg said. "Maybe they were the first two of their kind. If so, and the male is dead but the Heesh evolved anyway, there should be some little ones running around."

That afternoon Dan went out with Allie to collect specimens of plants. He was the expert, but she knew enough to help, and Carlos insisted that no one brave dinosaur territory alone.

"I don't think I'm a greedy man," Dan said, "but here I am amid hundreds of species of plants no one has ever seen before, and I keep telling myself, 'They're mine, all mine!' "

"I'd rather have you find lettuce and tomatoes and onions," Allie replied. "And cucumbers. I'd trade my second-best microscope for a fresh green salad."

"What I miss is sweet corn. The Late Cretaceous is no place for a vegetarian. I can't build up an appetite for leaves."

Dan dug a seedling out of the ground while she kept watch for predators. "*Lyriodendron*," he said, pointing out the shape of the leaf, which had a broad base and narrowed to two broad fingerlike lobes at the tip.

They heard a guttural shout. "The Heesh," Allie said. "Let's see what the freaks are up to."

Keeping an eye on the trees around them and branches above them, and holding their lasers ready, they made their way through a tangle of plants to the source of the noise until they almost stumbled over a Heesh male. He was crouching behind a bush and holding a rifle loaded with darts. Startled by their appearance, he jerked his weapon up but halted before firing. "Ishinol," he whispered, and motioned with his hand to have them crouch down.

A shout sounded from not far away, then another shout from a different direction. Allie cupped her hand over Dan's ear and whispered, "They're driving the Ishinol this way."

"It may be the Prime Mother," Dan answered as quietly.

They waited. More shouts sounded, closer.

The Ishinol raced into the clearing, pivoted abruptly as if it had seen those who were hiding, and dashed to one side.

At that moment Oomis appeared in front of it. It scurried around a tree, away from her, and scrambled into the lower branches. She snapped off a useless shot from her own dart gun and shouted at the Heesh male. He peered into the tree and fired an automatic burst of fléchettes, which whistled as they carried tranquilizer darts into the foliage, but it was hard to guess what he had been aiming at. Dan saw the Ishinol scamper across branches to another tree and disappear. Two more Heesh males appeared. Oomis roared at them, and they ran in the direction the Ishinol had taken.

Suddenly Oomis yanked her whip from her side and slashed the first Heesh male viciously across the face. As he howled with pain, she raised her whip to strike again. He dropped to his knees in an attitude of supplication, covered his bleeding mouth and cheek with one hand, and raised the other to implore mercy. The tip of the whip cracked against the outstretched hand, gashing it.

"Hey!" Dan roared. He leaped to grab the end of the whip and tugged violently, jerking the handle out of Oomis's hand. Oomis aimed her dart rifle at him.

"No!" Allie shouted, training her laser gun on Oomis.

The Heesh female trembled with rage but controlled herself. "No" was one of the few English words she had learned, and the danger of being burned was clear. She spoke furiously into a microphone near her chin and turned the earphone so that the humans could hear her words translated by her ship's computer. "Vermin! How dare you oppose me? You should be flayed and your skin used to cover a drum."

"You savage!" Dan answered heatedly. Allie had never seen him so outraged. "How can you injure anyone so viciously?"

"You are the savage, or you would know that a female has the right to punish a male who fails. That miserable specimen cowering at your feet let the Prime Mother escape!"

"Your shot missed her too."

"I do not argue with inferiors. Get out of this area and don't come back! I will not tolerate interference." Oomis added a few words over her radio that the ship's computer did not translate.

Dan recognized that the confrontation had implications that were more than personal. In addition, Oomis had reinforcements near, the two males she had sent after the Ishinol. She might have just summoned them. He spoke into his radio. "Carlos, do you read me? Good. We have a problem." He reported what had happened.

"Tell her we will settle this question later," Carlos answered. "I will get hold of Marfor and negotiate with her. We don't want to start a war between the expeditions. Come back to the ship."

"You will hear from us later," Dan said to Oomis. He let go of the whip. Oomis picked up the handle and coiled the whip but didn't raise it to strike again.

"I will make you pay," she snarled.

Dan returned her glare with one of his own and walked away with Allie, slowly, to avoid any impression that they were fleeing.

As they left, the two Heesh males returned, and Oomis gave orders. "Haban, follow them and report to me where they go."

The order was not translated, but Dan and Allie saw a male start after them.

"Halt!" Dan ordered. Haban might not understand the word, but its meaning was clear, and Dan had his laser rifle leveled at him. Haban dodged behind a tree, waited until Dan and Allie had taken a few steps onward, and moved to another tree close behind them.

"We'd better watch our backs," Dan muttered to Allie. "I'll do that while you keep an eye out for danger ahead of us."

"I was right about not trusting them," she answered. "I think Oomis wants to take care of you personally."

"The feeling is mutual."

Carlos took Nick in a flier to meet Marfor near the Heesh ship. He had seen close-up photographs but wanted to inspect it himself. As he and Nick got out of the flier, Marfor came out of the ship with Nim, who carried a small radio for computer translations. Nick carried one too. The four of them stood facing each other.

The rim of the saucer-shaped Heesh ship was elevated above a circular substructure that rested on pistons, which were longer than an array of rocket cones within the circle, and that had guidance nozzles around it. The rim might provide stability in atmospheric flight, which the *Pegasus* could not manage, while most living and working took place in the thick saucer inside it. The top of the ship had been rolled back to let a watchtower, electronic equipment, and weapons be raised. The weapons had the narrow snouts of lasers. Carlos could see no missile launchers or barrels for artillery. We are roughly equal in armament, he thought, but if they take to the air, they have maneuverability, which we lack.

"Thank you for agreeing to meet me here," Carlos said. This was a time for making peace before an incident of hostility festered like a boil until it erupted. "It appears to me that the goals of both of our expeditions are in jeopardy. Has Oomis reported to you, Senior?"

"She has, Colonel. Your man was very wrong to interfere with her discipline. It was none of his business. How would you like it if one of us meddled in your affairs?"

"We would resent the interference. We would not threaten the person who interfered with a dart gun. We would protest to you and try to negotiate the difference reasonably, as I am doing now." Carlos wondered if this gargoyle, who had come to seem almost human to him, could think in human terms.

"Oomis was threatened in turn, and her whip was seized. That was a personal insult. Her whip is a badge of honor as well as a badge of office." Marfor rested a hand on Nim's shoulder as if she felt weak and needed support.

"And Oomis responded with an insult, calling my crew members vermin." Carlos shook his head. "I don't think we will get anywhere adding up insults. We might try to understand what was behind them. My man, Dan, is kindhearted and was outraged at seeing a fellow creature hurt so badly. Why did Oomis react to him so strongly?"

Marfor laughed, but feebly. "Several reasons. Her rights over her attendant male had been challenged, contrary to Heesh law and custom, both of which it is her duty to uphold as a senior matron of the Hall of Guardians. She is jealous of her rights and quick to anger. Second, she was challenged by a male, who is by definition in our society an inferior person." Marfor closed her eyes and took a deep breath before adding, "Finally, and most important to Oomis, she regards your race as an abomination."

"You are very frank," Carlos said. He was reminded of the diplomatic formula that an exchange of views was "frank" when it was going badly. "How do you feel yourself about our race and our equality of males and females?"

"Your race looks as outlandish to us as we must look to you, but you are civilized. I judge that from your conduct, not your technology. It is conduct that matters, not appearances. The equality of males is hard to accept, but I can accept you as an equal without discomfort."

"As I accept you," Carlos answered. "With that as a basis, I think we can solve our problem. I will censure Dan for acting so hastily, on impulse, without thinking. How you handle Oomis is your affair. Beyond that, I think we should avoid contact between our two races, except for the radio and meetings with you, to avoid any chance of friction."

"How do you propose to arrange that when we are both working in the same area?"

"Set a boundary." Carlos produced a map that Rusty had drawn. "There is a creek between our ships. That can be the boundary. The Heesh can have exclusive rights to the your side of the creek, where the male Ishinol was killed. The humans can have the other side. The life that we are investigating is the same on both sides."

Marfor stepped forward to take the map and stumbled. Nim caught her and kept her from falling. Marfor looked at the map and said, "I will accept the boundary, but if we see the Prime Mother cross the creek, we must have the right to follow."

"Agreed, and if we see the Prime Mother, we will call you." Carlos looked at her closely. She had seemed tired and clumsy. The down that covered her head and hands looked dull, lusterless. "Are you feeling all right?"

"Not quite. Our ship's doctor, one of our males, says my

temperature is high, but he cannot find a cause. I'll get over it."

Carlos liked Marfor, and he didn't want to take a chance that she would become so ill that Oomis would succeed her in command. "I would consider it a privilege if you would allow our ship's doctor, who is a female, to examine you. When she studied the blood sample from Nim she found a virus that humans don't have, and she synthesized antibodies to counteract it. You may have caught a virus from us."

"What is a virus? Our computer has no translation."

"It is a very small microorganism that can cause serious illnesses. Some kinds are carried in the air."

Nim was reluctant to enter the dialogue between commanders, but negotiations had ended, and he was afraid that Marfor, not at her best, would overlook an important point. "What else did your doctor find in my blood?" he asked.

"She analyzed your chromosomes and sequenced your genes. She can tell you exactly how you differ from an Ishinol, or from us, at the basic level of genetic coding."

Not comprehending, Marfor stared at him and said, "Thank you for the offer of medical help. I will think about it."

"I refuse to believe that those wretched creatures have medical knowledge superior to ours," Oomis said. She held the handle of her whip in one hand and the lash in the other, flexing the lash back and forth in a loop in her frustration.

"Our medicine is not good enough to cure me," Marfor answered. Her temperature had risen, her balance was unsteady, her eyes were watering, and there were painful swellings in her armpits. "I would rather take a chance on the humans than take a chance on dying. They do know more biology than we do. We learned nothing from their blood. They apparently learned a lot from ours. I will have their doctor do what she can for me."

She called Carlos to ask that his doctor examine her. It was an admission of inferiority, but need outweighed pride.

* * *

"I'm bringing you a medical case that should present some problems that will interest you," Carlos told Allie.

"You sound like you're softening me up," she answered suspiciously. "What sort of problems?"

"Figuring out how to treat one of the Heesh when all you know about them is that the head bone is connected to the neck bone."

"So now I'm a veterinarian, flying blind," she grumbled.

"It will look good on your résumé." He clapped her on the shoulder. "Aliens our specialty."

"I'd like to see this bunch of aliens drop like flies."

"You sound like Oomis in reverse." When that silenced her, Carlos said, "Marfor is sick. It could be something she caught from us. The Heesh medic can't figure out what's wrong. I hope you can find the cause and cure it."

"If she's caught a bug, maybe I can fix it. Bring her in. Old Doc Steele doesn't make house calls."

When Marfor appeared, accompanied by Nim, Carlos led them directly to the biological laboratory aboard the *Pegasus*. She should have a wheelchair, Carlos thought as he watched her supporting herself on Nim's arm. She must not have recognized much of the equipment in the room, but she appeared to be too weak to be curious about it.

Allie overcame her aversion toward touching one of the Heesh and checked Marfor's pulse, heartbeat, and temperature although she had no idea what the normal readings should be, let alone what diseases would produce what symptoms. The swellings in the armpits suggested an infection. Infections she could handle. She took a blood sample as Carlos watched.

"I suggest you lie down while I analyze this," Allie told Marfor. "One thing you need is rest."

Dan brought a cot for Marfor, who looked at his size and couldn't help thinking that a fight between him and Oomis would be an equal match. Nim was given a chair to sit beside her. Allie tested the blood for antibodies and found one that was not listed by the ship's computer but resembled one that was on record.

"What Marfor has is bacterial, not viral," Allie reported, "and she didn't catch it from us. It resembles tularemia. Humans catch it from infected rabbits or from ticks or fleas that have fed on rabbits and transmit it to our blood. I don't know what this came from. Something that lives around here. Or did live. The male Ishinol that Meg dissected had ticks. If they were the source, we're all lucky we didn't get it. Or maybe it doesn't affect humans. Senior Marfor, did you dissect the body of the Ishinol?"

"I did. Nim worked on it too."

"Let me examine your skin."

Allie took one of Marfor's forearms, which was bare under a short sleeve. Gently brushing aside the down, which was not as soft as it looked, she saw that the skin beneath it was a lighter brown. Examining it swiftly, starting with the wrist, she found a reddish spot of inflammation near the elbow. There was no tick, but a tick could have dropped off after sucking its fill of blood.

"That's not conclusive but it's suspicious," she said. "In any case, we know the cause of your illness. I'll use the bacteria to design an antibiotic against them."

While she went to work with her analyzer and synthesizer, Nim inspected his own arms. "I don't find anything," he said.

"If you had been bitten, you would be sick by now," Carlos said. "Something occurs to me, Marfor. If there is a tick aboard your ship, it will look for another meal of blood. You might have to fumigate the ship."

"Evacuate the ship and fill it with a deadly gas?" Marfor asked. "I don't want to do that. I'll have the techs make a search."

"And if you find your Prime Mother, watch out for ticks."

"The Prime Mother wouldn't infect us," Marfor protested.

"The Prime Mother doesn't know she's the Prime Mother."

Allie produced a bottle of pills for Marfor. Since the antibiotic in the pills was designed to attack one specific bacterium without other effect, it shouldn't cause harmful side reactions. The dosage was only a guess, but Allie prescribed one pill every six hours for five days.

"That ought to work," she told Marfor, with more confidence in her voice than she felt. "Let me know, will you?"

Nim supported Marfor as they left. Next day Marfor called Carlos to say, "Your treatment works. I feel better already."

"You made history," Carlos told Allie.

"Everyone here makes history every day. It was just a job. Don't expect me to develop a cozy doctor–patient relationship."

Chapter Four

At first Meg was discouraged by her failure to find many specimens of vertebrate life. "Hunting live animals is a very different game from hunting fossils," she told Nick. "Both are hidden, but fossils stay put."

"Also, you never had to shoot a fossil, like the hadrosaur," he answered.

Except for triceratopses, dinosaurs were rare, but late one afternoon Meg's luck changed. From the air she and Nick saw a stenonychosaur feeding on a small mammal, and she shot it.

"Two for the price of one," she said.

Nick understood her. "All you have to do to catch a mammal is follow a stenonychosaur around."

"And be careful he isn't following you."

They landed so that Nick could attach a cable to lift the stenonychosaur into the air. A slim two-legged dinosaur built for speed, it had gray scales with orange markings, eyes that faced forward in a long low head, many sharp teeth, and formidable claws on all fingers and toes. Two meters tall, it had a long thin tail, useful for maintaining balance when running.

"No animal native to this time could run away from it," Meg said. "Mammals had to hide, and this one didn't." She slipped on gloves to grasp the bloody half-eaten body of the dinosaur's small prey and open its long narrow jaws.

"What is it?" he asked.

"A didelphid, an opossum. Notice the five incisors at the front of the upper jaw and four in the lower. Both jaws will have a canine, three premolars, and four molars. Just like opossums at home. It could eat anything, which is one reason it will survive the coming extinctions. Genus *Alphadon*, I think. I'll have to check references in the computer to determine the species."

"A naked tail," Nick observed.

"Yes." She looked for a maternal pouch, which opossums, as marsupials and distant relatives of kangaroos, possessed, but nothing but shreds of skin and flesh was left of its underside, and it may have been a male.

Nick and Meg took turns pursuing their specialties, each aided by the other, if only as a guard. Returning from a trip, they worked in the lab. Enough work piled up there to keep teams of scientists busy for years. They welcomed rainy days, which confined them to the lab, but then they welcomed the sun again so they could go outdoors and add to their collections.

Nick was setting traps for insects that flew at night. Meg set out traps for mammals too, baiting them with seeds, bits of meat, and following an inspiration, cheese. She wanted multituberculates, which were thought of as the rodents of the Cretaceous age. "You trap rats with cheese, don't you?" she asked Nick when he laughed.

It worked. The strong odor of cheese must have been inviting. She caught two species of multituberculates that looked like mice with small ears. They had sharp incisors for biting and complex grinding teeth topped by ridges or the rows of tubercles that had given them their name.

"Let's keep them as pets," she urged Carlos. "I'll call them Willy and Milly. They'll take up hardly any space."

He agreed. To keep them alive, Meg had to determine their diet. "They're supposed to be herbivores, but they'll eat anything," she announced after a few days. "I think that's one secret of surviving the asteroid. These tiny animals have lasted for millions of years, and they will last until rodents evolve as more successful occupants of the same ecological niche."

Sometimes, ever watchful for predatory dinosaurs, she and Nick went out in the truck and halted it to walk through the forest to hunt on the ground. Most such searches were fruitless, but they turned up a turtle near the creek. Meg's most unexpected triumph came when she was fishing the creek with a small strong hook and a line that could hold a shark if any had been there.

Something tugged the line hard and jerked the rod and reel out of her hands. She grabbed the rod before it was dragged into the creek, caught the handle on the reel before the line spun out, and tried to play her catch as she would any large fish. She kept losing line and said to Nick, "You try it. You're stronger."

He looked around for danger, saw none, laid his laser rifle on the ground, and quickly grabbed the reel. Just as quickly, Meg picked up the laser.

A long snout, hooked at the tip, surfaced in front of small eyes in a broad skull. "It's not a fish!" Nick exclaimed.

"It's a champsosaur," Meg said after a glance. "It has nearly a hundred fifty sharp teeth in those long jaws. I'll shoot it before it decides to attack." She fired her laser into the water just below the head, catching the creature in the chest and killing it.

With difficulty, Nick dragged the champsosaur onto the bank of the stream. The body, not counting head and neck and tail, was more than a meter long. "It looks like a crocodile," Nick said.

"Like a gavial because of its snout," Meg answered, "but it's not any kind of crocodile. It's not a dinosaur either. It's more closely related to the lizards. This is a great find!"

Nick was hunting terrestrial arthropods. Not insects; he had plenty of them. Now he wanted millipedes, which had existed for many millions of years before the Late Cretaceous, and centipedes, which were not known until after the K/T line. At a casual glance by one who didn't recognize them, they looked alike, long and many-legged, but centipedes had one pair of legs for each body segment while millipedes had two. Centipedes could scurry along the ground much faster and had poisonous claws that could inflict an excruciatingly painful wound. Nick wore gloves.

Meg joined him to act as lookout and guard. They worked on the edge of a clearing.

Carrying a small net in one hand, Nick brushed leaf litter aside with the other and turned over rotting wood to rip off the bark, for many centipedes lived under bark. A ground spider, one that didn't weave a web, scuttled swiftly away from leaves it had scattered. It was a target of opportunity, and he tried to net it but failed.

"Don't worry," he muttered. "I'll save a place for you in one of my best bottles."

"Nick," Meg said loudly, "we have company."

A Heesh male and female had entered the clearing on their right. Meg recognized them as Lippor and Dorkin. The spidery robot was with them.

"Have you seen an Ishinol?" Lippor asked through her translation link.

"No. I thought you were supposed to be on the other side of the creek," Meg answered.

"Dorkin saw an Ishinol's tracks on our side in mud leading to the creek. We assume it crossed and headed this way."

"How did you recognize the tracks?" Nick asked.

"Dorkin made casts from the feet of the Ishinol your captain gave us. These were the same, three toes the same distance apart, and an impression of a toe high in back where the mud was deep. The agreement between Senior Marfor and Colonel Lecompte gives us the right to follow."

"I know," Meg said. "Good luck."

"We won't disturb you," Lippor assured her. "We are in a hurry. Dorkin saw the tracks of a dromaeosaur too. It may have been following the Ishinol. Watch out for it."

The Heesh and their robot proceeded across the clearing. As they neared a stand of trees, a dromaeosaur emerged and raced toward them. As the robot moved to intercept it, the dinosaur started toward Meg and Nick.

Jumping to her left to avoid hitting Nick with a beam from her laser, Meg tripped and fell. She rolled to a prone position and tried to take a steady aim. The dromaeosaur was between them and the Heesh, and a shot from either side would endanger the other team. I have to hold my fire until it's almost on top of me with those terrible claws, she thought nervously. She gritted her teeth.

And she saw a blur of action as the robot, moving much faster than any animal that had ever lived, came up behind the dinosaur and seized it in two of its flexible metal arms. The dromaeosaur screeched, twisted around, slashed at the robot with the four-inch claws on its feet, and tried to bite one of the arms. It couldn't dent or even scratch the steel body. Failing to kill the thing that held it, the dromaeosaur kicked at it and tried to break free, but two more arms came around it and held it closer.

Lippor shouted a command. One of the robot's arms tightened around the neck of the dromaeosaur and strangled it. When it ceased to move, the robot dropped it to the ground.

"I couldn't shoot," Dorkin said to Meg. "I would have hit you too."

"I know." She regained her feet.

"Do you want this creature?" Lippor asked.

"No thanks. We already have one."

"Then we may pick it up later. Marfor might like to have it. We will continue our search for the Prime Mother."

"First things first," Nick commented as watched the Heesh leave the clearing. He crouched over the ground again.

"Survival comes first," Meg answered. She checked her laser to make sure it was in working condition, although she had lost some of her confidence in it. "We might have survived without the robot, but maybe not. That thing is more formidable than I realized. I wonder what other tricks it can do."

"Never mind. I've got a millipede!"

When the asteroid due in ten weeks struck the Earth, the *Pegasus* would have returned to space to speed past the terrible upheaval of its impact and the ensuing period of devastation and icy cold. Then the team would land to study surviving life. It would reclaim instruments left behind to record temperature, rainfall, wind velocity, seismic shocks, and the kinds of dust that filled the air.

"I wish I had an outcropping of rock to anchor my instruments," Rusty told Carlos, "but there ain't no rocks hereabouts. Let's drive a piling into the bank on our side of the creek and attach my gadgets to it."

"They'll wind up underwater," he warned her. "Heavy rains will bring a flood."

"My stuff is built to take it."

Carlos took her to the bank in the max with Nick and Dan to stand guard and help with assembly. The max had been fitted to drive a steel piling five meters into the dirt and attach a pylon of steel girders on top of it.

"An earthquake will shake it but won't knock it down," Rusty said. "Bolt my anemometer on top, will you, Dan? It will stand up to a 400-K hurricane. I'll attach the seismograph at ground level."

"Carlos!" Nick shouted. "Rusty! Dan! Look across the stream!"

On the opposite bank an Ishinol squatted beside a crude nest, a shallow depression scooped out of the warm sand. Hearing the humans, she bared her teeth at them and hissed, but she had been caught at a time when she couldn't flee. One by one she extruded eight eggs from beneath her tail, depositing them in a tight cluster.

"It's the Prime Mother!" Rusty exclaimed. Nick, she saw with approval, was taping the scene. "The Ishinol that hatch from those eggs will be the ancestors of the Heesh."

Carlos called the Heesh ship. "Message to Marfor. Your Prime Mother is on the bank of the creek between our ships, on your side. We are observing."

Oomis sat in the Heesh control center when the message arrived. She understood immediately that this was her chance to deprive Marfor of credit for finding the Prime Mother and win it for herself. "Haban, send the collector robot to the creek to take the Ishinol," she told her attendant male. "Then join me at the flier. There's no time to waste." Now I can bring Marfor into this, too late, she thought. She spoke over the intercom. "Senior Marfor, you are needed in the control center. A message has come from the humans. I am taking care of it."

The humans saw the Ishinol scamper into the forest. They feared that she would disappear, but she returned with a mouthful of leaves and scattered them on top of the eggs. Evidently the humans, motionless, didn't frighten her. Again she started into the forest, but stopped.

The Heesh robot scuttled out from between trees not far away and started toward her. For every foot that slipped on loose sand, seven other padded metal feet found purchase.

The Ishinol raced into the creek and started to swim across it. The robot pursued her, but it couldn't swim, and it lost ground as it waded in water that sometimes covered its head. Reaching the other bank, the Ishinol scrambled up it with a flurry of arms and legs. At the top, faced with a line of four people, she leaped without hesitation at Carlos, straight ahead of her, bowling him over. Instinctively he threw his arms in front of his throat and face to protect them. Claws ripped his chest and legs, and teeth sank into an arm. Yelling with pain, he tried to hurl the beast off.

Rusty aimed her laser above the Ishinol's body, to avoid hitting Carlos, and fired. A thin torrent of energy sizzled through the air. She brought the beam down like an incandescent knife to cut through the Ishinol's backbone and nerve cord. It shuddered and died. Rusty dropped her rifle and knelt by Carlos. His twisted face and eyes squeezed shut as he endured the pain of his wounds brought tears to her eyes. What if he died? The thought was unendurable. Wiping her eyes, she looked closely at his cuts. They were bad but didn't look fatal. No major blood vessels had been severed. She took a scarf off her head and wrapped it around the bloodiest wound, in one arm.

"The Heesh," Dan said. He pointed upward. The Heesh flier had arrived and hovered above them. "There's a big female inside it. It looks like Oomis, the one I tangled with. She saw that." He jumped aside, out of the way of the robot, which had reached the bank and climbed it. It scurried toward the dead Ishinol, scooped it off of Carlos, and cradled it in the thin cables of two hands. Pausing as if receiving orders, it pivoted and seized Rusty in two more hands. She struggled uselessly to break free and shouted, "Shoot it!"

But the robot had raced back into the creek and was wading across it. It held Rusty above its head behind it while it was in the water, and it lowered her like a shield when it climbed onto land. The men couldn't fire without hitting her.

Before it carried her into the forest she shouted desperately, *"Prenez les oeufs!"*

The Heesh computer had not learned French. Oomis's flier flew back to the ship. Nick and Dan, although puzzled by Rusty's shout, drove the max across the creek and collected the eggs before returning to take Carlos back to the *Pegasus*.

Rusty was terrified but hardly scratched by her wild ride through the forest in the grip of the robot. A skin-like rubber padded the finger cables that held her, and flexible joints and limbs absorbed the shock of metal feet pounding the ground. Holding the Ishinol in two arms and Rusty in two more, it used its other arms to brush branches out of the way. When the robot carried her up a ramp into the Heesh ship and set her on her feet, she felt shaken but not bruised.

I hope Carlos got my message in French, "Take the eggs," she thought. I hope he'll guess what I had in mind. How badly was he hurt by that horrible little monster? The cuts looked deep when I knelt beside him, but not so bad that Allie can't patch him up. Then he'll act. Carlos would never abandon me. Why did the robot grab me?

Two Heesh males, the feathers of their crests raised high from an emotion that Rusty could not decipher, barred the way out of the ship. Their faces, large round eyes without brows or lashes, mere slits for nostrils, and massive protruding jaws, made them frightful and frightening. Hieronymous Bosch could have painted them as demons in hell. Even in her present straits Rusty thought of portraying them in a surrealistic scene.

After a wait, another male beckoned her to follow him. He led her along cabinet-lined corridors to a cabin in which three females sat in high-backed chairs behind a table that held a translation terminal. Marfor sat on one side and—Lippor, wasn't it?—on the other, while a female larger than either of them, as tall as Dan, sat in the center. That would be Oomis, whom Rusty knew, unfavorably, by reputation.

Attendant males stood behind them, and Rusty recognized Nim. There was no chair for her.

A silver band around Oomis's head held a small golden egg above her forehead. Above that brutish face the ornament looked as incongruous as the wigs that English judges used to wear as symbols of dignity and authority, but Rusty sensed that it was equally as serious a symbol. Was she on trial?

Lighting in the cabin was dim, and the large eyes of the Heesh were wide open. Their stare was disconcerting. Rusty could not claim to read expression on a Heesh face, but the broad thin lips of all three females curved downward at the sides, and the lips of the big one in the middle were parted slightly, showing her teeth.

Sudden motion made Rusty raise her hands protectively. A poota flew from a perch like a blue bat, circled around her head, and settled on Marfor's shoulder.

Two males carried a small table bearing the corpse of the Ishinol to a place between Rusty and the table for the Heesh females. The Ishinol sprawled on its back, drab and scrawny in death.

Reaching forward with fingers extended like claws, Oomis roared at Rusty, "Killer! Abominable creature! You are guilty of the most unforgivable of crimes!" A loud translation from a terminal expressed her fury as clearly as her words. She pointed at the Ishinol. "I saw you myself, and there is the evidence."

Rusty understood what she was talking about but was taken aback by the vehemence of the denunciation. "I have committed no crime," she protested.

"You murdered the Prime Mother!"

Rusty stared with outraged disbelief at the remains of the shabby creature that was held in such superlative honor. "Killing an animal is not murder, and I had no choice." The nightmarish unfairness of the proceeding in which she found herself trapped made Rusty angry. "Marfor! Who is in command here?"

"Senior Matron Oomis of the Hall of Guardians has convened a court of correction," Marfor answered. "The administration of justice honors the Cosmic Egg. Oomis has full authority to decide questions of morality and law. If you have anything to say for yourself, I will phrase the issues on your behalf."

Marfor sounded sympathetic, as she should be after having dealt with the humans on terms of growing understanding and warmth and having been cured of her illness by a human. Carlos plainly liked her, and she might like him.

"Here's an issue," Rusty said. "Heesh laws do not apply to humans."

"There is no precedent," Marfor said to Oomis. "Perhaps we should clarify the question before proceeding. We should see if the humans have any valid arguments."

"Talk to those disgusting mammals?" Oomis asked. "What do they know about the cosmic plan? Vicious creatures! I would like to drop this one into a cage of mammals in a zoo to teach her how vicious mammals are."

Rusty lost her temper. "I saved my captain from a vicious creature you call your Prime Mother."

Marfor winced at what she knew Oomis would consider unforgivable blasphemy. Not that it would make much difference when Oomis had a chance to vent her hatred of the humans. And fear? Yes, fear too, no doubt. She could avenge her fear with self-righteous triumph.

Oomis yanked her whip from her belt and waved it in the air. "Show respect to the Prime Mother or I will whip respect into you! Fool! She was not trying to harm your captain. She wanted to escape."

This inhuman thing is crazy, Rusty thought with alarm. Nevertheless she answered firmly, "Your Prime Mother didn't have to claw him and bite him to escape. She tried to kill him."

"He should be proud of his wounds. Any of us would be proud to die for the Prime Mother."

"Surely you understand that I care more about my captain." It would not help to say that she loved him. "I did my duty."

"Her motive is worth considering," Marfor said, but with an air of hopelessness.

"Her reasoning is insane," Oomis answered. "Motivation is disregarded in a case of murder. She must be punished."

Rusty's alarm grew. If she was punished immediately, Carlos couldn't save her. She spoke defiantly. "Any harm that comes to me will be avenged."

"How?" Oomis asked with scorn. "I will take you home with us for final judgment by the Matriarchy. You will be punished far beyond the reach of humans."

But Oomis had overlooked one overriding fact that she would have to confront. Because she didn't know Carlos's condition, Rusty felt that it was more important to play for time than to enlighten her. Calmed by the thought that Oomis could be forced to back down, she said, "With all due respect, Senior Matron Oomis, I urge you to defer your decision until you hear from my captain."

"It would be interesting to hear what he has to say," Marfor said. This could be her last chance to save this human. "We need not be hasty."

"Our task here is done. We have all we will ever have of the Prime Mother. The desecrated remains of her revered body must be taken home for burial with the most solemn honors. There would be no purpose to our staying in this miserable time one moment longer. Prepare for launch, Senior Marfor." Oomis gestured to her attendant male. "Haban, we will lock this creature up."

To take me into exile, at best, in a strange world, Rusty thought. Oomis is as bullheaded as a triceratops, and Marfor can't divert her. Hurry, Carlos, she prayed.

His cuts were painful, but Carlos felt the pain less than his fear for Rusty and his fury at the Heesh. As soon as Allie had disinfected and bandaged the wounds he felt ready for battle. Nick and Dan had brought the Ishinol's eggs when they flew him back to the *Pegasus*, and at first Rusty's urgency about the eggs when her life might be in danger puzzled him. Obviously she had said "Take the eggs" in French to prevent the Heesh from guessing that her friends would collect them, as if they were worth as much as she was. Eggs? Egg line! Carlos understood. And he finally had a clue to the mystery of the separate evolution of Heesh and humans and the puzzle of the divergence of time tracks. It all depended on the success of what he would do now.

Within an hour from the time Carlos had been attacked by the Ishinol, Nick sat behind a heavy laser on the max robot, which was concealed at the edge of the forest near the Heesh ship. Heesh males were carrying trash out of the ship and dumping it. Dan stayed behind the cover of other trees with the laser in the truck. Carlos wished he had missiles, but lasers would do. He took a third position and called on the radio frequency that the Heesh monitored.

"This is Colonel Carlos Lecompte of the *Pegasus*. Inform Senior Matron Marfor that I demand return of the captive member of my crew."

After a minute an answer came. "This is Marfor. The captive is under the control of Senior Matron Oomis of the Hall of Guardians, who has been conducting a hearing."

"Let me talk to my crew member."

Rusty's voice came over. "Carlos, this is dreadful. Oomis has accused me of murdering the Prime Mother and plans to take me back to Naneg for trial."

Carlos thought of red-haired Rusty, so bright, capable, loyal, cheerful, and affectionate, everything he admired and wanted in a woman, being kidnapped and taken to strange and hostile surroundings for a travesty upon justice. She would be beyond reach or rescue, doomed to an unguessable fate. He had trouble controlling his temper, but there was reason to believe that his plan to save her would succeed. It had to.

"Marfor, I need not remind you of your debt to us or of the chance for a friendly relationship between our races that is at stake," he said, as calmly as he could. "How can you allow this to happen?"

"Oomis has higher authority in a case like this. She is listening. I can arrange no more than that. If you have arguments to free your crew member, Rusty, state them."

"Your legal position in condemning a human action by Heesh laws is untenable, but I will not waste time arguing. I demand, again, the return of Rusty. I have means to enforce my demand."

Marfor answered firmly. "Are you threatening us?"

"I have weapons in position to burn holes in the hull of your ship. She will not survive in space."

Oomis spoke up. "If you disable our ship, we will disable yours. Would you doom yourself and your ship to save this female?"

"I would."

"A very civilized attitude," Oomis answered with sarcasm, "but I have judged your female to be guilty of murder of the Prime Mother."

"Nonsense," Carlos said. "Your Prime Mother brought death upon herself." He produced the argument that should be conclusive. "Consider one question. Does she have an egg line?"

"Of course she does," Marfor said, "or we would not exist."

"You may cease to exist. We have the eggs. I will give them to you in exchange for Rusty, or I will destroy them."

There was a pause before Marfor answered. "To say that we, who exist, would not exist, contradicts fact."

"It is an equal contradiction that both Heesh and humans exist," Carlos answered. "I think that the truth of this paradox depends upon your decision now."

For awhile Carlos heard no more. He suspected that the communicator had been turned off while Marfor conferred with Oomis. Finally she spoke again.

"We are analyzing the theoretical threat to our egg line. Return to your ship. If we find your argument logical, I will bring Rusty to your ship and exchange her for the eggs."

Oomis strode back and forth in rage. "I will not be beaten by these nauseating animals!"

Marfor looked at her with distaste. "You won't be. We gain everything by the trade they offer. Surely the very existence of our race is worth one human female."

"I think you wanted to free her all along."

Marfor ignored the accusation rather than lie by denying it. "The issue is clear. Without the eggs there will no egg line. There will be no more Ishinol, no Hanishan, and no Heesh. Mammals will take over our world."

"But if we ensure an egg line, why are there any humans?"

"They don't come from our world, or they come from a world that will arise from this one if we don't reclaim the eggs. This may be a critical moment offering two possibilities, of which only one will come true. I don't think the humans have thought of that. They may be destroying their own race."

Oomis looked surprised, then thoughtful. "That would be worth our giving up one female now. That parody of a male, with her red hair! All right. Trade her."

Told that she would be exchanged for the eggs, Rusty felt relief so great that she could scarcely refrain from gloating in front of Oomis. She was proud of herself and Carlos, too. She knew enough Heesh words to know that the matrons had debated the threat to their egg line before Oomis had agreed to give her a reprieve. Her own quick thinking in calling to Carlos to take the Ishinol eggs had led to her release. She was proud of Carlos for comprehending the importance of the eggs in time to save her, for acting swiftly and decisively, and for his willingness to risk the loss of his ship. It had been a sound gamble but still a gamble.

Trailed by the spidery collector robot, Marfor drove to the *Pegasus* with Rusty on the seat beside her and Nim behind them, manning a heavy laser. She saw a triceratops wandering through the forest from shrub to shrub in its endless search for food to fill its bulk. It lowered its horns toward her, and she turned to circle around it. This was no time to play tag with a dinosaur.

In the end, Rusty knew, Marfor had been the one to persuade Oomis to yield. "I think I have you to thank for getting me out of there," she told her.

"All I did was pound a spike of logic into Oomis's brain," Marfor answered. "It would be easier to convince the Prime Mother." She stopped talking, guiltily conscious of unflattering thoughts about the Prime Mother.

"Our flier is up there," Nim said. The others looked up. "It's probably Oomis."

"What does she want?" Marfor asked. "I don't trust her."

"I thought she was following us, but she's circling over the forest. She acts like she's looking for something."

The flier was back overhead when Marfor reached the Pegasus.

"She's probably making a record of this," Nim guessed.

Carlos was waiting in his truck when they reached the ship, and Dan sat casually near the laser on the max robot. Rusty leaped from her seat and ran to Carlos, who reached down to lift her up beside him. He hugged her, and she kissed him. Released from his arms, she looked at his bandages and kissed him again.

Marfor and Nim watched the expression of human emotion by a demonstration that seemed peculiar and unsanitary, and they glanced at each other without comment. There was business to transact. "Where are the eggs?" Marfor asked.

"Here." Carlos got out of the truck and took a box from its back. It held eight eggs, twice the size of hens' eggs, each crudely protected from breaking against the others by a padding of leaves.

Marfor left her own truck to examine them and said, "The collector robot will take them. Your padding was thoughtful, but my truck will bounce around a lot on rough ground. The robot's sensors make instant adjustments in the length of its legs, and it moves smoothly."

Carlos put the box on the ground. He backed away as the robot approached and took an egg in the tendrils of each of its hands. Its fingers are padded and its arms, like its legs, are shock absorbers, he thought.

"Our ship will leave now," Marfor said. "I am sorry that our encounter with you ended in hostility. I had hoped that our two races would develop friendly relations."

"We have made a fresh start," Carlos answered. "I too am sorry we can't continue our acquaintance. Two great civilizations should have much to offer each other. Good-bye and good luck."

"May the Spirit of the Egg glow for you." Marfor returned to her truck and drove away, followed by the collector and its invaluable burden. The Heesh flier stayed above them until they reached the forest and then speeded on ahead.

* * *

As soon as the Ishinol's eggs had been deposited in individual nests of plastic foam, Marfor went to the control room of her ship with Nim. Oomis, looking more ready to condemn than praise her, waited with Lippor and their attendant males.

"Now we hop ahead a few thousand years, to a time when the world will have recovered fully from the asteroid strike." Marfor said. "We'll wait a couple of months for the eggs to hatch and make sure the infant Ishinol can fend for themselves. Mammals won't have evolved enough to threaten them. We can go home proud of what we have accomplished."

"It's a disgrace to go home with nothing but the corpse of the Prime Mother," Oomis said. "If we can't take her, we should take her eggs with us."

Marfor looked at her with astonishment. "I thought you understood. The Ishinol have to be left to start their evolution very close to the period we are in now to give time for their egg line to lead through many changes to the Heesh. Tell her, Lippor."

Unable to avoid calling Oomis wrong, Lippor said unhappily, "I see no alternative to Marfor's plan. The evolution will take many millions of years."

Oomis glared at her but said, "So we must stay in this backward time another two or three months? All right. But there is one thing we must do before we leave." Hunting for the triceratopses while Marfor delivered Rusty, she had found them disappointingly near her own ship and had known that she could not herd them to the right place to goad them into charging the human ship. There was a simpler possibility. "We must punish the humans for interfering with justice. When we launch, we will hold a horizontal course above them. Our rockets will consume them."

Shocked by the proposal, Marfor objected. "They haven't harmed us. We made a bargain, and they fulfilled their part. I will not permit treachery."

"You? What have you to do with it? I represent the Hall of Guardians, and I have sole authority to decide questions of morality and law and to decree punishment. I warn you, Marfor, do not question my right to speak for the Spirit of the Egg. Whatever has happened since then, the humans killed the Prime Mother. They must be punished. Go to your controls. Get us up and above the human ship. If you don't do it, Lippor will."

For the first time in her life, Marfor chose to defy a decision made in the name of the Spirit of the Egg. Her sense of justice and her conscience rebelled at the enormity of the plan to destroy the humans. She wheeled, strode to the controls, and moved a switch, carefully chosen. Nothing happened. "Something's stuck inside," she said, and took a screwdriver from a drawer. Detaching a panel from the control board, she pushed wires aside and gouged a small chip of circuitry. "There," she said. "The ship can still be launched and landed, and maneuvered in space, but we cannot control the vernier rockets that would hold us at low altitude. You will not be able to satisfy your insane hatred of the humans, Oomis."

"Insane!" Oomis yelled. She started toward Marfor with her arms extended. Nim slipped between them, and she cuffed his head so hard that he fell to the deck. "You are insane to defy me, Marfor!"

Marfor tensed to fight the larger female. Oomis would beat her badly and might use her whip, but the blow to Nim drove caution from her mind. Contempt for Oomis and a growing hatred that had festered within her erupted in a tirade.

"I say you have lost your mind! You can't bear to think that your doctrines have been shattered. You can't believe that the Cosmic Egg gave rise to humans as equals of the Heesh. You are imprisoned in dogma, unable to look outside the cage of your prejudices. You are blind to the chance for greater knowledge and understanding that the humans give us. What is this Prime Mother we found? She is a vicious animal, a mindless predator, an immensely distant ancestor who is necessary to us but is an ugly dirty dwarf, a creature who belongs in this savage time and deserves no more than a page of recognition in ours. We should stay here and learn more about the humans while we have the chance. One human is worth a hundred Prime Mothers!"

"Heretic!" Oomis shouted into Marfor's face. "You condemn yourself. I speak for the Hall of Guardians, and I won't allow you to bring your heresy back to Naneg. The ship will return, but not you. Get off it!"

I went too far, Marfor thought. The prospect of exile in this dying age dismayed her, but she refused to apologize and retract what she had said. There was one hope. "Lippor, you have learned too much about our long line of bestial ancestors to give them reverence. You can cause Oomis to take a temperate view."

Lippor has acted like a friend to me but she fears Oomis, Marfor thought. She steeled herself for the answer.

Marfor may be right about the nature of the Prime Mother, Lippor thought, but she has challenged accepted doctrine, which she has no right to do. Oomis is being irrational and vindictive, but the Hall of Guardians is charged with upholding doctrine. With exile in a world of ravenous dinosaurs? Lippor looked at Oomis, fingering her whip, and thought with dread of being forced to follow Marfor out of the ship.

"I am sorry, Marfor, but Senior Oomis is not exceeding her powers," Lippor said.

"Leave now!" Oomis shouted.

Nim rose from the floor to say, "You will be condemned for this at home, Senior Oomis. It will be seen as vengeance, not justice."

"You too! Off the ship!"

Nim spoke up to make sure that he would be marooned with me, Marfor thought. She felt warmly grateful that he was so fond of her that he would share her doom. "We will leave," she said, "but we are entitled to take our personal belongings. Come, Nim."

Her personal locker held little and his less. Along with clothing, a picture of Marfor's daughter, and their personal lasers, they took useful items like knives, flashlights, lighters, binoculars, canteens, knapsacks, and first-aid kits, as if they were going on a simple fieldtrip. Marfor added her computer and a selection of memory cubes.

"Let me copy something while we still have access," Nim said. He tapped the ship's main memory. "There. Now we can translate if we have any dealings with the humans."

"You read my mind," Marfor said.

When she confronted Oomis again she said, "I'll take the truck and its heavy laser. You won't need it anymore. Or is this a sentence of death, Oomis?"

"Take the truck." With heavy sarcasm Oomis added, "Good luck in synthesizing fuel."

Marfor whistled. Her poota, bright blue with cheerful orange spots, flew to her shoulder. It stayed there as she and Nim drove down the ramp to a world that suddenly looked more menacing.

Outside in the truck Marfor said to Nim, "Oomis will expect us to seek help from the humans. They may drive us away after our recent dispute, but we may not survive long without them. Oomis may try to stop us before we find out." She drove toward the *Pegasus*. "Oomis still wants to punish the humans, too. We had better get to them before she thinks of something."

Nim heard a noise and looked up. "That's Oomis in the flier. Why is she following us again? Has she already thought of something?"

"Maybe she has. Keep your laser ready in case she attacks us. I hope she follows us to the ship. Maybe they'll shoot her down."

Marfor entered a clearing, saw a triceratops there, and veered back into the forest. From her limited experience, a triceratops was surly if bothered but wasn't dangerous if given plenty of room. This one screeched and chased the truck.

Nim tried to level the heavy laser to burn it down, but the truck was bouncing on dead branches. The beam swung back and forth, up and down, with the truck's motion, far off target. A triceratops was faster than a truck over the rough ground in the forest, and it rapidly closed the distance. For a moment the beam passed across the shield behind its head, and it screamed with pain as the skin on it was blistered, but it kept coming as if something worse was chasing it.

"It's crazy!" Nim exclaimed. He struggled to hold the laser steady and managed to slow the dinosaur down when he seared its legs. He continued firing.

"There's another one!" Marfor shouted. She dodged between trees, driving with one hand while trying to use her hand laser with the other. She couldn't miss a target so big but she couldn't seem to burn anything vital while she was jostled in the truck. She stopped the truck to take steady aim.

A third triceratops caught them without warning from the other side as she fired. It crashed into the truck, knocking it over and throwing Marfor and Nim to the ground. They scrambled for hiding places behind trees and ferns, and Marfor was conscious that the poota was no longer riding her shoulder. She watched two triceratopses sink to their bellies, fatally burned, while the third one trampled the truck into twisted metal, lifted it with its horns and tossed it aside, and stamped on the computer, smashing it flat. It raised its head and looked around. As suddenly as it had been consumed by rage it was calm. Ignoring the two dinosaurs that had been killed, it moved placidly through the trees.

Nim rose to his feet, limped over to Marfor, and asked, "Are you hurt?"

"Bruised, that's all. How about you?"

"I twisted an ankle and may have sprained it. That and scratches."

"What got into those beasts?"

"Who knows?" Nim looked up. "The flier's gone. Could Oomis have sent them after us?"

"She must have done so somehow. We weren't bothering them." Marfor considered the possibilities and quickly found one that was plausible. "She could have herded them with bolts from the laser on her flier. If I'm right, the knowledge doesn't help us now."

Curses upon Oomis might make her feel better but would be as useless as blowing bubbles into the wind. Deciding what to do next would be useful. Marfor whistled. Her poota flew from a branch high in a tree to land on her shoulder. "Let's take inventory."

The small items they had brought with them were scattered but largely undamaged. The truck and the computer were junk. Test firings showed that the personal lasers could still be used.

"As long as the power cells last, we won't have to fight dinosaurs with knives," Nim said. "Then what? I hope we can rely on the humans. If Oomis did this to destroy us, she should be satisfied."

"I don't think so," Marfor answered. "She wanted to destroy the humans most. I don't see how she can do it." She ran a hand lightly, affectionately, over Nim's crest. "Lean on me, Nim. We'll walk to the human ship."

Familiar thunder turned their eyes to the sky. Their ship was riding billows of flame and smoke out of the Late Cretaceous, away from them forever.

Chapter Five

Everyone aboard the *Pegasus*, Meg and Nick in the watch pods and the others in the control room, heard the rumble of the Heesh ship's rockets in the distance. They watched the ship rise into the sky and disappear. "That's that," Carlos said. He felt depressed. "Too bad. So many opportunities wasted. The Heesh and humans could have gained much from each other."

"Or fought the worst war of all time, if creatures like Oomis run things there and could reach us," Dan commented skeptically. "We have human weeds just like her. They would love a crusade against what they would call monsters."

"I'm going to miss them," Meg said over the intercom. "We were beginning to get along well. They're no uglier than lizards or a lot of other life on Earth. I've always liked lizards because they're so close to my dinosaurs."

"We should have killed those eggs with a heavy dose of X rays before we turned them over," Allie said. "I keep pinching myself to make sure I'm still here. I've studied the chromosomes from the first Ishinol we found. I read them to indicate that they mature in two years. If half of every generation survive, there will be trillions of Ishinol in a hundred years. Did you know what you were letting loose on the world?"

"Not our world." Carlos had not told his team everything he planned. "We'll take care of that when we finish the work we came for. What's on your schedule, Dan?"

"Ferns. They're like the ones at home but different."

"I'm going to look over the site of the Heesh ship with Rusty and poke through the trash they left behind." Surely something could be learned from it. "I'll take the truck and drop you and Allie off."

Carlos drove away full of gloom over lost opportunities. "I'm tempted to destroy our pictures of the Heesh," he told Rusty. "People will think we faked them. Nobody will believe we met an alien race from an alternate world back here."

"They will if you say the aliens arrived in a flying saucer."

Carlos laughed. It was the first time he had laughed since Rusty had been captured. She always knew how to cheer him up.

"Remind me that destroying records is against regulations," he said, smiling.

"It's definitely against regulations."

He had dropped off Dan and Allie and reached the creek when he stopped as if he had seen ghosts in broad daylight. Marfor, her clothing rumpled and the down on her skin dirty, was wading toward him, laden with gear, holding her laser in one hand and supporting Nim with the other arm. Only Marfor's Necklace of Twelves gleamed with its normal soft, immaculate sheen. Nim limped. He had one arm around Marfor's neck and also carried a laser. The blue poota huddled on Marfor's shoulder.

A suicide squad? Carlos wondered. Not on foot and with a minimum of equipment, not looking as if a gang had beaten them up. "Marfor!" he exclaimed, and he helped her and Nim out of the water. He pointed up. "Why haven't you gone?"

Without a computer to translate for her, Marfor could command only a few English words, but his meaning was clear. She, too, pointed up. "Oomis," she said. "Marfor, Nim, no."

"Let me try," Rusty said. "I've been learning the language." She had pronounced Heesh words as she listened to the tapes but she hadn't used them in a dialogue. Conversations with Dorkin had always been in English, on her part, and in Heesh on his, with the computer translating. When she tried to question Marfor she discovered that her vocabulary was too limited. "I think they've been marooned but I don't understand why. We could link our transmitter to the computer aboard the ship, but let's go back there. Marfor and Nim need medical attention."

Marfor squeezed Nim's arm with relief when Carlos said "Come" and gestured to the backseat in the truck. They stopped for Allie, who exclaimed "No!" at the sight of the Heesh, and Dan, who stared, finished uprooting a fern, and shook his head as he came to the truck.

"Castaways," Rusty explained.

"With a pet?" Allie asked, pointing to the animal on Marfor's shoulder.

"Why not? Wouldn't you take your pet? Pets are a good sign. They show a liking for other animals."

"Who wants to be a Heesh pet?" Allie asked.

"That's not what I meant, and you know it. It's more likely to be the other way around. Marfor and Nim were stranded here. They can't survive long without us."

"They need help already," Carlos said. "Take a look at them. Apparently your old friend Oomis tried to get rid of them and came close to doing it."

Shipwrecked sailors, Carlos thought as Allie frowned. There's no doubt in my mind that I should rescue them, and it will be a triumph for me if I bring back these amazing aliens, but there are problems. "We'll have to call a full conference," he said.

As the truck neared the *Pegasus*, the Heesh robot came from behind it in the forest unexpectedly and scurried past it without pausing. Puzzled, Carlos speeded up the truck to follow. When the robot reached the ship, it leveled a heavy laser and burned a hole through the hull, shredding the heat-resistant tiles on the surface and turning the steel behind it into boiling vapor.

Carlos snatched his laser rifle from his shoulder. Before he could fire, Nim shouted, "Rakak!" The beam died, and the laser fell from the robot's hands. It stood silent and motionless. Nim turned to Carlos and swept his hand in a horizontal path past his neck, a sign that the robot had been deactivated.

"I think he shouted a code word to override the robot's program," Carlos said. "Let's take a closer look."

Having Dan keep his rifle ready in case the robot should suddenly revive, Carlos drove up to it. It had the look of any machine in good condition that was not in use, lifeless but ready to be brought to life again at the touch of a switch. Dan kept an eye on it while Carlos picked up its laser and turned to inspect the damage to the *Pegasus*.

A hole ten millimeters wide pierced the hull. The hole could be sealed against the loss of air in space, but full protection was needed against the white heat of friction when the ship plunged into the atmosphere again. Carlos decided what he would do to repair the damage, but first things first.

He told Meg and Nick in the watch pods what had been happening. "We heard you talking with the Heesh and saw you come back with them," Nick said. "When the robot showed up, we thought it was with them. We had no idea it was a threat to the ship."

"I understand," Carlos said. "I'm bringing the Heesh aboard. Stay on line for a conference."

First the injuries of Marfor and Nim had to be treated. Reluctantly, wondering if she would have to make a career of patching up these ugly aliens, Allie was pressed into medical service again. She disinfected cuts and scratches and put Nim's ankle under the X ray. The joint was above ground level. It appeared that the Heesh, like their nearest dinosaurian ancestors and many mammals, walked on long toes, with the foot elevated.

No fractures were found. Allie wound bandages around the ankle to strengthen it. She filed the X ray in the best medical tradition, without comment. Later, she promised herself, she would get complete X rays of both the male and female Heesh and run the two of them through more sophisticated scanners. The demands of science came before personal prejudice.

When those in the crew who were not on watch were gathered in the wardroom with the two Heesh and the translation program was spinning silently in the computer, Marfor explained her predicament. "Oomis declared me a heretic, disrespectful of the Prime Mother, which I was, and subversive. Under Heesh law she has the power to impose punishment. The existence of humans contradicts everything in which she believes, and she ached to destroy you. She wanted to bring our ship over yours with rockets flaming. I destroyed a circuit to prevent that, and she exiled me and Nim in this time."

"Then I think she tried to kill us, except that we can only guess how she managed it," Nim said. He told about seeing the flier above them and about the encounter with the triceratopses.

"I think she goaded them into attacking us, probably with laser beams," Marfor said. "She may have seen one of them crash into our truck, and she probably thinks they trampled us. Then she must have returned to our ship and sent the robot with a command to burn a hole in your hull. How serious is the damage?"

"It can be repaired," Carlos answered. "If I can't find a piece of steel in storage, I will cut one from the bulldozer blade on the max robot and weld it over the hole in the ship, then smear ceramic compound over it." He looked at her thoughtfully. "You and Nim seem to have saved our ship twice, once by keeping Oomis from flying over it in the Heesh ship and then by deactivating the robot."

"Marfor tried to help me when I was a captive," Rusty added. "We should take them with us."

Good for her, Carlos thought. I don't have to be the first to say it.

Allie stared at the ground. She knew what common decency dictated, but the Heesh brought back memories of childhood nightmares of fleeing from devils after she had heard a vivid description of hell. She had been suspicious of the Heesh from the first, afraid of them and what they might do. Treating them had been a professional duty, not an act of compassion.

"We can't abandon them among dinosaurs," Dan said, and Allie glared at him. He was remarkably altruistic after his confrontation with Oomis.

"Think of what we can learn from them!" Nick said from his pod. Meg topped him: "Think of what the world can learn! A whole new civilization is a lot more sensational than the last of the dinosaurs."

"Allie, don't you want to follow up on your patients?" Carlos asked.

"Sure," she said with resignation. "Count me in."

Carlos grinned, but he had to hear from the castaways too. "I'm willing to take you with us," he said to Marfor. "Do you want that? To be honest, the way you look bothers us. We know we look ugly to you. Do you want to be surrounded by billions of people who look like us?"

"Billions?" Marfor asked. She had a clear grasp of the magnitude of a billion, a number beyond the clear understanding of many. It made the humans sound like ants.

"There are eight billion humans on our world. We've managed to hold it to that, but we're very crowded."

"We're piled on top of each other like coffee beans in a grinder," Allie said.

Marfor, who didn't know what coffee was, stared at her, uncomprehending. "There are only four hundred million Heesh, and we feel crowded. Nevertheless I would like to see your world."

"We have only three small cabins aboard the ship, and none for you. I would have to give you quarters in storage space. It will be uncomfortable, and we'll be on short rations."

"Whereas if we stay here we will live in luxury," Marfor answered. Carlos hadn't known she was capable of irony.

"Marfor and I together can double the work I could do alone," Meg said. "Up to this period her paleontology and mine are the same. She'll have to learn my technical vocabulary, of course. It would take too much time to wait for the computer to translate everything."

"But what happens when we get home?" Nick asked. "Scientists will want to pick you apart, not literally, but study you night and day. A lot of people may hate the sight of you. Others will want to put you in a zoo. You don't belong in a zoo."

Two Heesh would be lost among eight billion strangers, Carlos thought. They would face enormous difficulties in being accepted as normal individuals, with whatever rights humans ordinarily enjoyed. What status would they have? None, except what they created for themselves.

Marfor hesitated, as if she understood the problem and was thinking it over. She whispered to Nim, who nodded. Then she said, "I will come as ambassador from my world to yours. As the ranking representative of the Heesh in this period, I have full authority to act in emergencies, and these are extraordinary circumstances. The question of future contacts between our worlds can be left open."

"A good idea if our government agrees," Carlos said. He was impressed with Marfor's speed in finding a solution that might work. "It will give you diplomatic privileges. Until then, consider yourself and Nim members of my crew."

"Thank you." Marfor hesitated. "I feel obligated to bring up one matter. I persuaded Oomis to exchange Rusty for the Prime Mother's eggs with the argument that evolution would then favor the Heesh, and humans would not exist. I don't believe that, but I don't understand how you can evolve. Do you?"

"I have a card up my sleeve," Carlos said. Marfor was silent, puzzled by the idiom, so he added, "That's an expression from a gambling game. It means I have a way to win when I ought to lose. You will understand in time."

He would not explain his plan. If he did, Marfor might sacrifice herself to ensure that there would be no humans to engage in possible conflict with the Heesh.

"I would also like to take your robot. Nim, can the program you deactivated be wiped out?"

"Easily. Programs can be displayed on a screen behind one of the plates and can be deleted."

"Can you delete all programs and disassemble the robot? I would feel more comfortable if it were in pieces." Carlos didn't want to have the thing come to life and stalk the ship like a mechanical monster.

"That will be easy too. Simple tools can handle disassembly."

"Good. We'll fix up some quarters for you and box the robot as a present for engineers at home."

"With ribbons around it," Rusty added. The Heesh needed an explanation of that expression, too. A lot of common expressions would have to be explained if the Heesh were going to understand English words that hopped into idioms whose meanings were not obvious to a stranger to American culture.

"We put gifts in boxes and wrap the boxes in paper covered with greetings," Marfor said. "Adding ribbons seems frivolous, a waste of time and material, but I like the idea. It would make gift-giving more festive."

"They were fools," Oomis said. She and Lippor and their attendant males stood outside their ship and watched a small Ishinol, only two days old, race after a mouse-sized mammal that had popped out of a hole in the ground and catch it in its claws.

The Heesh had landed two thousand years after the meteorite struck. Males had guarded the eggs for two months while they incubated, had called the matrons to watch while they hatched, and had placed morsels of meat from small local mammals within easy reach for a first meal. The Earth had recovered from devastation but mammals had scarcely begun to vary in form. The Ishinol, like the reptiles from which their line had sprung, could fend for themselves as soon as they left their shells.

"Think of it, Dorkin!" In high good humor, Lippor brushed a hand over his crest affectionately. "There are four males and four females. They have no predators to fear, if they avoid crocodiles. They can feast on mammals all day long. Each of the females should lay another batch of eggs in two years or so. If the females multiply by four times, or even two times, every two years, they will overrun the world."

"Until they are forced to eat each other," Dorkin said. He watched an Ishinol search for the entrance to a burrow and hide in weeds waiting for a mammal to emerge. Even as an infant, even covered with soft down, it was an ugly creature, not one he would want for a pet. Not one he would choose for an honored ancestor. "Then they will adapt in different forms in the eternal contest between predators and prey until one line leads to us."

"Marfor told us that's how it would happen," Lippor agreed. "How it did happen. I get mixed up watching something get started and know I've seen how it ended. Mammals will never be more than small things that run and hide."

She had a thought that she was afraid to express while Oomis was within hearing. Marfor had made this scene possible and should be watching it. Marfor had often been on her mind, a burden to her conscience, during the short period it had taken the Heesh to jump forward in time. She should try to forget her but couldn't.

"Tape this scene too," Oomis ordered. She had had pictures taken of her, alone, among the eggs as they hatched. She had picked up one of the infants, very carefully to avoid being bitten or clawed, for a close-up. Now she moved slowly toward the Ishinol that was watching a burrow, careful not to frighten it into flight, and stretched out her arms as if she, Oomis, was personally giving the world to the Ishinol.

How unjust, Lippor thought. Oomis will claim the credit that should be Marfor's. I should have known that this would happen.

She glanced at Dorkin. He was expressionless.

Using Lippor's code for access to computer memory, Dorkin had been copying audiovisual records of the expedition. From puzzling gaps in what some of them showed, Lippor assumed that Oomis had edited them to make sure that she would always appear in the best light. She wouldn't edit this one, but Dorkin would copy it anyway for completeness.

Aided by the castaways, the *Pegasus* team studied the ecology of the Late Cretaceous. Carlos was confident that the trip was already a success but he would have to report on life and extinctions at the K/T line, and he was determined to be thorough. Each day he measured progress by the quantity of data added to computer memory. There would be time later to pursue his private plan, which promised much greater consequence than all the rest of what they were doing.

Dan was quietly ecstatic at working with living plants instead of fossilized pollen and impressions of leaves. Ferns, horsetails, cycads, conifers, and many primitive flowering plants would survive the meteorite. Although different kinds of plants grew together, the angiosperms, the flowering plants, were generally nearest to the creek, especially palmettos. There should be palm trees around, but he hadn't seen any. In April magnolias showed a few inch-wide flowers scattered among the leaves, nothing like the profusion of blossoms that would become their glory in later times. Farther from the creek were dawn redwoods and tall auracarian conifers with broad crowns of leaves.

Nick collected insects, worms, and snails. Along with seeds and roots, these would keep mammals from starving at the K/T line. His greatest prize was three ammonites from the inland sea, and he was disconsolate that he could not provide a steady diet of small fishes and plankton to keep them alive in a tank during the months before they reached home. The ammonites were not the polished coils of shell that were sold to collectors but had rough surfaces. Nick found them when he dropped his trap in water more than fifty meters deep. He preserved two of them for display at home and dissected the third. It was a large Lytoceratid, chosen for its size, and he was in luck. It was a female and contained an egg sac.

Nick persuaded Carlos to let him and Meg take the flier to see what could be found in a limestone formation three hundred kilometers from the ship. "I want to make a point," he said.

He made it when they returned.

"Look at this," he told the others, holding a rock in his hand. "It contains a fossil trilobite." The fossil was about fifty millimeters long, flattened and roughly oval, with a shieldlike head, a central ridge down the thorax, and segments along both sides. "Lots of them are jumbled together. They've been in that rock for about three hundred million years. The point is that the sixty-five million years we have traveled leave ninety percent of life on Earth still in the dim past."

"Let someone else travel back and study it," Allie said. "Sixty-five million years is enough for me."

Nick's eyes took on a speculative look, focused on nothing. "We don't know why trilobites became extinct, or a lot of other creatures," he said. "There have been several mass extinctions. The more we know about them, the less likely we are to become extinct ourselves."

"I blame asteroids every time," Meg said. "Or predators. Trilobites had no way to destroy the environment."

Meg began to repeat herself with the mammals she trapped. Tiny multituberculates, with sharp batteries of teeth in jaws two centimeters long, were widespread. She caught a small condylarth of the group ancestral to both horses and cows, and a live *Purgatorius*.

Meg left the live *Purgatorius* in a cage and showed Marfor the remains of the one that had been killed by the male Ishinol. Marfor examined the rat-sized animal with more than professional interest. She had watched the tape that showed her ancestor killing it. Apparently there were no hard feelings. It had happened too far in the past and had involved two species that could be found only in that past. "Evolution can bring wondrous changes, but it's hard to believe that humans are descended from this insignificant creature," she said.

"From this or something very much like it," Meg answered. "Humans belong to an order of mammals called the primates, and there are some fifty more genera. Others have become extinct, like this one, *Purgatorius*, which is the first one known. The big toes of primates, except humans, are opposable, and usually the thumbs are too. That helps them hold on to branches when they climb. This one could, as we know, and it could run fast too."

"From this early one, primates would seem destined to spend most of their time in trees," Marfor observed. "What brought your species down on the ground?"

"Who knows? Distant ancestors came down from the trees, and we can only guess why. No one could have predicted it."

"Some kinds of Hanishan took to the trees, but none of the ancestor of the Heesh did."

Carlos walked in during the discussion. "Don't forget to show her the teeth," he said. Meg had shown them to him. Vertebrate paleontologists would be big on teeth no matter where they came from. Sometimes those were the only fossils they had to work with.

"Of course I will," Meg said. "The teeth are what let me identify this animal as *Purgatorius*. Each half of a jaw has three incisors in front, where most primates, even the early ones, have two. They are not spade-shaped like mine but come to a point. The single canine is standard. There are four premolars, compared to our two, and three molars. It has a total of forty-four teeth compared to thirty-two in humans." She pointed to the one in a cage. "We really must take this one home alive, Carlos."

"Very well," he agreed, "but only one. We don't want them to evolve all over again."

"It might be instructive. With a different environment and different competitors, who knows what would happen?"

"Only one," he repeated. "What will you do with the carcass you're looking at?"

"Freeze it for detailed dissection at home. When that's done I'll put it in a chamber with carpet beetles. The larvae will clean the bones of every bit of flesh as they feed on it. We don't go into the chamber unless we have to because there's nothing that smells worse than rotting flesh, but there's no easier way to get clean bones and teeth."

Carlos left when Meg and Marfor took a magnifying glass and settled down to the technicalities of the distinguishing characteristics of teeth as if they were two high school girls discussing a new boy in their class, except that they didn't giggle. He couldn't become fascinated by names like metacone and paracone applied to ridges on a molar.

But he felt a deeper appreciation for the problems that Marfor faced in learning the vocabulary of a new language. She had to learn not only everyday words like "come" and "go" but the technical jargon of her specialty. To direct the work of paleontologists, Carlos had learned the basics, but he had discovered that he forgot words unless he used them regularly himself.

A change in the plants that herbivores were accustomed to eating had left only a few kinds of dinosaurs to succumb to the effects of the meteorite. Meg never found the small triceratops she wanted to take home. She settled for an infant dromaeosaur, one of the last that would ever be born, and caged it behind a double wall of bars that it couldn't reach through with its sickle claws. She would give odds that it could wipe out a den of wolves.

Although Marfor and Nim helped greatly with the work and never complained about their makeshift quarters in the main equipment bay or unaccustomed food or isolation from their own kind, the humans found it harder than expected to accept them as equal members of the team. "They look like feathered orangutans," Allie said. "With those long arms they should be swinging from trees."

"They have feelings like ours," Rusty answered. She was their strongest defender. "They're smart. Look at how fast they're learning English. I'm getting to speak Heesh pretty well, and so is Carlos, but they're way ahead of us."

"You could chatter with monkeys pretty fast if you had to do it to survive," Allie answered.

Allie stopped making derisive comparisons to lesser primates when Marfor staggered them all with a remark she made after she had learned English well enough to carry on a conversation. "I've been wondering what Oomis will tell the Heesh at home about humans," Marfor said. "The knowledge could cause trouble. The cosmology she defends so fiercely has no place for other intelligent forms of life. We haven't found any life at all on planets around the stars we've visited."

Carlos looked at his crew, all stunned into silence by Marfor's casual revelation. They were scarcely breathing. He asked softly, "Have the Heesh visited the stars?"

"The six nearest stars that are like the sun," Marfor answered. "There were no water worlds like Naneg, uh, Earth. There were planets so hot that iron would melt and frozen balls of rock and planets of swirling gases but none that would support life. Nim went on one such trip when he was a technician."

"That I want to hear about, but how do you get to a star and back in a lifetime? It would take us forty years to reach one, if we could manage the logistics."

"There is a dimension that has the effect of shrinking space." Marfor interpreted Carlos's silence to mean that he didn't know what she was talking about. "Haven't you discovered that? You will soon. We learned about it before we learned to travel in time."

"Theoretically space-time has ten dimensions," Carlos said. "The only ones we have learned to use are four dimensions of space and, since encountering you, two of time."

"You've made the . . . breakthrough is the word, isn't it? Not that space jumps do much good. You find that the energy it takes has all been wasted when you get there. Who wants dead planets? After being disappointed six times, I doubt that the Heesh will try again soon. Do you agree, Nim?"

"Nobody volunteers twice," Nim said. "I was in the engine crew, with nothing to do but watch dials, which I didn't have to watch because they had alarms attached. I studied math and computers. When we reached the star we found four planets, all dead except for volcanos on one of them, and an asteroid belt about where Earth would be."

The humans eyed Nim with respect. This skinny freak with a flamboyant crest had actually circled a star.

"Nim, you'll make our astronomers break into tears," Carlos said.

"Yes," Rusty agreed, "but why were you there? Were you looking for life? Your doctrines of the Cosmic Egg seem very conservative to me. Do they have room for life off Naneg?"

"Some Heesh would say no, but others say yes. How can you limit the powers of the Cosmic Egg? Astronomers had shown that Naneg was not the center of the universe and then that our sun was off to one side of our galaxy. When they showed that there were trillions of other stars, and billions of them were like the sun, it seemed likely that many of them had planets that could support life." Nim glanced at Marfor, who remained silent. "Since we believe that the Heesh fulfill the cosmic plan, there might be Heesh on other planets too. Our trips to the stars were intended to find them. When we found no life at all, many Heesh were disappointed. Others were comforted by the thought that Naneg and the Heesh had been uniquely favored by the Cosmic Egg."

"Now we must make room for humans in the cosmic plan," Marfor said. "Knowledge of your existence will be bitter medicine for many Heesh, but there are no theoretical objections."

But if Heesh physical science was ahead of that of humanity, their biological science lagged. The *Pegasus* team discovered that for the second time when Nim grew listless and developed a high temperature. He started to shed down from his skin. Allie took a sample of blood and ran it through her analyzer.

"He has measles," she told Carlos. "We've all been immunized but most of us carry some of the virus around with us. He picked it up from one of us. It's brand new to the Heesh, I suspect. It could kill him, except that I can knock it out."

"Come out swinging," Carlos said. "Then you'd better immunize Marfor."

Impressed before by the treatment of her own illness, Marfor was impressed again by the antibiotic that Allie synthesized to bring Nim relief and the antibody templates she added to stimulate his immune system into controlling any future outbreak of the virus. "We have medicines," Marfor said, "and we have vaccination, but nothing that will knock out a disease so fast when it has taken hold."

Allie found herself teaching biology. She decided that she enjoyed having such eager students as Marfor and Nim, no matter that they looked like goblins. Their knowledge of biology was about that of humans of the early twentieth century. They knew about chromosomes but hadn't begun to map genes, whereas Allie's computerized equipment could churn out a map of a hundred thousand genes in two hours and start running off the nucleotide sequences.

The Heesh knew nothing about determining the structure of a virus to synthesize a counteragent.

"We had to learn it in self-defense," Allie told them. "About a hundred years ago everyone was worried about germ warfare. We had to learn how to cure any kind of brand-new disease, along with some nasty old ones, in a hurry."

Warfare? The entire *Pegasus* crew sat fascinated during this discussion. The Heesh had violence, and they had police and censorship under the Hall of Guardians, but they didn't have warfare. They had developed on one continent and spread gradually to the others, always united by the doctrine of the Cosmic Egg. They had developed weapons to defend themselves against predatory beasts and then to advance against them, and they had no qualms about hunting wild animals, but they had no warfare.

"Now you face the curse of the dominant species," Dan said. "Overpopulation. A lot of human wars have been started by men who wanted more land, more wealth, and, although I hate to say it, more women."

Nim laughed. The humans found his "Ork! Ork! Ork!" irritating. "You don't have overpopulation when females run things," he said. "Males tend the eggs and raise the children, but females have to carry the eggs for four months. That was a handicap back when they were swinging clubs and spears, and they still think they have better things to do. Any male who tried to force himself on a female would be lucky to live through the battering she gave him."

"Do your police include males?" Allie asked.

"No. A male isn't strong enough to subdue an unruly female," Marfor answered.

"That's an excuse repeated so often that many Heesh believe it," Nim said. "The truth is that ranking females don't trust males to enforce against other males the laws and customs that keep females in power."

"Are you claiming they would? The guardians have whips," Marfor explained. "Sometimes they slash the crest of a male who gives them trouble. They cut part of it right off. I wouldn't trust a male to do that."

"Disfigure another male? Of course not," Nim said.

"Some males will have their crests slashed if they react the way I think they will when they find out that a human male can have females under his command," Marfor said.

One night Carlos found Marfor and Nim sitting together silently staring at the stars. He sensed that they were depressed and asked if anything was wrong.

"We are trying to persuade ourselves that the adventure thrust upon us makes up for isolation from our own kind," Marfor answered. "Most of all, I miss my mother and daughter. They will think I'm dead when Oomis brings the ship back without me. I would give all the excitement of seeing Earth if I could be there when my granddaughter is born."

Carlos saw her sentiments as a bond with humans, and he sympathized. "I'm sure you will get back home," he assured her. "There must be a way to do it."

At the end of two months the Heesh remained curiosities to the *Pegasus* team but had been accepted as different but equal. Growing acquaintance with them had made time pass swiftly. Sometimes, when Nick played his guitar, Nim kept the beat by drumming on a cup with a spoon. But the Heesh couldn't sing. They could chant but used only a few tones, for their small ears were not adapted to a wide range of sounds, and they were completely incapable of harmony. When they tried to sing, their voices rasped, out of tune.

But Marfor made Rusty envious after looking at a painting Rusty had made of the creek running through the forest at sunset. "You draw as well as anyone on Naneg," Marfor said, "but why don't you use a full range of colors?"

"I thought I did. There's everything in that sunset from violet to red."

"The spectrum goes farther. Let me use your light pen." Marfor took a sheet of treated plastic and slid the control button of the pen along its track continuously to paint bands of every color that Rusty had used, the primary colors and their combinations, and others at each end of the scale. "We like these," she said, pointing to bands that Rusty couldn't see.

Instruments aboard the ship confirmed Rusty's assumption that the Heesh could see colors that reflected infrared and ultraviolet light.

"I wish I could do that," she told Marfor, "but it's what the painter expresses that counts, not the colors. Some powerful art has been painted in black or gray."

"Let's not have a debate about what constitutes art," Carlos said. He had been through that with Rusty before, and he sensed that she was becoming defensive.

"It's nearly time to launch," he said one day. "We're cutting it close. I'm going to declare a holiday first."

Ever since he had been chosen to lead the *Pegasus* team, Carlos had cherished a wish that he could try fly-fishing in dinosaur country. He had cast artificial flies in the waters of Norway, Scotland, Canada, and Idaho for salmon and trout. To escape from the niggling demands of the daily routine, to find time for contemplation, there was nothing like keeping a lazy eye on the surface of the water to catch the ripple of a fish rising and trick it into striking at a hook concealed in thread and a bit of feather. In a different season he would use a wet fly, drawing it beneath the surface.

Meg had found salmon-like fishes in Hell Creek. Nick had found dragonfly nymphs nearly ready to emerge from the water, split their thoraxes along the back, wriggle out with nearly adult bodies, and spread their wings. The nymphs were food for the fishes. Therefore, Carlos reasoned, the fishes would snap at artificial flies resembling the nymphs.

Fishes were unpredictable and might bite at or ignore anything. Nick helped Carlos design a nymph that did not yet have the elongated body of an adult dragonfly nor full wings. Carlos had brought a fly rod and reel but no wading boots. Experience had taught him that dragonflies worked best along the shores of lakes, not in the running water of streams, and a pool beside Hell Creek looked promising. Meg and Nick, the experts, concurred. Fish were feeding on nymphs there.

The obvious problem was to avoid offering himself as bait to a dinosaur while he was oblivious to everything but fish. Ordinarily he would seek solitude to savor to the full the lonely pleasure of the sport and to prevent others from frightening a fish. Now he needed a guard. He had made the rule that members of the team should travel only in pairs, and it was a sound rule. Rusty could stand watch. He could trust her to keep quiet while he was absorbed and to spring into action with her laser as needed.

"Guard me for a couple of hours, and I'll return the favor when you want to sketch something," he told her.

"Fine. I'll try to watch the forest and not you."

The two of them left the others, including Marfor and Nim, to do what they wished, which turned out to be more of what they had been doing. They took the truck to the creek and walked along its tangled shore to the pond. For an hour Carlos worked his way along its bank, forgetting about dinosaurs, the Heesh, and everything but outwitting a wily prey. Repeated casts brought not a nibble. Refusing to concede that a fish was smarter than he was, he changed his carefully designed fly to one that was small and bright and resembled nothing that had ever lived. At his first cast he felt a tug and watched the line spin out. When he reeled it in he had an eight-inch fish, which he flipped ashore.

Rusty cheered. "Write it up," she urged him. "You'll be the envy of every angler in the world."

How true, he thought smugly.

When they returned to the ship he presented his prize to Meg. "Please mount it for me. This specimen goes on my wall. Scientists can eat their hearts out."

Before they left Hell Creek, Carlos placed a radioactive beacon at the grave of the male Ishinol. "I'll need to find this place again," he told Rusty.

When the *Pegasus* reached an altitude of twenty-five thousand kilometers in space, Carlos held the ship north of what would become the Caribbean Sea. Humans and Heesh drifted into places behind windows to watch the most awesome event in many millions of years of Earth's history.

They saw a warning glint of light reflected from the sun as a mass of rock twelve kilometers in diameter hurtled earthward at seventy-one thousand kilometers an hour. "There's more than one!" Rusty shouted with excitement as a telescope focused on the object. Six rocks the size of large meteorites, more than a kilometer in diameter, and a few smaller ones accompanied the main asteroid at various distances from it. They raced toward Earth together like a barrage of mountains hurled in a cosmic bombardment. The crew at the windows waited for what they knew would happen.

Light flared as the asteroid followed its shock wave through the air and rose to a temperature hotter than the surface of the sun. The smaller objects burned as brightly as they aimed at different places on an Earth that rotated as if trying to dodge them, but these displays were lost in the hellish radiance of the main impact. The asteroid plunged into a shallow sea, and a fireball rose from the planet. Molecules ripped to ions spread glowing plasma through the highest reaches of the atmosphere. A pall spread over the Earth, a shroud of steam from the sea and debris torn from bedrock and from the disintegration of the asteroid and its companions. Dust and darkness gradually encircled the globe.

Rusty cleared her throat. "Could we survive what's happening now? Earthquakes, tidal waves, volcanos, forest fires, hurricanes that could blow down a mountain. Soon dust will blot out the sun and the cold will come."

"Those furry little ancestors of ours were tough," Allie said.

"If we had been left behind, I suppose Nim and I would have tried to find a cave, or dug one, for refuge, but we would have had to be lucky to survive," Marfor said.

"To survive not only the impact but the deadly competition for food that will follow," Nim added gravely.

"What would we have done if you hadn't been able to repair the hole the robot burned in the ship?" Nick asked Carlos.

"Fill the water tank and stock up on food, such as it is. We wouldn't need a cave. The rounded cone of the ship's hull could stand tornados without blowing over, and it's fireproof. An earthquake could shake us down, but an earthquake could also bring the roof of a cave down on our heads." He smiled. "And we would pray around the clock."

He looked at the gray-brown cloak of dust blanketing the Earth below them. "We'll take a look at the damage and see how animals are doing after things have settled down. We'll find out how they came through without our technical resources. First we will return to Hell Creek, two years earlier than our first landing."

"Why will you do that?" Marfor asked.

"I may have a surprise for you." Ever since exchanging the eggs for Rusty he had had a plan. Now he would act.

The patchwork on the hull held up as Carlos brought the *Pegasus* through the atmosphere at white heat and put it down in the same clearing it would occupy two years later. It was hard to believe that this deceptively peaceful forest, hiding the battles for life within it, would be destroyed by the holocaust he had seen from space.

"Marfor, Nim, stay aboard with Meg and Nick," he ordered. "I'm going to take the flier out with Rusty, Dan, and Allie." He had picked the last two because they were the best shots with laser rifles. Mystifying Rusty, he had her carry two nets.

He flew them to the sand bank on which the Prime Mother had laid her eggs before being killed. "I think she would have returned to a familiar nesting site, the one in which she was born just about now," he said. "If I'm wrong, we may have a long search ahead."

Looking above the sand, he saw an unnaturally round arrangement of dead leaves. "Like the lid on a pot," he said, and landed near them. "Dan, climb out and see if there's anything under those leaves."

Dan brushed leaves aside and uncovered eight eggs twice the size of hens' eggs. "Break an egg and see what's in it," Carlos said.

Dan picked an egg up and tried to crack it with a stroke from his hunting knife. The shell was leathery, not brittle, and didn't crack, so he carefully gashed it. A neck stretched up from a small creature inside the egg, and a head turned toward him.

"It was ready to hatch," Dan called to the others. Seizing the neck behind the head, to avoid being bitten, he ran his other hand over the hatchling's scrawny body. It was wet but he could feel feathery down. "It's an Ishinol!"

"Watch out!" Allie shouted. "The mother's coming!"

Dan saw a stenonychosaur, nearly as long as he was tall, coming from the trees. He dropped the egg and the creature still in it and grabbed the laser slung over his shoulder.

"Don't shoot!" Carlos shouted. "Get back in the flier out of the way."

Cursing, feeling like bait, Dan scrambled into the flier. Nick slammed the door behind him. Dan saw Carlos taping a scene and turned to watch.

The stenonychosaur snatched the newborn Ishinol out of its egg with the three clawed fingers of one hand. Evidently she did not recognize it as one of her offspring. She crunched the neck with her teeth and tossed it aside.

"It's a mutant," Allie said. "To her it's a monstrosity."

The other eggs began to hatch. A claw would poke a hole through a shell from beneath and rip a gash through which a head would appear, followed by the body. Watching the eggs, the slim dinosaur went about killing the Ishinol one by one, but she took enough time to examine each one that two of them had a chance to skitter out of her reach.

"Rusty, watch where that one goes," Carlos said, pointing. "I'll track the other one."

Both of the newborn Ishinol dug burrows into the sand and disappeared from view.

"Now you can shoot mommy, Dan," Carlos said. "Rusty, you and I will go down and cover the openings to those hiding places with nets. When we're ready, Allie, heat up the sand with your laser and drive them into the nets."

It was done in minutes. Where eight eggs had rested in the sun there remained eight broken shells and six small ugly bodies. The two surviving Ishinol struggled in nets, trying to rip free.

On returning to the ship Carlos took in each hand a net that held an Ishinol. "Marfor, I have a surprise for you, a gift," he said. "I think we have here your Prime Mother and its mate."

Marfor was at a loss as to what to say. "But they're dead," she began, in confusion, then, "No, because this is earlier. They just hatched, didn't they." She stared at the scrawny bodies and at jaws gaping to be fed or to bite. "What in the name of the Egg will I do with them?"

"That may depend on whether I find something else. For the time being we'll keep them in a cage. And find something to feed them."

"Something with lots of minerals and vitamins," Allie said ironically. "The Prime Mother deserves the best."

"More than you realize," Marfor said. "Nim and I will take care of her."

Chapter Six

Oomis cursed Marfor as she watched Lippor prepare to land the ship at home. What a triumphant return she could have had if she had been able to sweep across the city, noisily visible, trumpeting her return to everyone! The only announcement that she could make before landing now was a message by radio. Marfor had made horizontal flight at low altitudes impossible. Rockets thundered during the landing, but their deafening notice of arrival ended too soon, and it occurred at the spaceport, out of hearing from the city.

At least Oomis had returned with the remains of the Prime Mother, which she would have to say had been killed by a demonic alien. But she, Oomis, had collected the remains, and she had cleverly seized the alien to trade her for the Ishinol eggs to ensure the evolution of the Heesh. Marfor and her attendant male had then taken the truck outside the ship for some unexplained reason. Unfortunately a triceratops had killed them. Let them be recorded as martyrs to science.

"Attention, everyone," Oomis announced. "No one will make any statements about our search. Our activities are privileged information for announcement solely by the Matriarchy." Which will rely on my version, she thought with satisfaction. "Because you endured hardships, you may have compensated with fantasies about what you thought happened. Any wild talk will cause your immediate detention in a mental hospital. If friends ask you about the search, say that it was routine and you were told it was successful but you don't know the details. Are there any questions?" She looked at Lippor, Haban, Dorkin, and the techs with her sternest expression. "No? Lippor, deploy the ramp. I will lead the way out."

Haban taped the triceratops destroying Marfor's truck, Oomis thought. I have deleted segments showing my laser beams goading the triceratopses. Haban is the only one who knows that I was involved. Very soon, I think, Haban will have to be silenced forever. I will have the pleasure of choosing an attendant male to replace him.

A senior matron from launch headquarters drove to the ramp to meet Oomis and congratulate her. "Where's Marfor?" she asked. "Did you find the Prime Mother? I want to hear all about everything."

"Marfor lost her life. Beyond that, I will report to the supreme matriarch first."

"Of course, of course," the senior matron said glumly.

Oomis took Haban, Lippor, and Dorkin and drove to the Hall of the Matriarchy. She wanted the other three to be with her so that she could intimidate them, if necessary, into confirming all that she reported. Where the techs went did not concern her. Probably to their homes, wherever those hovels might be.

Word of their arrival having been sent ahead, Oomis and her party were admitted to a reception room to see Supreme Matriarch Tellima immediately. Haban and Dorkin carried, concealed in a box, the corpse of the Prime Mother that the robot had recovered from the humans. Two aides, both senior matrons, waited with the matriarch.

"The spaceport director told me that Marfor died during the search," Tellima said. She glanced at the box as if it might contain the body of Marfor, but it was too small. "I am sorry to hear that, but I am glad to see you back. What is your report?"

"The Prime Mother is dead, too, but I saw to it that her eggs hatched to ensure the evolution of the Heesh."

"Do you mean that you found the Prime Mother, but she is dead?" Tellima asked with agitation.

"Yes, Your Supremacy." As a mid-level matron, Oomis had not seen much of the supreme matriarch in the past, but she knew her reputation as a decisive administrator who did not hesitate to use her power. Now she was upset by the

death of the Prime Mother and might want to make somebody pay for it. Nevertheless, Oomis was not intimidated.
She had chosen her course and followed it with confidence.
"We encountered disgusting aliens, who had come from a
world we do not know on a search of their own. One of
them killed the Prime Mother. I recovered her remains,
which are in that box."

"Open the box."

Haban flung himself on the box to open it. Tellima
looked without expression at the wiry body, which Oomis
had had cleaned and straightened out to lie as if at peace.
"So that is the Prime Mother," Tellima said. "What happened to the alien that killed her?"

"I captured her and traded her for the Prime Mother's
eggs. I carried those to safety and saw to their hatching to
ensure the evolution of our race."

"You did?" Tellima said with surprise. "I cannot think
of a more important service, Oomis. Do you have tapes of
the search for the Prime Mother?"

"Yes, your supremacy."

"I will review them with you, and learn what you can
tell me about the aliens. Lippor, do you have anything to
add?"

"No, Your Supremacy." Once again, Lippor thought, she
had taken the coward's course. She could have said that it
was Marfor who arranged to trade the alien for the eggs.
Now she was committed to Oomis's story. It hurt to have
Dorkin witness a silence that was the same as a lie.

Lippor glanced wordlessly at Dorkin. She had come upon
him using her terminal to make copies of recordings in the
main computer. If she had reported him, she would have lost
him, so she had merely asked quietly what he was doing.
"It's for your friend Marfor," he told her. "You couldn't
help her back there but you can protect her memory."

He was not telling her everything on his mind, Lippor
sensed, but he was right in guessing that she felt she
owed a debt to Marfor. She felt guilty at having agreed
to Marfor's abandonment, and she hoped that the chance
to make amends would come. She was glad that Dorkin
had a set of tapes.

* * *

Hell Creek was scarcely recognizable when Carlos had Rusty land the *Pegasus* there again, two months after the meteorite had struck. The creek trickled through mud and the rotting debris of vegetation. A few trees, stripped of leaves and pointing broken branches into the air, still stood. All that remained of others was jagged splintered trunks and the branches that had been torn from them. Some green leaves had appeared, but most plants looked brown and dead. It was hazy, for dust thrown into the sky by the impact and by volcanoes had not yet settled, and it was very chilly for a summer day.

Rusty's instruments reported that hurricane winds had blown as hard as 250 kilometers an hour. Many creatures must have been killed by falling trees or flying branches. Others had drowned in floods from heavy rains. Temperatures had dropped almost to freezing as dust blocked the rays of the summer sun.

"It will be years before the climate returns to normal," she said, "but we're past the worst of it. Any life that survived until now is likely to last, and to adapt."

"It will be hard to find animals that did survive," Meg said. "Cold-blooded dinosaurs like triceratops didn't have a chance. Warm-blooded ones like the dromaeosaur had no insulation and lost heat faster than their metabolisms could generate it. The mammals probably dug burrows as shelters to conserve heat. They'll still be in hiding."

"What would have happened to the Prime Mother and her eggs if we hadn't intervened?" Marfor asked.

"Assuming that the eggs hatched, I think the young Ishinol would have made it."

"So," Marfor said contemplatively, "if humans and Heesh had not come back to this time, only the Heesh would have evolved."

Carlos grinned at her. "Meaning that the humans created their own destiny? It's not that simple. I doubt that there was time for the Prime Mother's eggs to hatch before the meteorite struck. I'll explain my theory of what happened, but I want to show you something first."

He drove the truck and took the max robot to the site of

the male Ishinol's grave. Dan and Allie stayed on watch, "In case more strangers show up," he told them. Rusty, Marfor and Nim, and Nick and Meg joined him in the truck. It was hard going, even for the max, which cleared a path for the truck through tangles of trees and branches splintered by hurricanes. They passed the skeleton of a triceratops and the scattered bones of a hadrosaur. Both dinosaurs had been killed in violent storms or had died of cold and hunger and had been picked clean by famished predators.

Carlos looked at the jumble of branches and leaves that covered the patch of ground that the radioactive beacon pinpointed. "I wonder if anyone ever dug a hole before in the hope that he wouldn't find anything," he said. "Here goes."

The max brushed the litter aside, and a chain of toothed buckets ground into the earth.

"You aren't digging up my fossil, are you?" Marfor asked in alarm.

"Your fossil isn't there. It's trying to get out of a cage aboard my ship. I intend to prove it to you."

After the max had dug well below the level at which Nim had laid out the bones of the male Ishinol, after Nim and Nick had dug into all sides of the pit with pick and shovel without uncovering any remains, Carlos drove them all back to the ship.

"This is how I see it," he explained. "All of us guessed that humans and Heesh existed at the same period on different time tracks. The tracks came together at one point in the past. How could that happen? An event that started one time track should eliminate the other. How could both tracks not only occur but overlap? In short, what was it that we didn't know about time?"

"It's as if time can impose a will of its own." Nim spoke slowly. "The reasons that both expeditions came to this savage period became less important than imperatives we discovered after we arrived." Nim did not know the English word "imperatives," but the computer translated it from the word he used. "The Heesh had to save the eggs to ensure their future. The humans had to prevent the Ishinol from laying eggs to ensure their own future. You did that when you went farther back and caught the Prime Mother and her mate right out of their shells."

Carlos nodded in agreement but said, "There's more to it. I had to stop thinking about normal linear time. Separate linear tracks required a second dimension of time. Then both Heesh and humans created loops in time. That must be in a third dimension, which I guessed existed. The Heesh created one loop when they jumped ahead, skipping a segment of time, to leave the Ishinol to evolve. We created another when we jumped back to block the Ishinol. Both of us had to travel outside of linear time and two-dimensional time to do it. The two tracks had to meet where both futures were possible. Then the Heesh carried their stream out of normal time, like running a creek through an aqueduct, and started it again by taking their eggs to the future. We diverted the time stream to a different channel, the one we are in now, the one without Heesh." He added quickly, "Except for our guests."

"I have a thought," Marfor said. "There should be a way to cross from one time stream to another. If there is, and if Nim and I can return to our world, I know what to do with the Prime Mother."

Carlos almost laughed. If a way could be found to travel sideways in time between Earth and Naneg, there would be more important things to worry about than the Prime Mother. Well, perhaps not, in the view of the Heesh.

Furious but methodical work filled a month. There was not enough time to find and list every kind of plant and animal life that had survived the collision of the meteorite and its aftermath, but the tally had to be as comprehensive as possible. What had happened in this small corner of Earth had to illuminate changes around the world as a whole. The habitats of survivors of the catastrophe were investigated thoroughly. It was important to know how they had survived.

Very few specimens were kept alive aboard the ship, which wouldn't have enough food for more than a few of them. Others were killed and preserved for study during the long voyage home and afterward. The stomachs of animals would be opened to determine what they had been eating, and detailed anatomical and cellular studies would follow. Complete studies would take years.

Meg searched without success for another *Purgatorius.* "We know that they survived the meteorite," she said. "One fossil specimen was found near here, and I think there were three others in the same general area. Reptilians, especially dinosaurs, are my specialty. I've kept up with mammals but I don't remember all the sites."

To the surprise of everyone, one dinosaur was found alive. A stenonychosaur, emaciated, near death from starvation, rose on its hind legs to its full two-meter height and reached out with its claws when Meg and Nick found it hiding in a nest it had made beneath a fallen tree and broken branches. It was too weak to leap at them. They threw a net of steel links over it and took it back to the ship. This specimen would be kept alive.

"It may be the mother of the Ishinol," Rusty said. "The world will expect at least one live dinosaur from an expedition that went to find them. This and the dromaeosaur we have give us two. Two living horrors."

"Plus we have some great tapes of dinosaurs charging at us," Carlos added.

"Some mammals must have been caught in the early days after the impact, but they were small, and most of them hid in burrows where dinosaurs couldn't dig them out," Meg told the crew. "Some mammals crept out at night to chew twigs and feed on the inner layer of bark or nibble the large seeds of cycads. Others ate other seeds or roots or worms and insects and larvae underground."

"There's a lot of that left," Nick added. "Lots of nematodes, which I don't think are much good for food, and other worms. Insects are almost indestructible, with eggs and larvae as well as adults, although cold weather would kill a lot of them."

"But the mammals were still hungry," Meg said. "The ones we trapped came out to devour our bait."

"Plants are coming back," Dan reported. "Besides the seeds, I've found green shoots."

Nick found snails and small crustaceans in the creek. He dragged his trap through the sea at different depths but found no more ammonites, not even shells, which had sunk to the bottom. There were oysters, clams and brachiopods, sea stars, sponges, a few fishes, including a small shark, and a greatly depleted variety of plankton.

Microscopic life on land, particularly underground, had fared better than in the sea, where so much depended on sunlight that had been cut off by the shroud of dust around the world.

One prize discovery was a two-foot crocodile in the swamp near the landing site. "We have a lot of fossil crocodiles, but this is a new species," Meg said gleefully. When Rusty expressed surprise that a crocodile had been found in what would become Montana, Meg said, "North America swarmed with crocodiles. I found some in Colorado while I was a student."

Nim helped collect specimens while Marfor worked with Meg and Allie in the lab. Space was cramped, but Marfor had learned to use human scientific equipment and to stay out of the others' way. Her three-fingered hands were deft. "I don't think I could have handled all the stuff we're bringing in without you," Allie told her one day. She had stopped reacting to the Heesh as creatures out of a nightmare.

"I like the work," Marfor answered. She looked at a genetic map for a shrew-sized multituberculate and became thoughtful. "I must find a way to get back to Naneg. There's a lot of data here that the Heesh don't have."

Carlos checked the patch on the hull of the *Pegasus* and added a layer of ceramic coating. He looked at the Heesh robot, its arms and legs disassembled by Nim. Engineers at home would learn a lot from that contraption. He checked water and food supplies. With two persons added to the crew and live animals in cages, everyone would have to live on short rations until he could land a few million years up the road and gather fresh food. Finally, when time was growing short, he decided that the collectors had done about as much as they could and the ship would never be more ready.

"Strap in for lift-off," he told them one day. "We're headed home."

Carlos crossed the nightside of Earth when he brought the *Pegasus* back to his own time. Lights glowed cheerfully from cities that covered hundreds of square miles in the blackness below the ship. Until he saw them, Carlos didn't realize how much he had missed lights outside the ship during the dark nights of the Age of Dinosaurs, when neither the pale moon nor the distant stars could cheer a small band of humans in lonely isolation, when only volcanos had glowed against clouds in the distance, and now and then streaks of lightning had searched angrily for visitors alien to the age. Lights were the symbol of civilization. He was home.

"We did it!" Rusty exclaimed. "We got all we went for and a big bonus." She took Marfor's hand. "I can't wait to show you Earth!"

"So many lights," Marfor said as she and Nim stared at the world below them. "So many humans." How much better it was to return as natives, as the humans did, than to arrive as strangers with unknown problems to face. It was an adventure with an unpredictable outcome. Nim obviously shared her concern, for he was staring at Earth very solemnly. Glancing at her, sharing her mood, he managed an encouraging smile.

Nick put an arm around Meg and said, "I'm glad we went, but I'm more glad to be back. I don't think I want to do it again."

"Not even to see the last days of the trilobites?" she asked, and squeezed his hand. "We have to celebrate when we land. It was a great trip, and I wouldn't have missed it."

"Nothing to it," Allie said. "Just like riding a seesaw, sixty-five million years down and sixty-five million back up again."

"It was only the beginning," Dan said. "I'll be glad to get back to my lab and my office. We filled computer memory with data to study. Our colleagues will be fighting to look over the data and see the specimens we brought back.

We have reports to write. We'll be busy the rest of our lives."

"Starting after the party," Allie said.

Rusty looked at the Heesh. She admired their bravery at facing circumstances entirely new to their race, and she guessed their doubts. "Our friends will be very busy too. We must help them all we can. Let's get started. Carlos, can we put this horse in the barn?"

Carlos had her take the ship to a good reentry position and radioed to the base. "*Pegasus* reporting. Request permission to land."

"Glad you're back, *Pegasus*," the answer came. "The patrol spotted you in orbit. Your landing pad is clear. Come on down. We're eager to hear all about your trip."

Carlos recognized the voice of Wallcroft, the director of the Time Project, and said, "The expedition was unusually successful. Will there be media coverage for the landing?"

"Sure. Going back so far in time is big, and a lot of people are hung up on dinosaurs. I'll get the word out immediately."

Carlos paused. The world was about to hear much more than it could have expected. Some of it was so sensational that people at the highest levels of authority would want to hear it first and not be caught by surprise at public reaction. Carlos knew that he had earned high commendation for what the *Pegasus* Expedition had accomplished. He did not want to spoil his career by annoying his superiors. More important, he did not want to jeopardize a good reception for Marfor and Nim. Their arrival should be announced with due concern for protocol. Nobody knew who might be listening in on his radio exchange with Wallcroft.

"Sir," he said, "I recommend that we go to a voice scrambler."

"Agreed. Code Grasshopper."

When he had pressed keys for the encipherment of audio transmission, Carlos continued. "We have a lot more to tell about than dinosaurs. We can report intelligent aliens."

"From the Late Cretaceous? What are you talking about?"

"I happened to pick up a couple of intelligent aliens

along the way." Carlos liked to shake people up with an offhand remark. "I have them aboard."

The director answered sourly. "Great. You may be lynched. We'll need guards to protect them. After all the sci-fi horror films they've seen, with aliens invading Earth and adding humans to their diet or taking over their minds, most people are ready to kill an alien on sight. Tell me more about the ones you have."

Carlos decided not to pitch the full load of hay on Wallcroft yet. "These aliens are friends. They're people, except that they look peculiar and are covered with down."

"Well, keep them aboard until we can find out more about them. Can you land in six hours?"

"I can and will. *Pegasus* out."

Carlos looked at Rusty, who was frowning, and then at Marfor, whose wide mouth was turned down at the corners in the expression he had come to know meant serious concern. "Sorry, Marfor," he said. "You have run into human intolerance for anything that's different. We'll work to overcome that."

The computer calculated the course and cut in the landing rockets to bring the *Pegasus* down on its target while Carlos monitored the descent. A crowd of people able to assemble on six hours' notice, more of them than he had expected, stood behind the security line, and cameras had been set up. A return from the Age of Dinosaurs was indeed a popular sensation. Wait until people learned what else he had.

Before the landing pad had cooled completely, a van came from the operations building. "Come to the head of the ramp and wave with joy and triumph, then go back inside and hibernate while I learn the score," Carlos said to his crew. He waved with the others, went down to the van, and rode silently beside the driver to the office of the project director.

Wallcroft shook Carlos's hand vigorously and took his arm to propel him to a chair. "I suppose you're full of your trip," he said. "I want to hear all about it, but the monsters you brought back have first priority."

"I didn't bring monsters. They are Grade-A aliens. You'll enjoy meeting them." Carlos grinned before springing his next surprise. "One of them has been to the stars."

"What! Are you sure? We can't travel to the stars. Their technology must be way ahead of ours." If Wallcroft hadn't been shaken up before, he was now. "That could mean a lot of trouble. Don't let word of it get out. Hold on while I call the president."

"You can tell him that the second alien has high rank and is here as an ambassador."

"From aliens we've never heard of. Yes, that will interest him." Wallcroft made his phone call. He learned that the president already knew that the *Pegasus* had landed. After telling him that it had brought aliens with a high technology, one of whom claimed to be an ambassador, he received orders and passed them on to Carlos.

"Go back aboard and stay until the president's representatives get here. Get ready to put on a show when you debark."

Carlos returned to the *Pegasus* to brief his crew and the Heesh. "I hope the president's people hurry," Meg said. "I wouldn't trade our trip for all the fossils ever dug up, but I'm excited about getting home, and I'm eager to see my family and friends. I hate waiting."

Nick took her hand. "We must pay our dues to bureaucracy."

"You're waiting because of Nim and me," Marfor said. "It doesn't sound like we'll be welcome."

"Make yourself welcome," Carlos told her. "Remember, you are here as an ambassador from the Heesh to establish friendly relations between us and your government."

"Ork!" Marfor snorted. "As soon as I find my government."

"Our best brains will want to pump you about how to get to the stars, Nim."

"All I know is that it can be done. The math was too advanced for me, and I don't know the engineering."

"You can give us a start. When we know something is possible, we'll find a way to do it."

The two Heesh were subdued, plainly worried about an

unfriendly reception, and Carlos tried to cheer them up. "You two will be celebrities, and I predict that you'll be popular."

"Not with everybody," Allie warned. "It took a long time to win me over."

"The poota will help," Rusty said. "People like cuddly little pets, and they've never seen one that can fly."

"Pigeons, maybe?" Meg asked. "Parakeets?"

"Pigeons and parakeets aren't really pets."

In two hours Carlos was told that an undersecretary of state and a special assistant to the president had landed at the base. "They want to see the aliens right away," Wallcroft radioed, using the scrambler. "You have to parade them past the media first. Don't expect cheers. The media get nasty when they're kept waiting this long and all they get from me is 'No comment.' Put on a good show, but not a word about technology. The president will be watching. Come on out now."

Reporters and cameras and guards had been brought near the foot of the ramp. "Wait until I set the stage for you," Carlos told Marfor and Nim. He led his crew, all of them in blue work coveralls with the Time Project patch on the left breast, all of them grinning, to the foot of the ramp. None of them knelt to kiss the ground. He introduced them one by one, for many people might be watching now and millions would see later broadcasts after they heard what had happened, and they needed to be reminded of names forgotten while the crew was gone.

"I am happy to report a successful mission," he announced. "This team has learned much about the world of sixty-five million years ago and what led to the world of today. We can fill in many previously unavoidable gaps in scientific studies. We also have some surprises that may be of even greater importance. First I want to show you two live dinosaurs and something brand-new."

At his signal Dan and Nick returned to the ship and drove the truck down the ramp. It held three cages covered with plastic sheets. Like a magician revealing a pretty girl in what his audience had been led to believe was an empty box, Carlos whipped the cover off the cage that held the dromaeosaur. Full of strength and vigor after a diet of assorted mammals plucked from different eras during stops on the voyage to the present, it made a gratifying screech and leaped to claw at its bars.

"Dinosaurs are supposed to be large, and this one grows no larger than a man, but its claws would slice up a tiger," Carlos said. "It's a dromaeosaur." He waited while the cameras took close-ups. Uncovering the second cage, he said, "Here's another one about the same height, but it's slimmer and it's very fast. It's a stenonychosaur. It has a big brain for a dinosaur. Notice the claws. You wouldn't want to let this one run loose on the streets either."

Carlos was enjoying his performance as a showman. Give the crowd a moment of suspense. "In this other cage, we have two creatures descended from dinosaurs like the one you just saw. We didn't know they had ever existed. As you will see, they are covered with down, like feathers."

He uncovered the third cage. The two young Ishinol, a third of a meter long by now and slim but no longer scrawny, rose on their hind legs and faced the cameras.

"What are they?" a reporter asked.

"Ishinol," Carlos answered, as if that one word could explain everything.

"Are those baby dinosaurs?"

"No. There are other differences, but the down is the most apparent, like feathers on a bird. The Ishinol, like birds, are descended from dinosaurs."

"Where did you get the name for them?"

This was the big moment. "From friends whom you will now meet," Carlos answered. "I have saved our most important discovery for the last. We encountered another intelligent race." He intentionally avoided the word aliens. "They were on a mission of their own. Two of them returned with us. I have the honor of presenting Her Excellency, Senior Matron Marfor, ambassador of the Heesh, and her deputy, Nim."

Marfor and Nim appeared at the top of the ramp on cue and stood there while the cameras zoomed in on them. They wore short-sleeved shirts, so that their down would show, and long pants and boots. Marfor's Necklace of Twelves glittered on her chest, and the poota rode on her shoulder. Nim had oiled his crest lightly so that his red-and-yellow ridge of feathers glistened. Nothing disguised faces that might frighten humans. They waited calmly under what they must have known was the astonished and uneasy gaze of millions.

"Your Excellency, would you care to say a few words?" Carlos asked.

Marfor raised her hands and crossed them, palms up, in the gesture of greeting. Carlos knew that the three fingers of each hand would be distinct. "Greetings to Earth from the Heesh," she said in her baritone voice. Her wide jaw and mouth gave the words a slight accent, but they were clear. "I hope that our two peoples will develop the most cordial relations. An alliance could be to our mutual advantage."

Two reporters spoke simultaneously.

"Who are the Heesh?"

"Where do you come from?"

"The Heesh are a race that forms one nation on the planet Naneg," Marfor answered. "Naneg is in a different sector of space-time from this one."

"What's that thing on your shoulder?"

"It's a poota, my pet." Marfor nudged the poota, which spread its wings and launched itself into the air. It flew in tight circles and did one somersault while cameras hurriedly tried to follow its course. Intimidated by the strangeness of its surroundings, it soon came to rest again.

Wallcroft, the Time Project director, intervened. "That's it for now, ladies and gentlemen. The *Pegasus* team must be debriefed, and we should have more details for you tomorrow."

"Ambassador Marfor," someone shouted, "are you going to see the president?"

"That will be up to the president," she answered. Protocol here would not be very different from that at home.

Wallcroft managed to look pleasant, although he was disconcerted by their appearance, when Carlos presented Marfor as ambassador from the Heesh and Nim as her deputy. Two officials stood near him, and Wallcroft introduced them. "This is Mr. Holcomb, the undersecretary of state, from the office that deals with foreign nations, Your Excellency. And this is Miss Ormsbee, an assistant to the president. They want to talk to you."

"Certainly," Marfor answered. "I would like Colonel Lecompte and Miss Rourke to be present. They speak my language and can help with translation. I have come to think of them as my liaison with your world."

Good, the undersecretary thought, if this country of the Heesh amounts to anything. The secretary general and every major member of the United Nations will want to be in on the act, but our man puts us on the inside track. Of course I'll have to get an update on his security clearance.

"I hope you will forgive our ignorance, but we didn't know the Heesh existed," he said. "You can imagine what a surprise it is to receive an ambassador."

"We didn't know about you either until the ship I commanded encountered your expedition." Marfor did not want to misrepresent her position, so she added, "I could not get back home before coming here, and I saw the need for an ambassador from my government, the Matriarchy of the Heesh, so I appointed myself, as I had full authority to do."

An ambassador without credentials from her government? Most irregular. Unprecedented. And a matriarchy? That would have to be explored. The undersecretary glanced at the president's assistant. She did not seem to be disturbed.

Marfor understood the undersecretary's silence, for she knew how the Matriarchy would feel if confronted by someone who claimed to be an ambassador but had no credentials. The Heesh, of course, did not have to deal with ambassadors. The closest thing to them was delegates from regional matriarchies. "Our only contact took place sixty-five million years ago," she said. "I don't know how to make contact in the present. Carlos, please review the facts for these gentlemen."

They're on a first-name basis, both officials noted. That might be good, if Colonel Lecompte was as dedicated to the national interest as his record suggested. The thought was filed away while Carlos told about the encounter and the discovery of alternate time tracks, with mutually exclusive courses of evolution. He did not go into details about the origin of time tracks. That would have to be explained to officials, to scientists, and no doubt to the public, later.

"Her Excellency asked me to take her with us," Carlos said. He did not mention that she and Nim had been marooned, and he wondered how much editing of the facts, without actually lying, would be necessary. "Her own ship was locked to its time track and couldn't reach us."

"Let me make it clear what Carlos did," Marfor said. "At this nexus sixty-five million years ago, it appeared that one of our races would be denied its future. Carlos made it possible for both races to exist by ensuring that there would be two time tracks. Naneg is Earth on a different track."

He played God, the presidential assistant thought. That's what I call using initiative, but it shows a suspiciously friendly interest in the Heesh. Maybe it will pay off. "When you appeared before the cameras you mentioned a possible alliance," she said to Marfor. "How can we have an alliance if we can't reach each other's worlds?"

"There must be a way through unexplored dimensions of space and time." Marfor felt forlorn as she wondered whether she would ever see Naneg again. If she did, she was sure she would find changes. "If you solve the problem of travel between our worlds, your first reward will be our ability to travel to the stars, as my deputy, Nim, has done." She and Nim had agreed with advice volunteered by their human friends, that the term "attendant male" would arouse hostility among males on Earth.

The officials had learned about travel to the stars in their briefing on Wallcroft's call to the president. They discovered quickly that a space jumper like Nim didn't necessarily know how he had done it. "I'm sure the president will assemble teams to work on both problems, crossing between time tracks and jumping through space," the presidential assistant said.

The undersecretary of state came to a decision. "Your Excellency, I will recommend that the United States accord recognition to the Matriarchy of the Heesh." Recognition could always be withdrawn if the claims of these aliens proved empty, but the United States would have the first chance to exploit what could become a valuable relationship. "We will provide an embassy for you in Washington and allocate funds. Colonel Lecompte, I will see to it that you are put on temporary duty with the State Department to work with us and Ambassador Marfor. Let them stay at the base here until suitable quarters are arranged. Before I return to Washington I will ascertain their needs."

Dorkin, Lippor's attendant male, took a seat, held vacant for him during his absence, at a meeting of the council of the League of Males. A room in catacombs dug beneath the Grand Hall of the Egg was the last place in which a conspiracy would be hunted. All ten members of the council were present. Two of them, one who worked in the Hall of Guardians and the other in the Hall of Records, were ugly, with small eyes and narrow jaws, and had never been attendant males. Four others had been discarded as their crests faded with age. The remaining four attended matrons in the Hall of Rites, the Hall of Science and Technology, the Hall of Finance, and the Hall of Cousins. The last hall dealt with all members of the zoological class of Hanishan, wild or domesticated, who were not Heesh.

"I have passed word to each of you that we found an unsuspected race of intelligent aliens during our search for the Prime Mother," Dorkin said. "Surely Oomis informed the Matriarchy, but they have kept the information secret. We hear nothing but propaganda about how Oomis saved the Prime Mother's eggs and carried them to safety where the hatchlings could grow and propagate. Oomis is praised everywhere as the savior of the Heesh. She is grossly distorting her role. I tapped the ship's computer memory through Lippor's terminal, and I can show you the aliens and most of what really happened."

"You have done a splendid job with Lippor," the chairman said.

"It's been a pleasure. She's one of the best-looking females I've ever seen, and we get along well." Dorkin thought of the beauty creases above Lippor's fine broad lips, the youthful softness of her down, the hard muscles of her arms and legs. She was intelligent, amiable, and affectionate, and he was fond of her. "I may be in danger, and I hope she will protect me."

"We all live in danger," the chairman said. "What is more urgent about yours?"

"Oomis's male, Haban, was killed last night. Oomis had given him jewels, and they were taken, so it's supposed to have been a robbery. But Haban was the only one who was with Oomis when triceratopses attacked Marfor. He taped it. The tape doesn't show what Marfor was doing or why the triceratopses attacked. Why didn't Oomis kill them or drive them off? I saw Oomis quarrel with Marfor, and Haban might have known more about the attack than Oomis wants known. I will watch what happens to the techs who were aboard. Like me, they know about the aliens, who called themselves humans. The Matriarchy may be waiting to reveal their existence at another time, but they would have to change their doctrines. The Cosmic Egg held more potential than they preach. And a male commanded the humans. Males can be dominant! How could the Matriarchy explain that? If they decide to suppress that knowledge, all males who know about it could be eliminated."

"I will arrange for hiding places for you and the techs," the chairman said. "We will change your appearance, put a patch of imitation skin over your scar and dye your crest, so that you can move around in public without being recognized. Show us your tapes."

Dorkin listened to the council's grunts of distaste at the humans' repellent appearance as their pictures appeared. "This is important," he said as he transmitted a scene that Haban had taped, which showed the Prime Mother attacking Carlos, Rusty killing the creature, and Rusty being carried off by the robot. "Marfor traded the captive for the Prime Mother's eggs, which the humans had taken, but this is what the Matriarchy has broadcast publicly."

Close-ups showed the robot coming out of the forest, an egg in each padded hand. "Oomis claims she ordered the robot to collect the eggs from the aliens," Dorkin said. "Would she have sent it on such an important task without recording it from a flier? Of course not, and she didn't. Marfor took the robot and recovered the eggs."

"Can you show the humans giving the eggs to Marfor or the robot?" the chairman asked.

"No, but I saw her bring the robot back with the eggs. Here's where Marfor appears again." A scene partially obscured by leaves showed a triceratops smashing Marfor's truck. "Oomis claims she answered a call for help from Marfor but arrived too late. A lot was cut out of computer memory before I taped it, or else Oomis locked it under her personal code."

"Even so, your knowledge is a weapon. You were right about the importance of getting aboard the time ship."

"We were lucky," Dorkin said. "I knew that Lippor was a space engineer before I accepted her, but I did not know about the time trip until she told me. The most important thing I did was persuade her to apply for the trip."

"Oomis will be promoted to grand matron of the Hall of Guardians," the chairman said. "She may join the Matriarchy. We will have to surround her with our supporters so she will pick one of them to succeed Haban."

"I don't envy him," Dorkin said. "Oomis is big and rough. She will want a worm like Haban, not the kind likely to be useful to us."

"Could you act the part?"

"Not with Oomis." What a frightful thought! "I can't stand her, and I would miss Lippor, and it would show. Lippor is not as inflexible about female superiority as most females are. I may be able to persuade her to help us. She is likely to become a senior matron in the Hall of Transportation."

He unrolled a scroll. "This may help us. One of the humans paints pictures, and she transmitted this one to me." He watched them study Rusty's cartoonlike interpretation of Heesh society, with a female riding on a huge egg that was dragged along by males attached to it by chains. Nobody thought it was funny and smiled. "The only paintings we see glorify the Cosmic Egg and the Matriarchy. There is nothing imaginative, certainly no caricatures like this. I think the human was remarkably sensitive to our predicament of subservience. What would be the effect if copies of this were distributed?"

"Just what you knew it would be when you showed it to us. It will inflame males more than all the manifestos we publish. It shows how females use worship of the Egg to hold us down." The chairman settled back in his chair and clasped his three-fingered hands on his chest. "You were gone seven months. We are nearly ready to act. Our problem is to choose the occasion. With your information and tapes, I think I see one that would be ideal. We will save this picture until then."

Chapter Seven

Halfway up from the base of the dome of the Grand Hall of the Egg, above the scalloped ring of annexes to the hall, a circle of windows showed night and the full moon rising. Soft light from the walls suffused the rotunda beneath the dome, and a chandelier suspended from the center glowed upon jewels that met in swirling patterns to cover the surface of an egg, grandly imposing, twice as high as the tallest Heesh, upon a dais surrounded by a gold railing. Thin chimes of brass clashed with a steady beat. A procession entered, led by the supreme matriarch, Tellima, who halted well in front of the egg and waited while others took their places. Twelve matriarchs moved with measured pace to twelve low altars around the egg. Matrons ranged themselves around the sides, grand matrons in front. All of them wore long green robes and scarlet cowls, had their Necklaces of Twelves suspended on their chests, and showed their rank and the halls they represented in the embroidery of pearls at the front of their cowls.

All Naneg is watching, Supreme Matriarch Tellima thought with pride, knowing that artfully concealed cameras were recording the scene. There hadn't been such a crowd in the Grand Hall since she was installed. She raised her arms and proclaimed, "All honor to the Cosmic Egg! Let the fires be lit."

A matriarch behind her, to the right, lit a bundle of sticks on her altar in the time-honored way, striking sparks into tinder with flint on iron. As flames rose she said loudly, "All honor to the Cosmic Egg, mother of the universe."

The fragrance of incense that she sprinkled on the fire began to fill the air.

One by one flames were lit on the other altars. Each matriarch announced all honor to the Cosmic Egg, Designer of the Plan, Fountain of All Being, Teacher of Right Conduct, and on through the litany, with responses from those assembled. A cloud of incense grew and drifted through the hall. Many of the matrons, particularly juniors for whom this ceremony was their first, tingled with awe. The rites of fire had been handed down from ancestors before the dawn of written history.

"Oh, most revered Spirit of the Egg, we serve you in all ways," Tellima said loudly. "We try to fulfill every wish that you reveal to us. For many years we searched for the Prime Mother, whom you chose to bring the Heesh into being through the Hanishan according to your plan. Thanks to your guidance, we found her, and we are eternally grateful. Her spirit resides in a likeness of gold, which we bring here tonight as a tribute to you and an inspiration to us."

She turned and called out, "Grand Matron Oomis, reveal to us the likeness of the Prime Mother."

Oomis entered, followed by twelve senior matrons, who bore a narrow platform draped with wild Hanishan skins on which stood a golden replica of the Ishinol twice life-size. Senior Matron Lippor, newly promoted, represented the Hall of Transportation. Oomis led them to a low pedestal in front of the high dais of the Egg, raised her arms, and proclaimed, "All honor to the Cosmic Egg! Thus we fulfill your command."

The senior matrons lowered their platform to the floor, gripped the image on arms and legs and body, and lifted it to its pedestal. It was a hollow shell of gold but was still very heavy. They placed it so that it stood facing the egg, more upright than an Ishinol had ever stood in life, with arms outstretched. The matrons carried the platform away, leaving Oomis and the supreme matriarch beside the statue. A spotlight came on, bathing the gleaming gold in its radiance.

And a loud voice, unexpected, brought consternation to the matrons.

"Look at that thing, Heesh everywhere. Look at the beast from a savage time that is supposed to be our inspiration.

How splendid it is in a fake skin of gold! But look at its cruel jaws, the jaws of a dinosaur. Look at the murderous claws of an Ishinol, so faithfully reproduced. You have heard lies about how this thing was found. We have tapes that show the truth. Watch!"

Stunned by the desecration of the ceremony, Tellima stood for a moment motionless, voiceless, dragged down in a whirlpool of disbelief, outrage, and protest. Someone captured the transmitter, she thought. It must have been males. What happened to the females there?

Recovering her poise and her voice, she spoke rapidly to Oomis. "Go to the broadcasting station and stop this." She saw Oomis hurry out of the hall. Oomis would end whatever was happening. Tellima made a gesture, and a wall screen showed what was being telecast.

"This tape shows the discovery of the creature we are ordered to call our Prime Mother, and her death," the voice said. From its high tone it was obviously a male voice. "Watch the Ishinol attack a creature unlike any you have seen before. There are three more such creatures. See one of them kill the Ishinol with a laser. These creatures call themselves humans. They are as intelligent as we are. The Matriarchy has hidden their existence from you because they have no place in what we are taught about the divine plan of the Cosmic Egg."

Oomis will take a company of Guardians and regain control of the transmitter, Tellima thought, but the damage is done. Or will these males be satisfied merely to expose our secrecy and contradict our teachings?

"Our collector robot, under control by Oomis in a flier, is taking the body of the Ishinol," the voice continued. "Now the robot seizes the human who fired the laser. She is smaller than the others. She is a female, and the others are males. Human females are smaller than males!"

Tellima realized that she was watching the start of a rebellion by males. What was taking Oomis so long?

"This next scene shows the captured female on trial in our ship," the voice said. "Notice her long red hair. Hair! She is a mammal. Why hasn't the Matriarchy told us about a race of intelligent mammals? There's Oomis in the center of the court, and Lippor at her left. The one on her right is Marfor, who arranged to trade the female for the Ishinol's eggs. Oomis takes credit for saving the eggs to let the Heesh evolve, but it was Marfor who saved them. Marfor left the ship and didn't return. Oomis says that a triceratops killed her, but she leaves questions unanswered. Oomis can't be trusted."

Nor can any of us who saw the original tapes, Tellima thought. I could blame it on Oomis, disgrace her, say that she misrepresented the tapes. But we have made her a heroine. Where did the males get the tapes? It must have been a male aboard the ship. There were six of them. One did not return and one was murdered later in a robbery. The second one was Oomis's male and the most likely suspect, because Oomis treated her males badly, but we cannot overlook the others.

Tellima went to the position taken by those who had brought in the golden image and drew Lippor aside. "Go to the Hall of Guardians. Have them arrest your attendant male and the technicians who were aboard your ship for questioning by me."

"Immediately," Lippor said, and left.

Tellima saw the face of a male on the screen. She recognized him from Guardian reports as a suspected leader in the League of Males, possibly the chairman of its council. "You will read about all this in reports that are even now being distributed to every door," he was saying. "You will also read the demands of the League of Males. We will call a general strike if the demands are not met. The demands are simple: equal status with females and reorganization of the government and the Halls to give males equal authority with females."

Outrageous, Tellima thought. Preposterous. And yet the situation was so serious that token concessions might have to be made.

A junior matron of the Hall of Guardians came through the arching entrance and gave something to a senior matron, who passed it on to a grand matron. The last one went to Tellima. "This is being distributed throughout the city," she said. Tellima saw a list of the demands of the League of Males with the reproduction of a painting, a libelous, damaging distortion of the harmonious relations between males and females. The painting showed a female riding on an egg that was pulled by three males in chains. She recognized it as a clever piece of propaganda. Who had the talent and originality to paint something like this? She had never seen anything like it before. It would undermine the loyalty of males; there was no question about that.

Loud noises came from the speaker near the screen. The chairman of the League of Males was seen as he looked up and shouted, "Guard the door!" The camera that had been focused on him swung to the door, which disintegrated in smoke under laser fire. Uniformed Guardians leaped through the door to exchange fire with males who held lasers, and charred bodies fell across the bodies of three unarmed females and a male who lay bound on the floor. Oomis ran through the door toward the chairman. He retreated from his desk, turned to a window, and hesitated before attempting a three-story jump to the ground outside. Oomis grabbed the feathers in his crest with both hands, lifted him, and swung him sharply to one side, breaking his neck.

Oomis turned to the camera and said, "This foolishness has ended. The Matriarchy is in full control. All males will return to their quarters. Further instructions will be issued by the supreme matriarch."

The first thing, Tellima thought, will be to warn of punishment for any male who goes on strike. Now we must catch the traitor who took the tapes, if he is still alive.

An armed Guardian drove Lippor to her home in a fast three-wheeler. It was a large house, suitable to her new rank as a senior matron, with curved rooms arranged like eggs in a nest, and she hated to think of the small box in a rectangular warren that she would have to move to if she were disgraced. Surely she, who had witnessed the events in the distant past, would be implicated with Oomis in the deception exposed tonight. What could she say in the face of the evidence? That she had been threatened by Oomis? That the supreme matriarch had exacted a vow of silence? Lippor didn't know how to proceed.

Dorkin would comfort her and give her hope. But she had been ordered to have Dorkin arrested! He had always shown her the greatest affection. He could tell her what to do.

Entering the house, she looked in the reception room for Dorkin. As she had hoped, he wasn't there. "Check the rooms upstairs," she told the Guardian, to get her out of the way. She went to her study. Dorkin was seated, watching the broadcast, which had turned from the recapture of the transmitting station to a dull history of the long search through one ancestor after another to find the Prime Mother. He looked up at her solemnly.

Lippor felt all of her fondness for him well up in her. She pointed to the window and said, "Run. Hide. The Guardians are hunting you. Think of how you can help me. Hurry."

"Say nothing except to Tellima. I'll get in touch," Dorkin said. He scrambled through the window and vanished.

Few humans welcomed the Heesh.

They were ugly. They were skinny, with muscles like cables on their arms and tendons prominent in their necks, and their faces were deformed, pushed out of shape. Their grins, all teeth, were frightening. They looked like experiments upon human victims by a mad scientist. Official announcements called them the descendants of dinosaurs, not dinosaurs themselves, but the distinction was lost on many people. Except for their down and their erect posture, they looked reptilian. Everyone knew that many dinosaurs had stood on two legs. These things were nothing but fuzzy dinosaurs.

To fundamentalists of all of the world's major religions they were demons. The very name Heesh sounded like the hiss of snakes, shapes favored by the devil and his cohorts. Surely their coming foretold the arrival of Shiva the Destroyer, in Hindu cosmology, or the last days promised in Revelation.

Crowds blocked the street in front of the embassy given to Marfor and chanted, "Heesh go home! Heesh go home!" People threw rocks. Barriers were set up and a strong guard posted. An armed escort had to accompany Marfor and Nim wherever they were taken.

While the president, Zeke Parker, was deciding how to deal with an unaccredited ambassador, thousands of voters wrote to him and to their congressmen to denounce the government's favorable treatment of these weird creatures. Legal purists asked how we could recognize the sovereign status of a nation we hadn't seen. Congress, although aware that the conduct of foreign affairs was a presidential prerogative—and what could be more foreign than a planet on the far side of nowhere?—thought it should have been consulted.

The House Budget Committee hastily called hearings at which it was pointed out that expenditures to support the Heesh had not been approved. "What are we supposed to gain from this?" a congressman asked Carlos when he was summoned to testify. "We can't even find this alleged world, Naneg."

"Well find it, sir," Carlos answered. "Never sell America short." He had always wanted to throw that expression at somebody. "When we do find it, we will gain the technology to jump between the stars."

"What good will that do us?" the congressman asked.

"Possibly none, sir. Possibly a lot. We won't know until we reach the stars. But can we allow the Heesh to have a capability greater than ours? They have a great deal of other knowledge we can use. You are all invited to examine a Heesh robot that can use its initiative to follow generalized commands and can change them on spoken orders. It has great versatility."

The committee adjourned after several speeches but without action.

President Parker knew that his place in history depended on his handling of the Heesh. They could present an unparalleled opportunity or a trap into which he could stumble. Making excuses to delay seeing them while he weighed reports from the State Department on their activities, he learned that they had been received courteously, even eagerly, at laboratories and colleges and, on carefully scripted visits, at factories and farms. They appeared to be decent and reasonable. Gradually he decided that he must reverse the general trend of public opinion before the Heesh fled to a friendlier host, maybe the Commonwealth of Europe or the Celestial Dominion. Those powerful nations and others were badgering the State Department with demands that their ambassadors meet with Marfor.

Two things precipitated the president's decision.

First, there was what happened in a restaurant when Carlos and Rusty took Marfor and Nim out to dinner. The assistant secretary of state, who had approved the excursion, went with them.

An ambassador is not treated to dinner at a truck stop. Carlos chose a two-star restaurant that would serve fish or fowl upon request but was celebrated for choice cuts of beef. After many months in a dietary no-man's-land, he wanted tournedos, inch-thick slices of filet in a sauce of mushrooms and wine, for himself. Rusty would be happy with plain roast beef, medium rare. The Heesh, they knew, liked the meat of mammals. They had eaten a roast from a horselike rhinoceros in the Eocene Period and an ancestral species of cattle from the early Miocene.

The manager of the restaurant, notified that they were coming, bowed to the group on their arrival and escorted them to a table on one side of the dining room, as requested. A waiter offered menus immediately, but before Carlos could explain the choices, someone shouted "Heeshsssss." Others joined in the hissing until "Heeshsssss, Heeshsssss" could be heard everywhere.

The assistant secretary of state stood up and said loudly, "Ladies and gentlemen! Her Excellency, Ambassador Marfor, and her deputy, Nim, are here as our guests. The government hopes for amicable relations with their government. Please welcome them with the friendly courtesy for which Americans are noted."

Sure they are, Carlos thought cynically, but he clapped his hands to applaud the statement. Rusty clapped too, and so did others in the room. But hissing resumed, although quieter and shortened to a simple "Sssss, sssss."

The manager spread his hands in a gesture of helplessness.

Marfor was angry. Rising to her feet, she said in her deep baritone, "As ambassador of the Heesh, I will not accept rudeness. Ours is a great nation, worthy of respect." Silence fell as everyone waited to hear what she would add. She continued more moderately. "I am glad that some of you welcome my presence here. To those who cannot control other feelings, I will say that I hope your views will change. You should know now that the Heesh cannot be bullied. We cannot be routed by hisses. I will stay here with my friends for dinner."

"Good for you," Carlos said when Marfor sat down.

"I think you should order steak tartare," Rusty said. "That's raw meat."

They both watched the manager leave the room. "He's calling the media," Carlos guessed. "Cameras will be here soon. Not the best publicity, but it's publicity."

Marfor put up with the lights and cameras when they came. She agreed to a change in seating so that Nim would be beside her for pictures of the two of them together. "We have made good friends among your citizens, Carlos Lecompte and Rusty Rourke and others, and we expect to make more. I know that we look very different, but we have much in common."

President Parker nodded with approval when he saw the report on holovision. He had a strong sense of fair play, and he admired people who fought back against injustice. But what made him decide to support the Heesh with the full weight of his office was a report he received from his woman assistant the next day.

"Max Lannin is using the Heesh to go after you," she told him.

"Tell me something surprising," he answered irritably. Lannin led a political movement that was expected to oppose the president when he ran for reelection. Meanwhile he raised funds by exploiting people's fears. "What's he doing?"

"Fright mail of the usual kind, plus paid spots on holovision. He says you are making a fraudulent use of the taxpayers' money, which should be used for higher Social Security payments. That's for senior citizens, but they've grown tired of his usual line about a spendthrift government. Now he says you want to turn the country over to dinosaurs. Claims that they aren't dinosaurs are just hairsplitting or out-and-out eyewash. A lot of people of all ages may listen to that."

The president nodded his agreement and said, "We can't let Max get a leg up, can we? Have Colonel Lecompte bring Marfor and Nim to see me in the Oval Office."

When Carlos brought Marfor and Nim to his office, Parker shook their three-fingered hands without shuddering and invited them to sit down. He was familiar with the appearance of the Heesh, but he had to overcome an instinctive revulsion before touching them. "I am glad you are here," he said, "but the prejudice of many people leaves me out on a limb." Did they understand that term? "I must consider what is best for the country. I'm gambling that we can get to Naneg and persuade your government not only to tell us how to jump between stars but to share much other valuable information. Can you give assurances that your government will agree?"

"No, Mr. President," Marfor answered. "The Heesh may react to humans with hostility like what we have encountered here. The friendship that we have developed with Colonel Lecompte and his crew make me believe that the hostility can be overcome. I would like to be able to say so at home. But the Heesh probably already know about humans, whom a former colleague of mine would have portrayed unfavorably. The best I can do, with the help of humans who should accompany me home, is to try to persuade the supreme matriarch to reach an agreement with you."

"How are you going to get home?"

"I wish I could answer that. It seems to me that a nation that has learned how to travel backward in time can determine how to travel across it. That is the one hope for me personally and for the success of my mission."

She lays it on the line, the president thought. "Will you explain to me the powers of your supreme matriarch?"

"She presides over the Matriarchy, a council of twelve matriarchs chosen from grand matrons of the twenty-four

halls that regulate all Heesh activities. She picks the matriarchs. Those who are serving when a supreme matriarch
dies or retires elect a new one."

Like a consistory of cardinals chooses a pope, the president thought. The last thing from a popular vote.

Marfor was still talking. "She has considerable power
because she can make promotions within the halls and
approve or disapprove the nominees of the halls. She sets
the agenda for the Matriarchy and decides questions that
are not the sole province of one hall. In any debate, her
views have great influence."

Thinking of Congress and the Supreme Court, Parker
asked, "Does anyone else have similar power?"

"Several grand matrons, who are usually also matriarchs,
have similar power but it is less. They preside in the most
important halls. The Hall of Rites decides all questions of
cosmology according to the doctrines of the Cosmic Egg.
That hall must decide where humans and a world on a
different time track from ours fit into the cosmic plan.
The Hall of Guardians enforces laws and customs with
its police and courts. Most weapons are in the hands of
the Guardians. The Hall of Finance, from which Supreme
Matriarch Tellima came, handles government accounts and
supervises commercial activities. The Hall of Science and
Technology is also important. You will find allies there."

"Do you have a Hall of Defense? Who controls your
army?"

"We have no army. The Matriarchy governs the whole
world. We have no one to fight."

If she was telling the truth, he needn't fear an invasion,
even if it was possible to mount one from a base tucked into
an odd corner of space-time, the president thought. "What
is your hall?" he asked.

"The Hall of Ancients. Our field is reserved for us, but
we have little power. We search for knowledge of the past.
Ork!" Marfor's bark of laughter made the president sit
back in surprise. "I found much more than they expected
at home."

The president liked this strange female who answered
his questions so frankly and could laugh at herself. He felt

that he could trust her. "I'm going to turn public opinion around," he said. "I'm going to put my campaign manager, who is also my publicity director, to work on it. She will be in touch with you, Colonel Lecompte. And I'll get the social ball rolling."

When the president faced cameras with the Heesh in the Rose Garden later, he said, "I have discussed with Ambassador Marfor here the advantages to both of our governments from a cooperative relationship. Just as important, I think, is the chance for friendship with a different species. We all know the importance of sharing our lives in good-will with people of different races and religions. Now we can carry our progress in tolerance and equality an important step further. The Heesh are great folks. I hope everyone helps them feel at home here."

A reception for VIPs filled the Blue Room at the White House. Leaders in government, business, the media, education, and the arts overcame their squeamishness, with the help of drinks served to them as they waited in the reception line, and shook the three-fingered hands. These were smooth and dry, not rough or clammy. Except for a disconcerting show of teeth when they grinned, the Heesh could have been any celebrities. Guests were disappointed that they had so little time to talk to the Heesh before they had to make room for someone else in line whom an aide to the president was waiting to introduce. How many chances did they have to exchange pleasantries with "great folks" who were monsters? They would have to arrange opportunities to really get to know them better.

Very soon Marfor and Nim headed the guest list of every ambitious hostess. Carlos culled the invitations with the State Department protocol officer. Finally the ambassadors of other countries got to meet the Heesh, but as guests at parties, not as hosts themselves. Nim spread his "Ork! Ork! Ork!" of laughter everywhere. After a cautious private test that left both of them in a stupor, Marfor and Nim did not accept liquor, not even champagne, at parties. They liked orange juice.

"Thank the Egg that we can remember names," Marfor said.

"The titles are confusing," Nim commented. "Mr. Secretary this, Mme. Secretary that, and they don't wear badges. We have to keep track of who is a judge and who is a justice. The attorney general and the surgeon general are 'general' even though they aren't military people."

"The Heesh system is a lot simpler. We address Heesh officials as junior, senior, or grand, and their insignia tells which they are." Marfor added thoughtfully, "The number of generals and admirals troubles me. A society dominated by males may be more pugnacious than one run by females. There would be tremendous difficulties in attacking one planet from another, but we may have to form a Hall of Defense. Nim, I will ask you to find out what weapons the humans use."

They asked Carlos to assess their gains at social affairs.

"You're doing fine, and you're making influential friends," he told them. "A word of caution. Times are hard and a lot of people are down on fancy parties. You need broader support."

"Scientists," Marfor suggested.

"A very fitting start." Carlos nodded. "They do not form a large part of the population, but educated people listen to them. You've met a few already and gotten along well with them. We'll introduce you to more."

Biologists and paleontologists had talked to members of the *Pegasus* team and had tripped over each other in a rush to see the Heesh themselves. Tenured professors accompanied by squads of graduate students were studying the dromaeosaur, the stenonychosaur, the two Ishinol, *Purgatorius*, and the other animals brought to Earth, all of which were kept in the National Zoo. Marfor agreed to be the principal speaker at a convention of the National Paleontological Society. She drew a crowd too large for Madison Square Garden at a meeting that could ordinarily fit into a hotel dining room. Reunited with the *Pegasus* team, she praised them. "They were tireless workers, with the same dedication to the advancement of knowledge that I have found in your laboratories."

She made an amusing story out of the way she had planted a fossil to find it sixty-five million years later. "I have heard a saying here: if you want something done right, you should do it yourself. That implies that you should know what you are doing before you find out that you have done it, which is not what happened to me. I can't complain."

The president's publicity director had made sure that Marfor's speech praised the humans. She met with Carlos later and said, "Marfor got a good reaction. Now I'll get her before the International Organization of Women. That's only the beginning. I want books written as if she were running for office. One by Marfor and one by you. Maybe books by other members of the *Pegasus* team."

Carlos thought of a paper that Dan was writing. It was too full of terms like *Glyptostrobus europaeus*, identifying a conifer, to win a mass market. "We're all too busy to write books."

"You really are sixty-five million years out of date," the publicity director said. "Lots of professional writers would stomp on their mothers for a chance at a seven-figure job of ghosting. And I know publishers who can print them as fast as spin-offs from a royal wedding."

Marfor made a mistake. At the meeting of the International Organization of Women she said, "It's natural for females to run things." At the howl that arose from men, she tried to recover by saying, "I should have explained that in a culture in which females are bigger and do the fighting, they are given the leadership in primitive social structures and tend to hold power as civilization develops. That is the role that males have played here. It seems to me that there should be equality of the sexes."

"I won't let you forget that," Nim told her later. "I taped it to play when we get back home."

Next the publicity director persuaded the president's wife, who had male ancestors who had fought on both sides in the Civil War, to wear a necklace resembling Marfor's. She decided to portray her first ancestors on the American continent, both husband and wife, on the central medallion of gold. "Don't ask me what they looked like," she told a jeweler. "Have an artist draw something." The side medallions of silver carried symbols for other ancestors, whom she was glad to name when asked.

Women everywhere began to want Necklaces of Twelves. Professional genealogists were overwhelmed with business. Scarcely twenty generations, if ancestors had married young, covered American history, and not even royalty abroad could authenticate 144 generations. Thousands of women tried to imitate the Necklace of Twelves, using half of the medallions to honor men and the other half women. If they couldn't authenticate twelve of each, they faked them. It appeared that the *Mayflower* had been bigger than the Ark. Many women had boasted of their heritage and had formed organizations restricted to members who could document their ancestry. Now it was fashionable to parade their claims in public. Jewelers were glad to help.

Unexpectedly, for this idea did not come from Washington, a hob gang swooped down at a party on their flitters. The men paraded into the hall with Mohawk haircuts, crests dyed to look like Nim's. Other young men took up the fad. The decoration of barbered crests grew fancier until they looked like rainbows.

Reporters and photographers staked out the Heesh embassy. Marfor and Nim could not go anywhere without a caravan of media people. The publicity director couldn't win a battle against the freedom of the press, so she began to issue daily itineraries. Cameras watched the Heesh ride a combine during a wheat harvest. "This is more efficient than our system," Marfor lied. The Heesh inspected factories, mines, fisheries, and schools, and they found something flattering to say wherever they went.

A ritual visit to Wall Street did not go as well. Confused by the turmoil on the floor of the New York Stock Exchange, Marfor admitted that she did not understand the mechanics of capitalism. The economy of Naneg was regulated by the Matriarchy. Professors of economics wanted details, but investors cooled toward the Heesh.

The broadcasting networks were becoming nasty about the refusal of the publicity director to subject Marfor to an interview on a talk show. The problem had been to avoid showing one network preference over the others. The first one to present her would score a prime-time coup. As soon as she satisfied herself that Marfor could handle herself, the publicity director solved the problem as best she could by arranging for a panel conference. It would last two hours, giving time for celebrated anchors and show hosts to display themselves asking questions. A dozen big names were invited, and all accepted. Regular reporters could sit in the audience. Regular reporters didn't like that, but they were outranked.

The publicity director, a person of status herself, presided. A large clock showed five-minute limits for each question, the answer, and follow-ups by a member of the media. Each of them could have two intervals.

The first question was hostile. "Your Excellency, we have heard that you have no credentials from your government. What authority do you have to represent yourself as an ambassador?"

"When the Heesh and Americans first met, sixty-five million years ago, I was the senior representative of my government present. My instructions included a blanket authorization to take any actions necessary. It became clear to me that formal relations should be established with your government and that our ambassador should be the person of highest possible rank. There was no way to refer the question to my government, so I named myself. That action is in accord with Heesh law. When regular contact between our two nations is established, as I am sure it will be, my government may want to name another ambassador. I hope that by then the president of the United States will have named an ambassador to the Heesh. I hope that mutually beneficial relations between our nations will develop. My task now is to initiate that development."

Not bad for an explanation of a decision that came out of a whispered conversation with Nim after we had been abandoned and rescued, Marfor thought. She saw Carlos and Rusty, who were in the front row of the audience, give satisfied nods.

The first questioner followed up by asking Marfor what had brought her to the meeting place sixty-five million years ago. The Age of Dinosaurs, wasn't it? Was she an ambassador to the dinosaurs?

"Ork!" Marfor laughed. "Do you think that mutually beneficial relations with dinosaurs are possible? Dinosaurs existed for 140 million years and were never intelligent or peace-loving. We all know that many of them were ferocious, and it's worth remembering, to the credit of early mammals, the ancestors of humans, that they survived during much of the Age of Dinosaurs. The ancestors of the Heesh, who are as different from dinosaurs as mammals are, appeared at the end of that period. I took an expedition back there to find the first of them, whom we know as the Prime Mother."

That led to a question about the Prime Mother. Marfor did not say that the Prime Mother and her mate now lived in a zoo on Earth. She found herself describing the doctrine of the Cosmic Egg, the Origin of All Things and the Teacher of Right Conduct. "In your terms, the Cosmic Egg is the name we give to God. The Prime Mother was the vehicle by which the Cosmic Egg gave rise to the class of animals that led to the Heesh. She also inspired sages early in our history to state rules of conduct that would be in harmony with the Cosmic Plan."

"Were these sages females?" a woman reporter asked.

"They were." Marfor did not expand on that answer, which included the consequence that females were given dominance.

Before the two hours ended, the panel had drawn her out on government by the Matriarchy, a static society that left little scope for change until a questioning spirit led to scientific knowledge and technological development, and a social system that knew dissent but had little crime.

On the whole, it is not a picture that Americans will admire, Carlos thought. She was frank but what choice did she have?

He was right to be worried. Rumblings from religious leaders grew louder after they heard about the Cosmic Egg. Jews, Christians, and Moslems all accepted the text in Genesis that said, "God created man in his own image." It didn't say anything about creating the Heesh and cer-

tainly didn't say that the image was an egg. It also said
that God gave man dominion "over every living thing that
moveth upon the earth." Nothing was said about Naneg,
but Marfor had said the Naneg was Earth on a different
time track. Time tracks weren't in the scriptures either.
The Heesh weren't exactly atheists but they were close.
They followed dangerous heresies.

Meanwhile the fright mill continued to grind out
deception for the simple-minded. Ads illustrated with
a tyrannosaurus, jaws agape, charging at the viewer,
shrieked, "Once dinosaurs ruled the world! Don't let
them rule it again! The Heesh have given them a foot-
hold. The government wants to bring in more. Already
we know that they reject all of our religions. They would
destroy our morals. What happens to us if they are hungry?
We should lock them in a zoo like crocodiles. Write to your
congressman and support the Save America campaign with
your contributions!"

It was a waste of time to point out that crocodiles were
only distantly related to dinosaurs, that the Heesh were
more like birds with arms instead of wings, and that the
Heesh were civilized, more so than many humans. Their
concocted image as dinosaurs spread. No one had ever
called Max Lannin's campaigns sweetly reasonable.

He went after computer fans with messages on "elbods,"
electronic bulletin boards. This tactic backfired. When
Lannin's supporters asked, "Why is the government supporting dinosaurs?" informed and contentious readers of the
message hurried to transmit notes ridiculing the libel.

"I don't understand this country," Marfor told Carlos.
"The government has no control over people."

"The government enforces a lot of laws," he replied, "but
not censorship. The theory is that the truth will emerge
from conflicts of opinion."

Books ghosted for Marfor and Carlos appeared.

In *Mission to Earth* Marfor told about her background
studying fossils, her mission to find the Prime Mother,
which she called successful without giving details except
for a description, her reliance on Nim, and, once again,
her hopes for her embassy. She gave her full name, Marfor

Endos Limfor Astelis and so on as author, and explained it in the book.

Carlos, in *Well Met in Time*, dealt briefly with his own background, went into detail about the mission of the *Pegasus* Expedition and its members, told lurid tales about battling dinosaurs, and said a lot about the Heesh and their separate time track. He did not relate that he personally had set up the time tracks.

Both books became best sellers. They were issued as a boxed set illustrated with pictures by Rusty, but not the one she had given to Dorkin. Dominance of Heesh males by females was too delicate a question on Earth to be satirized in a vivid cartoon.

Finally the publicity director played her ace, Marfor's poota. Toy birds that flew under a child's control were common; now the president's campaign manager found companies to make toy pootas that would flap through the air on batlike wings covered with down. Pootas appeared on T-shirts. Poota Pals clubs wrote in for photographs guaranteed to bear the three-fingered handprint, taken near a joint of one wing, of the timid creature. A report that the poota liked blueberries brought to the embassy hundreds of cases of blueberries, which were given to people who could seldom afford them. The poota won hearts all over America.

Carlos was glad when the polls showed that Marfor and Nim had become popular with a majority of citizens despite the Save America campaign, but he was impatient. "Hype isn't my style," he complained to Rusty. "I ought to be commanding a ship, or a squadron, in space or time, not playing nursemaid to the Heesh."

"What you're doing with Marfor is more important," she answered. "We're making a friend we'll need if we find Naneg. Too many of the Heesh will react to us like Oomis."

"And the way a hard core of fanatics here still react to Marfor. We don't seem to be able to dent them. Fortunately they're in the minority."

"You can take credit for a lot of that. You really like Marfor, don't you."

"You know I do."

She kissed him and asked, "What would you think if I asked Marfor to be matron of honor at our wedding?"

She can't be serious, Carlos thought, but he could see no guile in Rusty's expression. She hadn't asked it to tease him. "It's a generous impulse," he answered cautiously, "but think how bizarre she would look standing near you and what a circus the press would make out of it. The bride should be the center of attention."

"Bride and groom together," Rusty said. "Sometimes I think that everything at a wedding focuses on a bride because it's her last chance to hold the center of the stage. I know it won't be that way with us. But you're right; we should be at the altar, and Marfor and Nim should be somewhere with good seats but not in plain view."

Meg was matron of honor and Allie was Rusty's only other attendant. Dan was best man and Nick an usher. Marfor and Nim sat in the second row at the church, away from the center aisle so that they would not appear in the usual pictures. Nevertheless the pictures favored by newspapers and holovision were those taken at the reception, at which the two Heesh were asked to pose with the nuptial pair. Marfor and Nim had already appeared on the covers of three magazines; now they appeared again with Rusty, grinning happily in her bridal gown, and Carlos, who wore a smile that looked forced. The Heesh kept their mouths closed and didn't show their teeth.

"It was an impressive ceremony, full of warmth, and we were honored to be invited," Marfor said when asked her reaction. "It made me feel at home. I wish Carlos and Rusty every happiness."

Marfor was getting good at gracious little speeches. This one made her popularity with the public rise.

"Great," Carlos growled to Rusty in private. "All this is sand in the wind unless we learn how to reach Naneg."

A junior matron led a detachment of Guardians to disperse female demonstrators outside the prison in which Heesh males who had joined the strike for equal rights were held. Grand Matron Oomis was present to make sure that this rabble would be taught a lesson. Six dedicated supporters accompanied her. The junior matron had brought two vans to haul away demonstrators who were arrested. Two vans would not be enough, Oomis thought. She was in no mood anyway to let the demonstrators get off so lightly. Females! Females, disgraces to their egg lines, had rallied in support of males whom they could have dismissed and replaced. Their reaction to the arrest of strikers was as odious as it was unexpected.

The prison for males was a three-story agglomeration of small cells inside a courtyard surrounded by a high wall in a neighborhood of six-story cylindrical tenements. Females jammed a narrow street outside. Two thousand of them, Oomis estimated, twice as many as the number of strikers, who had been packed into cells like oysters in a bottle. The number was ominous, for it showed that the strikers had support from females in addition to those who had let their attachment to individual males overcome their training and judgment, their loyalty to the Matriarchy.

"Free the strikers!" the demonstrators chanted. "Hear the males! Free the strikers! Hear the males!" Over and over they repeated the chant, a noise that crashed like waves of storm-driven surf against the locked gate of the prison.

Laser rifles slung over their shoulders, the Guardians in the junior matron's detachment held their whips across their chests and pushed their way through the mob, squeezing its members against buildings across from the prison. Several Guardians were taking pictures. Oomis recognized nobody among the demonstrators. They infuriated her because they had tucked their Necklaces of Twelves beneath their shirts to conceal their identities. How shameful to deny their egg lines!

Climbing to the top of a van, the junior matron shouted over a loudspeaker, "This gathering is unlawful. You are creating a public nuisance. Break it up! Go to your jobs or go home."

"Free the strikers! Hear the males!" the crowd chanted.

"Those who do not leave immediately will be arrested."

Nobody moved. "Free the strikers! Hear the males!"

Guardians picked demonstrators at random to drag them

to the vans. Nobody resisted. When the two vans left, the other demonstrators waited, continuing their chant. Their spinelessness added fuel to Oomis's fury. Did they think they would enjoy it in jail? She wanted to rage among them, flail them with her whip, draw blood, punish them with pain for their betrayal, drive them into panicky flight. Why weren't they throwing rocks? As it was, holovision would broadcast a deceptive image of restraint among these Heesh who were undermining the social order and desecrating their faith.

Oomis couldn't stand it. "Now," she said to her supporters. Flanked by two Guardians holding lasers ready, she and the other four raised whips and ran toward the mob. Stopping just short of the front rank, she cracked her whip and shouted, "Get out of here! Fast! I'll make you pay for this! Go!"

Some of the demonstrators edged aside uneasily, but their ranks held.

Aiming at the face of the nearest female in the mob, Oomis snapped her arm forward. The female ducked, raising her hands in front of her eyes, and the lash of the whip cut a bloody furrow across her hands and the down on her head. She screamed, turned, and ran.

Again and again Oomis and her companions struck at whoever was nearest. Demonstrators who saw what was happening retreated in panic but were trapped by those behind them. A female who was as big as Oomis herself ran toward her. A Guardian raised her laser but Oomis shouted, "I'll take her!"

The female crouched, endured a painful blow from the whip on her side, and leaped forward to seize the whip. Oomis bent low, seized one of the female's legs, and jerked it up while slamming her body into her, knocking her down. She raised her whip and slashed again and again at the head and body on the pavement, too close to snap the whip but able to cut with it, until her opponent rolled over on her belly and lay motionless, bloody and whimpering.

Oomis looked around. Demonstrators were running toward both ends of the street to get away. "Leave her there," she said of the female on the ground. "I don't think we'll see any more rallies. Now I have an appointment with the supreme matriarch."

Oomis was admitted to a private room adjoining the office of Supreme Matriarch Tellima, whose attendant male was applying makeup for her appearance before bright lights and cameras for a broadcast. Tellima, who had watched live coverage of the demonstration, did not share Oomis's illusion that its violent suppression would end female support for the males. *She is too inflexible,* Tellima thought, *a fanatic, too ready to crush every slight divergence from strict doctrine. She doesn't know that I know she is forming a corps of personal followers among the Guardians. One good thing may come of her fury today, added to her hasty violence, watched by everyone, when she broke the neck of the male whose broadcast defiled our ceremony. We have made Oomis a heroine for salvaging the remains of the Prime Mother and helping her eggs to hatch in the line that gave rise to the Heesh. Now she will be seen as bigoted and cruel, a creature of sudden dangerous impulses, more to be feared than honored.*

"The strike is hurting us," Tellima said. "Strikers remain willing to go to prison, and you saw today that they have support. Other males claim they are sick to avoid going to work. What are you doing about it?"

"Isolating the leaders," Oomis answered. "The males will grow tired of jail. Without leaders to inflame them, the strike will end. The Spirit of the Egg will reign supreme!"

"Have you isolated the Council of the League of Males?"

"Not yet. I cannot believe that their council could hide successfully without support from ranking females. I tell you this, Your Supremacy, I suspect everyone! Everyone is being watched."

Is she watching me? Tellima wondered. *How ridiculous.* "If I were a member of their council, I would not confide secrets to females when I am trying to reduce their power."

A junior matron entered and said, "Everything is ready for the broadcast, Your Supremacy."

"That will be all for now, Oomis," Tellima said. She

watched the grand matron of the Hall of Guardians leave before she let her attendant male finish applying makeup. Shadows around her large eyes to make them seem more luminous and compelling. Short lines to strengthen an already strong jaw. A dusting of reddish brown on her down, which was grayer than she liked and showed her age.

Her Necklace of Twelves gleamed from polishing. Those medallions show four supreme matriarchs, Tellima thought. One of them created an uproar by granting pensions to attendant males who were dismissed. She came up through the Hall of Finance, as I did, and I suspect that she asked as many silent questions about the doctrines of the Hall of Rites as I do. The problems I face are not questions of doctrine but questions of power. Oomis can't see that far. Sometimes a little power must be given away to prevent more from being lost.

"My fellow Heesh, I bring you greetings," Tellima said to begin her broadcast. "I come before you to ask for your cooperation in ending a crisis that is entirely unnecessary. I greatly regret that the males who have gone on strike were so impatient, for the announcements I will make would have been made soon anyway. One thing had to be done first. The statue of the Prime Mother had to be installed with reverent ceremony in the Grand Hall of the Egg. Then it would have been time to turn to other matters.

"The first is the existence of intelligent mammals." A picture of Rusty appeared on the screen beside Tellima, who counted upon the ugliness of the human, with her narrow jaw, small eyes, and all too obvious hair to inspire feelings of revulsion. "The Matriarchy planned from the beginning to tell you about these humans, as they call them-selves. The rites of the Prime Mother had to be celebrated first so that you would know that all was well despite the fact that a human killed her. Her spirit remains with us. And yes, the humans seized her eggs, but they turned them over to us. Again, all is well. The appearance of humans was a new revelation to all of us of the universality of the Cosmic Egg.

"The other matter concerns the demands of the males.

Let me assure all of you, females and males, that the Matriarchy is proud of males and values them greatly. I am saddened that some of them feel slighted. I will appoint a commission to study their status and make recommendations. Meanwhile I urge all males to resume their duties with full confidence that their concerns will receive thoughtful attention. We are all Heesh together!"

Among those who watched the broadcast was Dorkin, seated among other leaders of the League of Males in the secret chamber under the Grand Hall of the Egg. "Tellima is very plausible," he said, "but wait until we demand that males be placed on her commission. Obviously she hopes we'll lose our spirit while her commission dithers and mumbles forever."

"We will announce that the strike will continue at its present level at least until we see the report of her commission," said the new chairman, who had the replaced the one Oomis had killed. "Tellima knows that we can increase pressure by striking the Hall of Sustenance."

"Why don't we destroy the files in the Hall of Records?" a male asked. "A female who can't verify her egg line would have a hard time arguing her superiority. She wouldn't be able to confer a Necklace of Twelves."

They all looked at the member who worked in the Hall of Records. "They know their egg lines by heart," he said. "Anyway, there are duplicate records in case of fire, and those are in a tunnel in the mountains, well guarded."

"All we need to do is stand firm," the chairman said. "We won't get all we asked for, but we can get a lot. The strike is hurting the Matriarchy more than us. The females aren't fools, remember, and many of them can take over details the males were handling, but it's demeaning work for them. And don't forget we have many females with us. The bloody way the demonstration was put down today will help. Those were females being whipped. Other females will take their side."

Dorkin waited until late at night before going to Lippor's house. Knowing Oomis, he expected to find the house watched, and he saw someone leaning against a tree up the street. A former hunting guide who could stalk wild beasts at close range undetected, he slipped through shadows unseen until he reached the house next to Lippor's. Crossing the open space between houses looked risky. Dorkin climbed to the roof of the neighbor's house. Lippor's rooftop was no more than twice his height away. His muscular build and long legs enabled him to jump across easily. He dropped behind the house and entered it with his own key.

Lippor was asleep in the bedroom. He stood in the doorway and called softly, "Lippor! Lippor!" until she suddenly half rose from the bed. "It's Dorkin," he said. "Oomis is having you watched, but I had to see you."

"I'm glad," she said. "I need you. Dorkin, I don't know what to do. I think that males like you deserve more, but I don't like this strike at all. I couldn't support it if I did, because I would be demoted to greasing axles or something."

"You can help end the strike and help the males at the same time," he said. "Get yourself named to represent the Hall of Transportation on Tellima's commission investigating the complaints of males. Do what you can to persuade the commission to recommend real concessions, because the strike won't end without them." He paused before asking, "Do you see much of Oomis these days?"

"No. She's too busy."

"That's good. I think you should cut your ties with Oomis, for your own protection. Don't make her angry at you, but don't take the initiative to see her. Oomis is poison."

Chapter Eight

"You might as well send Judas on a diplomatic mission to the Vatican," Rusty said. "After all, I'm the one who killed the Prime Mother."

Marfor had learned who Judas was. "But you are also the one who saved the Prime Mother when you caught her alive right after she hatched," she answered. "Your team took pictures of that, along with Carlos collecting her mate. I can take them both to Naneg. You'll be a heroine."

Scientists and engineers had solved the problem of traveling to a simultaneous time on a different track. Instead of turning back in time, one twisted sideways. So much was obvious. Physicists had deduced the trick of it easily, but it had taken complex mathematics and massive computer power to turn theory into engineering. Marfor and Nim could return home, taking the Ishinol, with humans who would negotiate full diplomatic relations and would ask for the secret of space jumps and other advanced technology. Marfor wanted the *Pegasus* crew, whom she knew, to serve on the delegation. All of them wanted to see Naneg, although Allie raised an objection.

"I can't teach biogenetics and molecular medicine to the Heesh overnight," she said. "It takes years of study and lots of lab work. I can bring an analyzer and a synthesizer and a library of memory cubes, but for a long time they'll be flying blind."

"We learn fast," Marfor answered.

"The president will decide who goes," Carlos said. "The secretary of state may want to go himself. What a junket!"

"Don't let him leave Nick and me out," Meg pleaded.

"It would be like watching two acts of a play and leaving before the third."

Allie laughed. "This is a play without an end, but we should follow as much of it as we can."

"A whole new civilization would be worth seeing," Dan said. "And think of the new plants! There are probably entire families of plants that developed on Naneg but not on Earth."

"And different birds and fish and reptiles. The Hanishan, which we don't have any of. Not to mention mammals, which Marfor has told us are nothing but little pests but which survived dinosaurs and now the Heesh."

"Let's hear it for our side," Allie said.

Rusty took Marfor's hand. "You get the idea. I hope you'll insist that the president send all of us."

"I have already asked him to. How could I leave behind such a group of dedicated scientists, all eager to put Naneg under a microscope? You are friends of mine, and I would hate to leave you. Right, Nim?"

"As your deputy, I strongly urge you to hold out for having our friends join us. I think they will make a good impression."

"In time, but not at first. My friends, you know it does not reflect my personal feelings when I say that you may arouse as much antagonism on Naneg as Nim and I did at first on Earth."

"We can't help it if we're gorgeous," Allie said.

Marfor met with the president and secretary of state. They were pleased with Carlos's work as liaison officer with Marfor, but President Parker had doubts about appointing him ambassador. "I don't want to get off on the wrong foot. Your people give precedence to females. I had in mind sending a woman who is president of Harvard. That's a place for higher education."

"Can she speak Heesh?" Marfor asked. "Colonel Lecompte can."

"He doesn't have enough rank to head an embassy," the secretary of state said.

Quibbling of that sort made the president bristle. "He will have whatever rank I say he has, and I'm going to

name him a major general and ambassador to the Heesh."
The president prided himself on his judgment of people
and on his decisiveness. "He can take his *Pegasus* crew,
but we'll have to beef that up. I want him to arrive in
something better than that oil can he flew backward in
time. It has to have room for an assortment of experts to
find out all they can about the Heesh and trade information
with them."

The most modern cruiser built for the Space Corps was
taken. It was modified to cross a rung between parallel
legs on the time ladder and was christened the *Ishtar* after
the ancient Assyrian goddess of fertility and war. Except
for the mother goddess of Crete, she was Earth's nearest
equivalent to a cosmic mother. *Ishtar* was not an egg, of
course, but the Space Corps would never hold still for
naming its best ship the *Egg*. The corps liked a warri-
or goddess who carried a bow into battle while riding a
chariot drawn by seven lions. She was also the goddess of
love, including illicit love, but there was no need to dwell
on that.

Carlos and his team would arrive at Naneg in a ship
armed to fight its way out with missiles, lasers, and parti-
cle beams if it had to. The armament was standard on ships
of the Space Corps and had nothing to do with the present
mission, Marfor was assured. As a gesture to the Heesh, the
crew would include more women than men. There would
be humans of every color to show the Heesh that beings
who were recognizably different could work together as
equals. The president picked them as if he were balanc-
ing the mix to satisfy all constituencies when choosing his
cabinet.

Before the launch Carlos was summoned to a meeting
with the president. "It's important to learn the secret of
space jumps from the Heesh, but friendly relations should
produce much more than that. I have full confidence in you
to get things moving in the right direction, Lecompte. No
officer has ever had a greater opportunity to perform an
invaluable service."

Translation: If you mess it up, you can eat your medals.

*   *   *

Space near Naneg buzzed with useful satellites but was not patrolled. Nevertheless, Marfor thought it best for the *Ishtar* not to barge in and land when it arrived but to proceed with delicacy. She had been disgraced and was probably thought to be dead, and she did not know how welcome the humans would be. Carlos agreed, and she radioed a message.

"This is Senior Matron Marfor of the Hall of Ancients. I am in a space ship above Naneg. I request direct communication with the supreme matriarch."

Many of the Heesh heard that, Marfor thought. They will all listen for what comes next.

What they heard next was the voice of Junior Matron Heem. "Senior Matron Marfor died during the search for the Prime Mother. If she had not died, she would have had no way of returning. Who are you?"

"As I will inform the supreme matriarch, the search had unexpected results. If you think I had no way to return, why don't you track the ship I'm in?"

Senior Matron Mosnik came next. "We are tracking an unidentified ship. If you are Marfor, identify yourself completely."

That was a sound move, Marfor thought. They asked the Hall of Records for my lineage, which no one but my mother and daughter and I would know. "I am Marfor Endos Limfor Astelis," she began, continuing for all twenty-five names and adding the names of earlier ancestors whom her grandmother had chosen for her Necklace of Twelves.

"This is Grand Matron Shandor," said the next voice. "The supreme matriarch is busy. Where did you get a spaceship?"

"That is one of the things that the supreme matriarch will want to hear directly from me." Nothing had changed in the protocol for working one's way up the hierarchy, but normal administrative routine made her impatient under the circumstances. "Naturally I would not think of interrupting Her Supremacy while she is busy. I will await her convenience."

Convenience began to look like a rare commodity while

Marfor waited. Naneg, below her, filled her viewing screen invitingly. Fluffy white clouds beckoned across the blue-green sea to green land and a home that she had missed for more than a year now. How welcome it would be to replace the disorderly world of Earth with all that was familiar and comfortable! Paleontology had made her more at home in the savage world of the Ishinol than on Earth, with its office towers that made her dizzy, jammed walkways and streets, incomprehensible activities, and constant clash of opinions on every subject. Best of all, her daughter and the grand-daughter she had never seen would await her.

Nim watched her fidget and said, "We'll be there soon. I'm as eager to get back as you are."

"We're all eager to land," said Carlos, seated near her at the controls. "Every man and woman on the ship is staring at Naneg on a screen."

The trip between time tracks had worried him. Nobody had ever done it before. The assurances of assorted mathematicians, physicists, and engineers that it would go like clockwork—and what would be more fitting for a trip across time, ha, ha!—had not impressed him. Earth and Naneg were like the bows of ships sailing their time lines, and a curve that made allowance for moving terminuses would connect them. They did not know how great the divergence was or how long the trip would take, but everyone knew that time was conservative. Assuming that the tracks were near each other, a scan of space would reveal Naneg.

So it had, and Naneg's track was remarkably close to Earth's. The sister planets were invisible to each other by the usual methods of observation because their coordinates in the total complexity of space-time included normally exclusive time factors. Both planets appeared at the same time when the connecting dimension was found. Carlos had found Naneg as soon as he had twisted his ship into the newly discovered dimension. The trip took only two weeks.

One thing was surprising. The sun and other planets appeared, but there were only six stars against the blackness of space. He was still wondering about that when he entered

Naneg's atmosphere. It was as if alternate time tracks were variables limited to a single solar system, except that they could be extended to others by something like the Heesh exploration of the stars. Carlos put that puzzle aside. He no longer had to worry about the trip, only about what he would do now that he had reached his destination.

Finally the voice that Marfor awaited spoke. "All right, Marfor, this is Tellima. What's going on? Start with how you escaped from a triceratops and got here."

"I'm sure Oomis showed you pictures of another race, the humans. They saved me and took me back to their world. They brought me here and have a lot to talk to you about. They also went back in time and found the Prime Mother and her mate, removed them from the time track in which they would die, and gave them to me to bring to you. I repeat: I am bringing the Prime Mother. May I land?"

"In the name of the Egg!" Talk about humans and time tracks could wait. "Land at once and bring the Prime Mother to me. I'll have the plaza in front of the Hall of the Matriarchy cleared for your ship."

"May I bring some humans with me?"

"Yes. I have a strong stomach."

Carlos heard that. "Our turn," he said.

After orbiting the planet for a gradual descent, he landed vertically on the pavement in the center of the plaza, which Marfor pointed out to him. The Hall of the Matriarchy followed the plan that he was to learn was usual for important buildings. This one had a golden egg-shaped dome in the center, four stories tall, with two-story buildings like a cluster of silver eggs around it. He was glad that his rockets hadn't scorched it. Trees around the plaza had sacrificed their leaves to the blast of air stirred up by the landing. Carlos had an escalator lowered from the hull.

As soon as the pavement had cooled a delegation approached the *Ishtar* from the hall. They dragged Lippor away from whatever she was doing to help greet me, Marfor thought. They brought my mother and daughter! Thoughtful touches like these have helped Tellima reach the top. Guardians are posted at streets leading to the plaza, but I don't see Oomis among them. Good. There are holovision cameras. Very good.

"All hands stay aboard the ship until further notice, except for the *Pegasus* team," Carlos announced. "They will come with Ambassador Marfor and her deputy and me. Prepare to lower the Ishinol at my order."

He had put on a dress green uniform with medals across his chest and two stars on each shoulder board, insignia of the rank that the president had thought would suit an ambassador to another planet. It was fun to be a two-star general despite the way brigadier generals groused at his being jumped over them in promotion. Both the men and the women with him would be dressed formally in white turtleneck shirts, green jackets, and black pants.

Marfor came down the escalator first. As Nim and the *Pegasus* team arrived and stood behind her, a grand matron faltered at the sight of the humans but welcomed them all by crossing her hands, palms up, and pronouncing, "In the name of the Egg." Immediately she asked, "Where is the Prime Mother?"

"In a moment." Marfor crossed her hands in response to the welcome and then in greetings to her mother, her daughter, and Lippor. Lippor, she saw, now wore the insignia of a senior matron. She doesn't look comfortable at seeing me again.

"You'll be on Necklaces of Twelves for thousands of generations!" her daughter exclaimed.

"The only necklace I care about is the one I will confer on my granddaughter in a few years. Tell me about her."

"She's strong and bright, and Homlik is taking good care of her. It was a perfect hatching. I named her Nellis."

Reassured about her egg line, Marfor returned to business. She nodded to Carlos, who signaled the ship to have both Ishinol lowered in a cage on wheels. They had nearly reached their full size of a meter long. Perhaps alarmed by the rocking of their cage as they were lowered by a winch, they began fighting, clawing and snapping at each other, leaving bloody scratches on their freshly cleaned down. As they reached the ground the male cowered in a corner of the cage while the Prime Mother gripped the bars and screeched a challenge to the world outside.

"That is the Prime Mother," Marfor announced to the watching world. "The other one is her mate." The supreme matriarch, she knew, would be watching on holovision.

Marfor was glad that the Prime Mother had won the fight. She was also glad that everyone had seen that the Prime Mother was a savage beast dragged from the quagmire of evolution. The Heesh in the delegation had confronted the alien humans, grotesque creatures, with scarcely a shudder, but they showed dismay as they gathered around the Ishinol cage, staying well clear of claws that reached through the bars. After they had had a good look, a screen of steel links was draped over the cage.

"I will honor you, you, you, and you," the grand matron said as she chose four junior matrons to escort the cage. They would order a truck for it and a hoist to get it on the truck without being clawed. She led the way into the Hall of the Matriarchy.

Marfor dropped back beside Lippor and whispered, "Where's Oomis?"

"She's hunting for Dorkin. Many males have gone on strike demanding equal rights, and Dorkin is one of the leaders. He is in hiding."

Glancing at Nim, Marfor saw from his almost imperceptible nod that he had overheard. "We must have a private talk as soon as possible," she said to Lippor.

"I wronged you, and I want to make amends," Lippor said.

"Help the humans." They would be as unwelcome as rodents. "Anything you can do for them will be a favor to me."

Tellima and several others awaited the arrival in the reception rotunda of the hall. She kept the travelers waiting until the Ishinol had been transferred to a dolly and could be pushed and dragged in with them by the junior matrons. Tellima immediately went to the cage to see the Prime Mother, which tried to reach her with her claws. What would she do with this thing and her mate? Why couldn't Marfor have died when she was supposed to die?

This was a cruel trick for the Spirit of the Egg to play.

"I'm glad you're back," Tellima said to Marfor, not realizing that the humans could understand her. "Your mission is a greater success than we had dreamed. I am happy to confer on you the rank of grand matron."

"Thank you, Your Supremacy."

"You may present the humans and act as translator."

"This is Ambassador Carlos Lecompte, who led the expedition that rescued me and the Ishinol. He speaks Heesh well. Now he hopes to establish diplomatic relations and an exchange of ambassadors between the Matriarchy and the United States of America, which is the most powerful nation on his planet, Earth."

"Indeed? How many nations does your planet have, Ambassador?"

"Thirty-eight, Your Supremacy. There were more in the past, but many combined with others." He studied the supreme matriarch's appearance. The same height as Marfor, she was a little thicker in the body but still all arms and legs. Her eyes were narrower and her down was touched with gray. Naturally she wore a Necklace of Twelves.

Tellima wondered if she would be expected to exchange embassies with thirty-eight countries. "I see from your leadership of this group that it is true, as we have heard, that your males are dominant."

"Not necessarily. Males are dominant in the armed forces, from which I come, but share the highest offices with females in other activities." He was not sure that he was suited to twirl gracefully in a waltz of diplomatic palaver. No doubt the niceties were important to his business here.

"Is the leader of your country a male or a female?"

"A male," Carlos answered with honesty and embarrassment. "In some countries the leader is a female." Offhand he could think of six.

Tellima went to the others, for she had the gift of kings and queens and presidents and premiers of exchanging a few polite words with many at a gathering, and she was genuinely interested in these caricatures of the Heesh. Despite their pinched faces, the hair on their heads, and the peculiar swelling of the chests of the females, humans were not as repulsive as she had expected.

"This is Rusty Rourke, the wife of Ambassador Lecompte," Marfor said. "She is the one who recovered the Prime Mother."

"After killing her first, I believe," said Tellima. "I have seen the pictures our expedition took of you. Your red hair is unmistakable. Well, we are indebted to you now. What is a wife?"

"A female who has contracted to live with a male."

"Can she end the contract?"

"Yes, and so can the male. In some countries the custom differs."

"Your world sounds confusing," Tellima said. She soon learned that Meg Ingraham had taken the last name of her husband, Nick, upon marriage, but Allison Steele had not taken the name of her husband, Daniel Lundgren. Evidently they had a choice. "Does a male ever take the name of his wife?" she asked.

"Some men add the names of their mothers," Carlos put in, thinking of his mother's native Mexico.

Ah! That was civilized. Tellima turned to Dan, whose size and blond hair fascinated her. He looked as tall as Oomis, and heavier. He had been introduced to her as a botanist but Tellima asked, "Are you also here to guard the others?"

"I hope not," Dan answered. "I'm a peaceful man."

"That's because nobody gets in his way," Allie said. His glance made her want to bite off her hasty tongue.

After chatting with Meg and Nick, Tellima offered quarters to Marfor and Nim, since Marfor's had been occupied since her supposed death. "I will ask you to come again tomorrow for talks at much greater length, just between the two of us," she said to Carlos. "I presume you will be comfortable aboard your ship."

"Quite comfortable. I will await your summons. Let me add one thing. My crew would like to explore your city and learn about the Heesh. Please consider when that will be possible."

"Soon. The Hall of Guardians will provide guides. You

speak Heesh well, but I assume that your crew does not. A computer learned your language, as I recall, and the memory can be linked to terminals wherever your compatriots go."

The Ishinol were fighting, Tellima saw as the delegation left. Let her attendant male figure out what to do with them. Figuring out how to handle the humans would be her problem. As if she didn't have enough troubles! She was sure of one thing. It wouldn't be dull.

That night a friend called Nim to invite him to join a small gathering of males at a public house to celebrate his return. They drank fermented kalnay juice, mildly intoxicating, and heard him describe the United States as a land of oases of wealth in an overpopulated slum, with large areas in which entire cities had been abandoned for lack of water. He learned from them about the strike.

"Construction has halted," the friend said. "Females can run the machines, but there's no one to tie and untie loads for the cranes or pour cement into the mixers or carry things around. Females are standing in long lines at the Hall of Records to get paperwork done without male clerks. You should see the females sweeping the floors at factories! Trash is piling up in the streets. Go in the back room and you'll learn more."

Dorkin waited for Nim there. "Lippor said you were in hiding," Nim said, noticing that Dorkin had concealed his scar. "Is this place safe for you?"

"If I don't stay too long." Dorkin grinned. "I no longer know what a front door looks like. The males are growing tired of the strike, and it needs a lift. I hope you can work through Marfor to arrange two things. Get the human males and females out together in public where everyone can see that the males are bigger but they treat each other as equals anyway. And put those miserable Ishinol on display!"

"The first is being arranged, and I don't see how Tellima can hide the Ishinol when everybody knows they're here. What are the stakes in the strike?"

"The League is asking equal opportunity for males. We want to have junior and senior and grand masters as well as matrons. We want the League to be named a formal advisory body to the Matriarchy. We want to add the category of companion males to that of attendant males. The companions would have equal status with the females they accepted and would not perform personal services unless the females shared them. We want the Hall of Records to keep lineages by male as well as female descent."

"You'll never get the females to give up their Necklaces of Twelves." Nim thought for a moment. "You may get males in the records, though, because males who look to the past will have standards to meet, if we're allowed to hold prominent posts."

"You're thinking the way Marfor does. Duty to the honorable ancestors! I think a lot of males will be like a lot of females, smugly satisfied to parade around in the trappings of ancestral glory and claim privileges they haven't earned. If male lineage is taken seriously, however, all males will gain status."

"I remember my father," Nim said. "He did more for me than my mother did. He should not be forgotten. His record should be kept as faithfully as hers."

"If Tellima agrees to exchange ambassadors, we have a new demand, places in the embassy staff. I'd like to go myself and see a world where males and females are equal, with a tilt toward the males."

Nim was still content to be with Marfor, but he was not as satisfied with his status as he had been before seeing Earth. He sympathized with the goals of the League of Males. They should win wider support when the humans and their customs became known on Naneg. Dorkin deserved a trip to Earth.

Carlos practiced talking Heesh with Rusty next morning until he was summoned by Tellima. Marfor joined him but no one else. A chief executive must always rely on others, Tellima thought, and she must rely on Marfor to correct any misrepresentations by this human.

"I have been thinking about an exchange of embassies," she said to Carlos. "It could be a mistake for the Heesh to deal with only one government on your world when there are thirty-eight. Is there no agency that represents all of them?"

"To a limited degree, there is," he answered. "It is called the United Nations. It is a forum for debates and for action on common problems, but it has no power to enforce decisions unless the stronger nations agree to support them. Grand Matron Marfor addressed a meeting of the United Nations and found some of its members hostile. The customs of the Heesh undermine their religious beliefs. I would suggest that you send an embassy to the United States first and then decide where to add others."

"I will think about it. Humans undermined our orthodoxy too, but we were able to account for you as a revelation of the powers of the Cosmic Egg. Meanwhile our first reports about you encouraged our males to disrupt the social and economic order. What do we have to gain from diplomatic relations with you?"

"We have much to learn from each other. Your computers and robots are better than ours. Our biological and medical knowledge is more advanced than yours. Yesterday you met Allison Steele, a molecular biologist, who has brought devices and texts for your scientists, if you are interested."

"She cured me of a disease I caught while working and one that Nim caught aboard their ship," Marfor said.

"Are you spreading disease here?" Tellima asked Carlos angrily.

"I doubt it. Marfor's disease was caught from an Ishinol, with an insect as vector. We have removed all vectors from the Prime Mother and her mate. When we found them, they were newly hatched, too young to be infected anyway. As for the humans here, the health of every one of them was thoroughly checked. If any of them carry hidden germs of disease, however, we also brought the means to make you immune."

"I don't like this at all. I have enough problems without a plague. Have your expert come talk to my doctors today. What do you want besides an exchange of missions?"

"An exchange of knowledge. You can make space jumps to the stars. We cannot. We want to learn how to do so from you. In return we will give you the knowledge of how to travel between time tracks."

"What about your medical knowledge?"

"That is yours, as a gesture of goodwill from us." With as much garbage as Allie can stir into the mixture, Carlos thought, if this creature proved uncooperative.

"The entire council of the Matriarchy will have to consider this," Tellima said. "I will want you to appear there."

"Gladly."

"May I ask about something else, Your Supremacy?" Marfor said. "What will you do with the Prime Mother and her mate?"

"The Hall of Science and Technology has them. They will build a compound and duplicate their natural habitat as nearly as possible. We can't put the Prime Mother in a zoo. There will be places where the Heesh can catch glimpses of them."

Carlos started to say something but stopped. "What is it?" Tellima asked.

"I was going to ask you about leave for my crew, but I don't want to trouble you about that now."

"They can leave your ship in groups of ten, three groups at a time. I will have guides for them tomorrow."

The grand matriarch was the kind of executive who made decisions promptly, Carlos thought as he thanked her.

Oomis will see me next, Tellima thought as Carlos and Marfor left. Oomis will make excuses for failure to find the leaders of the League of Males. She will want me to turn Naneg into a police state. There is no need for that, if I can arrange a compromise with the League of Males. Nor do I want Oomis running around with her whip. I can put her where she can't do any damage by making her responsible for planning a battle fleet for space, in case the humans cross between time tracks in force. A peaceful race would not have thirty-eight nations.

The logistics of warfare would favor the side nearest to its base, if armaments were equal. The space-time ship of the humans did not seem to be as advanced as Heesh ships. Peaceful relations would be best, of course.

* * *

Except for mining, Naneg's equivalents of Africa and South America were devoted largely to game preserves and hunting. The rest of the world had plenty of space for four hundred million Heesh. "They're a space race," Allie said, attempting a pun on the words. Even the tenements adjoined parks. No building stood more than six stories tall.

"Why are all the buildings so low?" Allie asked Marfor.

"We don't need tall buildings. We have plenty of space. On Earth I saw your ranch-style houses, all on one floor, for humans who had lots big enough for them. Even a six-story building looks unattractive to us. We like domes, and a series of domes rising that high must spread out and is too massive. You also waste space and power for elevators. You save horizontal space, of course, but we don't need that."

The capital city was laid out in curves, its principal avenues spiraling outward from the plaza and gardens around the Grand Hall of the Egg. Such an open arrangement required the Heesh to travel long distances from one place to another in the city. Matrons, the Guardians, and emergency services were allowed private vehicles; everyone else used computerized cars or buses or trucks that ran on tracks. Central tracks ran down the main streets; tracks at the sides of all streets received cars to be entered or left. A passenger entered the first empty car, punched the destination on the controls, and used an ID card to have the fee charged to a bank account. The car chose the route, switched from track to track, and stopped for cross traffic at intersections. On reaching her destination, a passenger abandoned the car to the next user. The Hall of Transportation monitored traffic and the computers that sent cars where they were needed.

"Wouldn't it be wonderful to have no traffic jams or parking problems?" Rusty asked Carlos.

"If you don't mind standing in the rain while you wait for a bus," he answered. "Our system at home may be a mess, but I like control over what I'm doing."

Batches of ten from the crew of the *Ishtar* had no control over the tours they were given. Taken first to the Grand

Hall of the Egg, they stood on a balcony to stare at the giant egg in the center of the hall and the golden Prime Mother in front of it while they listened to an obligatory lecture.

"The universe hatched from the Cosmic Egg and follows the Cosmic Plan," a junior matron told them through a translation robot. She didn't qualify her statement by saying "We believe." She was repeating axioms. A muffled gong sounded at irregular intervals as groups of worshipers, females ahead of males, approached the giant egg. They dropped incense into a glowing brazier and held their arms outstretched and hands flat, one on top of the other, in front of them while a priestess chanted a prayer.

"All nature is united by the Cosmic Plan," the junior matron said. "The plan has been brought to completion on Naneg by the evolution of the Heesh and their supremacy. To guide the Heesh and keep them in harmony with nature, the Cosmic Egg inspired right thinking and right conduct. Females and males are bound to each other by mutual respect, with the females given precedence because they continue the egg lines. They honor the Cosmic Egg by conduct that honors their egg lines. Males honor the Cosmic Egg by aiding the females as necessary."

The matron took the tourists past a room in which juvenile males and females together were memorizing the Book of Precepts, reciting it aloud in unison. The translator gave the passage being repeated: "Hear the words of the matriarchs to know what actions are good and bring harmony."

Most of the tourists took pictures of the large egg and worshipers in front of it.

As their bus took them through other parts of the city, they saw oak trees and ginkgoes indistinguishable from those at home to anyone but an expert botanist, trees like dogwoods but with orange blossoms, and flowers different from any that they knew. Stopping at a restaurant for lunch, they were served some kind of roasted Hanishan, which tasted like a cross between chicken and iguana. The final destination was the zoo, where they saw as many varieties of Hanishan as there were mammals on Earth, birds resembling those on Earth, and very few mammals. These were like rats or weasels and were seldom visited by the Heesh.

Heesh who happened to be at the zoo edged close to the humans with the queasy fascination of people at an alligator pit. The guides refrained from having computers translate Heesh remarks that they heard, which ranged from "How ugly they are!" to "How can things like that be intelligent?" and "Why don't they go back where they belong?" Each race took pictures of the other. The humans also took pictures of the pootas that flew close to their owners.

Allie, on orders from the supreme matriarch herself, tried to teach Heesh doctors the elements of molecular medicine. They didn't even have electron microscopes, let alone nucleotide sequencers or differential analyzers for molecular geometry. The best she could do was outline the principles, show the Heesh how she synthesized antibodies for several viruses presented to her, and leave them with a few rules of thumb. "Let me talk to your medical students, who have years ahead to work on this," she said. "I will leave some texts, but you will need many more, and years of laboratory work."

Meg and Nick worked feverishly at the Hall of Ancients. "Do you realize how they've turned paleontology into a branch of religion?" Meg asked. "Your invertebrates and even big things like dinosaurs are in side galleries. What they really care about is showing how they evolved from the Prime Mother and her Ishinol offspring."

She and Nick and their escort traveled in public cars or buses. Once, as they entered a bus, a female Heesh watched them sit in front and came up to them.

"You with short hair," she said to Nick. "Are you a male?"

"Yes." He didn't like her manner. "Why do you ask?"

"Males sit in the back of the bus. Move back where you belong."

Repressing his surge of anger, Nick looked behind him. Three males, whose crests stiffened as they watched intently, sat on rear seats. Several females sat ahead of them.

"Human males sit where they please," he said.

The female moved as if to strike him, but the escort, who was also female and may have agreed with her, said, "The humans are guests of the supreme matriarch. We must not offend them."

The female turned abruptly and sat down, on the other side of the bus, in the middle. Nick winked at Meg and wondered if the example he had set had furthered equality on Naneg.

"I'm glad you stood up for your rights," she said. "That may be difficult here."

Carlos prepared for a meeting with Tellima and the Matriarchy in full session. He persuaded Marfor to introduce him and Rusty to the twelve matriarchs, one at a time, in advance. He wouldn't be popular, any more than a gorilla would be popular among humans, but they might accept him as intelligent and reasonable. Only the matriarch from the Hall of Rites refused to meet with him. He made a point of asking the others about their Necklaces of Twelves and complimenting them upon their egg lines. Some appeared to be pleased but others turned down the corners of their mouths as if to ask, who are you to judge our lineage?

"There's an old saying that honey catches more flies than vinegar," he told Rusty. "Did you notice that they have bees here?"

"And butterflies. I'd hate to live in a world without butterflies."

A senior matron in botany who was a specialist in algae, an ancient form of life that continued to thrive on both Earth and Naneg, became friendly with Dan. She was impressed by his size, intrigued by the fact that a male could become a leading expert, and flattered by his interest in a subject about which she knew more than he did. He was primarily a leaf-and-pollen man. She invited him and Allie to join her and a colleague, whose specialty was orchids, for a social evening.

"This is the first time any of us humans has been invited to fraternize," Dan observed to Allie.

"We're prize specimens. She wants to show us off. I'll wear a short skirt to show them what legs should look like but go easy on the lipstick."

Their hostess, Sislinan, met them at the foot of the *Ishtar*'s escalator. A junior matron who rated a private car, she took them to what appeared to be the Heesh equivalent of a night club. A female maitre d' didn't need to check their reservation when she saw the humans. A male led them to a table while another male carried a translation terminal. Dan and Allie could speak a little Heesh but were not fluent. Conversation among patrons already seated stopped as everyone watched the small procession.

"Let's be gracious when they ask for autographs," Allie said.

"They're not all happy to see us," Dan answered. "Look at the frowns. We're celebrities but we're freaks. And notice how few other males are seated. If I've become any judge of crests, they are particularly handsome."

"Gigolos? Some of the females do look frayed."

A waiter brought drinks. They tasted like quinine water, not bad, but Dan was suspicious of unfamiliar stimulants. He caught Allie's eye and shook his head to warn her to sip sparingly. An appetizer of minced clams in a small mound of barleylike grain followed. Edible, but not the start of a three-star rating by a gourmet. The main course was shark fin, delicately fried and sprinkled with ground nuts. Dessert was a blob of unfamiliar berries in an unidentifiable gelatin. A world without mammals, except for vermin, had no milk or cheese or ice cream.

During dessert, while conversing with as much animation as a translation terminal allowed, Dan and Allie and their hostesses heard a hush fall over the room again. A large Heesh who wore a blue shirt and pants and had straps across her chest and around her waist was being escorted to a table. A whip hung at her side. Three other females with her wore the same uniform.

"Not so good," Dan said softly to Allie. "That's Oomis, the one I tangled with."

"I haven't forgotten Cuddles."

For their hostesses' benefit Dan said, "I've seen that big one with a whip before. She was with Marfor's team when it met ours sixty-five million years ago. Oomis is her name, isn't it?"

"Yes. Oomis is now a grand matron of the Hall of Guardians," Sislinan said. "She has been suppressing rebellious males."

Oomis saw them. Striding to their table, she jabbed one long finger toward the face of Sislinan and demanded, "Why are you with these spawn of a rotten egg? You disgrace us all."

The terminal on the table faithfully translated her words, and Sislinan's answer. "They have the favor of the supreme matriarch herself."

"She deals with them because she must. You do so by choice, demeaning yourself and violating the doctrine of the Cosmic Egg that places the Heesh above all other beings. Let shame and loss of status be your reward."

Oomis turned away and insisted that she be given a table as far as possible from the humans. Some of the Heesh in the room slapped their tables with the flats of their hands.

"I think they're applauding her," Allie said.

"Forgive this rudeness," Sislinan said. "They will forget Oomis when the entertainment begins."

While males were still clearing away the dessert dishes, the lights in the room, already dim, diminished to a faint glow. Two large females came onto a stage. They were evidently popular celebrities, for much table-slapping greeted them. They wore nothing but loincloths, giving Allie and Dan their first sight of Heesh bodies covered with down. Facing each other three meters apart, they stretched out their arms. Dan realized that they were about to engage in hand-to-hand combat, boxing or wrestling or judo or whatever the Heesh did.

One of the pair covered the distance between them in a single leap and slapped her opponent hard and fast, receiving a slap in return. Their hands are not made for hitting with fists, Dan thought, but the slaps with long bony fingers locked together look vicious. They grabbed at each other's arms and legs, loosened their grips when they were slapped, and grabbed again. One of them jerked the other off-balance and slammed a knee under her jaw. The second one staggered and threw her arms around the body of the first to stay upright. They pushed each other back and forth until the audience started to whistle, when they broke apart. Then, as one of them moved cautiously forward, the other one seized her wrist with a hand that flashed through the air, yanked her farther forward, and turned to throw her over a hip to the floor. Table-slapping began, for the contest had ended.

Dan looked up to see Oomis standing beside him.

"Can you fight, yellow-head?"

This creature needs a lesson, Dan thought with annoyance, but we're all diplomats here. "I am enjoying a pleasant evening," he said calmly. "I am not here to quarrel."

"Look at a male; see a coward," Oomis taunted him. "Let's see you crawl."

As fast as a snake strikes, her long arm lashed out to slap him from cheek to ear. Before he was fully conscious of how much the blow had hurt he was out of his chair, driving his fist at her belly. But Oomis was faster than any human he had ever seen. She dodged to one side and took only a glancing blow that didn't hurt her.

"Up on the stage," she said. Tossing her whip on her table, she went to the stage and stripped to her loincloth, throwing her uniform aside, but keeping her boots. Then she folded her arms and stared at him, large eyes unblinking and lips parted over sharp teeth. Her body was as straight and looked as tough as the trunk of a tree covered with brown fuzz instead of bark. Her arms and legs were sinewy and linked to knots of muscles.

Dan knew that he could not avoid fighting her without branding the human race as cowards. He stood up. "Are there any rules?" he asked Sislinan.

"Just get her down. I hope you do. A lot of us don't like Oomis. Watch out for her feet."

"Put a scissors lock on her neck," Allie said.

"I haven't wrestled in years," he answered. But hard work during his months in the Late Cretaceous had put him in good condition, which he hadn't yet lost.

"You're supposed to strip to the waist," Sislinan told him.

He frowned. Allie grinned and said, "Give the voyeurs a treat."

"Wrestlers don't wear much at home, and boxers wear less," Dan said irritably, but with resignation. He stripped to his undershorts and shoes. Walking to the stage with his head high, he heard rumbles, almost growls, from the audience. They are repelled by my naked white skin, he thought. The little hair on my chest and arms and legs is a poor substitute for their pelts of down. Oomis may be disgusted but she won't be distracted. She is appraising my broad shoulders, my flat belly, and smoothly sculptured muscles.

He stood in a slight crouch, with his arms extended, three meters from Oomis and waited for her to make the first move. The crowd in the restaurant was silent, as if many of them disapproved of what was happening, but no one wanted to interrupt a conflict that would be the talk of Naneg.

Oomis sidled closer. Dan readied himself to pivot if she kicked at him. She had struck with her right hand and would kick with her right foot. Instead, surprising him completely, Oomis jumped straight up in the air. As he raised his arms instinctively, she scissored her legs and kicked at his face. One hand deflected her foot, which scraped against the ear already bruised by her slap, and she landed lightly to dance away.

Close with her, he thought. Use my strength against her speed. He shuffled forward, reaching out with his arms, watching her hands, not her eyes. She slapped him again and again, stinging him with blows like drumsticks on a drum, blows too fast for him to block, enjoying herself as she tantalized him.

Dan sensed a regularity, a rhythm, in her blows, and he knew he had her. Timing his own move to hers, he seized her right wrist in his right hand and pulled her arm across in front of him. Reaching above her elbow with his left hand as she tried vainly to pull away, he shoved her upper arm, bending the arm at the elbow and twisting it with a hammerlock as she was forced to turn her back toward him. He raised her arm higher, wrenching her shoulder. She leaned forward to lessen the pain and kicked backward, striking a shin. He clamped his other arm around her in a headlock, dragged her to one side, and tripped her so that she fell to the floor.

Dan let go and stepped back. As he understood it, the fight was over. But Oomis kicked at him from the floor, striking one of his knees painfully. Angrily he dropped on top of her. Trying to wriggle away, she rolled onto her belly, but he held her easily with one hand, slipped an arm under one of hers and behind her neck, and pressed her head against the floor.

"Is that enough?" he asked, forgetting that she couldn't understand him without a translator.

Oomis reached behind her with her free hand to claw at his eyes.

Pressing his face tightly against her back to protect it, Dan clamped an arm around her waist and stood up. He released the half nelson at her neck and lifted her, face up, over his head with both hands. Turning completely around once, so that Oomis whirled helplessly in the air in full view of everyone, he threw her to the floor. She moved slowly, unable to rise.

Dan returned to his table and said calmly, "I've enjoyed the evening, but I think it's time to go."

Nobody applauded. Oomis had shamed the Heesh as well as herself.

"You may have blown our mission out the tubes," Carlos said gloomily to Dan.

"I had to fight her. I had no choice."

"Maybe so, but I have to confine you to the ship. I'll tell the Heesh I'm punishing you for conduct unbecoming a guest. That may help." Carlos looked at the big man's contrite, unhappy expression and said, "Between us, I'm glad you beat her."

"He doesn't act very glad," Allie complained to Dan when they were in private and he had reported Carlos's decision and his comment. "He ought to back you up all the way. What does he think it would have done to our precious mission if Oomis had left you lying injured on the floor? The Heesh would have laughed at us. They would have thought she had proved we were inferior."

"I think they're smarter than that. They won't think that they are inferior because I beat Oomis. Carlos did the right thing, considering the delicate situation we're in. But so did I. Nothing ever gave me greater satisfaction than giving that arrogant fanatic her comeuppance."

Marfor confirmed to Carlos his fear that Dan's defeat of Oomis had aroused ill feeling. "Everyone blames her," she told him, "but they do not like to have the Heesh look weaker than humans and they do not like it at all to have a male beat a female."

Heesh males might feel differently, Carlos thought, but Heesh males couldn't help him. "How does Tellima feel?"

"Mixed. My mother reports that Tellima detests Oomis and is glad Dan taught her a lesson, but Tellima favors your proposals and is afraid Dan may have turned some of the matriarchs against you."

Tellima was delighted that Oomis, feared as a bully, had been bested in a trial of strength and agility. Oomis had picked the fight and deserved her disgrace. Tellima censured Oomis publicly for discourtesy to guests. All of Oomis's aunts and cousins together couldn't win her a seat on the Council of the Matriarchy now. But Tellima knew that Oomis was too ambitious and zealous to remain in obscurity. As for the humans, Tellima had known from the start that their proposals had to be debated by the council. She summoned Carlos to a council meeting.

All of the most important persons on the planet are here, Carlos thought as he confronted a circle of grotesque faces staring at him with large eyes. They look like witches gathered on Bald Mountain. Who guessed when we went to the Late Cretaceous that it would lead to this? Carlos Lecompte, apprentice negotiator. I hope I've made some friends here. Dan must have made some enemies.

"We will discuss two questions," Tellima told the council. "First, do we want to establish formal relations with a human nation on Earth. Second, do we want to exchange the technology of space jumps for the technology of traveling between time tracks. Ambassador Lecompte, state your position."

"Thank you, Your Supremacy," Carlos said. "I thank all of you for the generous hospitality and the enlightenment we humans have received on Naneg." Slathering on a little grease might help. He should ignore Dan's fight with Oomis as too trivial to be worth mentioning. "Since the Heesh and humans have found each other, there will inevitably be continuing interest and further contacts. I think that friendly and cooperative relations will be productive. We have much to learn from each other. The appearance of Grand Matron Marfor on Earth has already stimulated my people to keep better records of their ancestors and give them greater honor." That should go over well. "But the customs of one race may not suit the other." The Heesh males were on their own. "The greatest benefit will come from the exchange of science and technology."

"We need more human biology and medicine," said a matriarch from the Hall of Healing. "We need human teachers."

"We do not need more human contamination of doctrine," the matriarch from the Hall of Rites answered.

"We were getting along better without the humans," said a female from the Hall of Resources, whose mines were idle. "They brought encouragement to the males who went on strike."

"I would like to send the humans home and erase them from our records and forget them forever," another female said.

"Impossible." It was the matriarch from the Hall of Learning. "Somebody always remembers. Scholars discover what happened and write new records. If there are problems, it's better to deal with them openly. I agree with the ambassador that there will be further contacts. Are we going to let them remain able to reach us while we can't reach them?"

"That raises the question of trading extradimensional technologies," Tellima said. "You are out of order."

Nevertheless the thought that humans could visit them without return visits from the Heesh weighed on the matriarchs' minds during further discussion. When the matriarch from the Hall of Science and Technology, who saw much to gain, moved that the Heesh exchange ambassadors and delegations, the motion passed on a vote of seven to five.

"Now we will consider trading space technologies," Tellima said. "Matriarchs, what are your opinions?"

"It seems clear to me that we are at a disadvantage if the humans can reach us at will, but we can't reach them," one matriarch said.

"The human offer is generous," added another. "The technology of star jumps has little value. A jump takes tremendous energy for the knowledge you gain."

"Can you use the same technique to travel between planets?" Carlos asked.

"No. A star is the node for the necessary distortion of space. Care must be taken to reenter normal space well away from the star, or you will be drawn into it. When you are back in normal space, you deal with normal gravitation. Planets have small nodes, but the star's mass is so much greater that it overwhelms them."

"Nevertheless, all knowledge is useful, and we of Earth would like the opportunity, at least, to gain it. Someday, I predict, life will be found around another star."

"Spoken like a Heesh," said the matriarch from the Hall of Science. "I move that we exchange these technologies and look for others that can be shared."

The motion passed eight to four.

How obvious, Carlos thought when space jumps were explained. They worked on the same principle as quantum jumps of an electron from one orbit to another in an atom without appearing in between. All that was needed was a way to home in on a focus, the node that had been mentioned, and reach its vicinity.

Eager to return home with a team of Heesh experts on taking shortcuts to the stars, Carlos had to wait for Tellima to assemble specialists for a delegation to study

life on Earth. Marfor would return as an officially designated ambassador, fully documented. The League of Males
asked Tellima to designate Dorkin to join the embassy to
Earth as an independent observer. She agreed in return for
a concession: strikers would return to work at the Hall of
Finance. Since Dorkin was going, Lippor wanted to go too,
and Marfor named her as a deputy.

Now that Dorkin could appear in public without fear
of being arrested, he came with Lippor to see Carlos and
Rusty in preparation for the trip to Earth. He brought one
of the handbills that had been printed with Rusty's picture
of the female Heesh on an egg dragged by males.

"Do you remember this?" he asked her.

"Of course. I transmitted it to you."

"The League of Males distributed a million copies. It
stiffened the spines of a lot of males who were afraid to
join our strike. We owe you a debt. Now we wonder whether you could paint something else for our propaganda. The
Heesh have no experience with such things."

"Oh, no!" Rusty said without prompting from Carlos.
"We are in a delicate position with the matriarchs. We cannot offend them by interfering in a Heesh controversy."

"I suppose not," Dorkin agreed reluctantly. "Too bad."

"Please don't say where you got the painting you used."

"I told my friends it was painted by a human, but I didn't
say it was you, and I won't. Tellima might figure it out anyway. We met only six humans in the Age of Dinosaurs."

"If I paint any pictures here, I will keep them in my
room, where none of the Heesh will see them and put two
and two together."

Marfor did not tell the rest of her staff until they got
into space that Nim would be her first deputy. They were
accustomed to the influence of attendant males who could
speak for ranking females, but few of them were pleased
to have the arrangement formalized and corresponding rank
awarded.

Since the humans had brought advanced biomedical
equipment, Tellima sent back with Marfor an advanced
computer and the specifications for the most versatile Heesh
robot, the spiderlike machine with eight arms.

Chapter Nine

Almost as soon as the *Ishtar* brought Marfor and Nim back to Earth with an entourage of experts, pickets appeared in front of the Heesh embassy. Beneath pictures of the gaping jaws of a tyrannosaurus, their signs read "Save America! Ban the Heesh!" They chanted the same slogans as they marched in a small circle outside the embassy gate. Once they tried to block a limousine containing Marfor and Nim from leaving. The police quickly moved them aside. Not many people watched, but newspaper and holovision cameras took pictures for the world to see.

"Opening a closed mind is as hard as cracking a coconut with your teeth," Rusty told Marfor. "Oh. You don't know about coconuts yet."

"But I do. Naneg's palm trees include coconut palms."

Carlos soothed her. "Don't worry about the crazies. You lost the initiative while you were away. Now you can regain it. Remember, the president is behind you. Your experts can start feeding us ideas that will make life easier for Americans."

"I'll ask to see the president to agree on what to do first."

"Right. Offer him a platter of goodies."

"Another thing I want to do is buy a bigger embassy. After learning something about Earth finances the last time I was here, I brought a lot of gold along. The Heesh embassy should be second to none. I represent a world, not just a nation."

"Don't blow that horn too loudly," Rusty advised her. "Other nations are proud and would resent it. You need friends wherever you can find them. I will bet a ten-carat diamond against a kumquat that other nations are incensed at being left out. Oh. You don't know carats or kumquats."

"No, but I get the idea. Ork! There are so many details! Carlos, I will ask your help in finding a hotel for the Heesh who came with me. They shouldn't have to stay aboard the *Ishtar*."

Carlos nodded his agreement. "Hotel rooms and shuttle buses. Security cars too. The crazies can be shouted down, but they shouldn't be ignored. The president will have the Secret Service take care of that."

"So I do have to worry about the crazies. I think I'd rather face dinosaurs. I'm glad you'll make the arrangements." She shook her head with disgust. "Let's get past housekeeping details. I should give two receptions soon." Marfor had already decided on one, but Rusty's remarks made her amend her plans. "The first one should be for ambassadors from other nations to smooth matters over with them. Then I should entertain the people the president had me meet, the people who entertained me, and the experts in law, finance, manufacturing, the sciences, and other activities my people will deal with. A social acquaintance helps in business dealings. There's an old Heesh saying: A spoonful of kalnay juice is better grease than a tub of nashon oil. Oh. You don't know nashon oil."

Smiling at the sly dig, tit for tat, Carlos said, "Like olive oil, is my guess. For the receptions you want, you'll have to rent a ballroom."

"And I've never given a reception. The idea makes me want to hide in a closet."

"You'll be good at it," Nim assured her. "You didn't rise in rank in the Hall of Ancients just by learning to tell one bone from another. You've done everything well since you hauled us back through time."

Nearly everyone who was invited came to the receptions, even the ambassadors of nations that were still trying to limit women to roles established by patriarchal ancestors. They had to see the enemy at firsthand. Marfor had brought with her on the *Ishtar* enough kalnay juice to let the Heesh have a familiar drink and let humans sample it, if they chose. She and Nim sipped glasses of water tinted to resemble white wine. On the advice of the assistant secretary of state, guests were served a vintage white wine from California and choice liquor, no cheap stuff like ordinary bar scotch. Guests at both parties became happily animated. Only one ambassador had to be helped to his limousine.

Then work began.

Lippor, as the senior space engineer among the Heesh, learned how to modify a time drive to cross between time tracks. She added theoretical and technical details to what Carlos had been told about star jumps and identified the stars whose planets the Heesh had found barren.

A junior matron from the Hall of Rites, who resolved to cling to a raft of faith in a torrent of blasphemies, ventured forth to a divinity school. Shocked by a prayer that began with "Our Father," she was happy to learn that a sect in India believed in the Cosmic Egg.

Dorkin set himself the task of learning systematically about the relations between males and females on Earth. He was learning English too, but with difficulty, and persuaded Dan to go with him as interpreter. Among all humans Dan was Dorkin's favorite because he had given Oomis her comeuppance.

"You bet women are equal to men," a man told him. "They're ferociously equal."

"We have to keep banging on the lid," a woman answered. The women Dorkin talked to seemed pleased that females dominated life on Naneg but reluctant to describe the organizational and political techniques they had developed to aid females on Earth.

More useful to Dorkin were meetings with labor leaders. They taught him about variations upon strikes, the sit-in and the slow-down, about picket lines, and about fringe benefits that had never occurred to the League of Males. I'll go back stuffed with ideas, he thought.

Heesh experts in biology and medicine accepted glumly what Allie had already told them, that their ideas were antiquated and that it would take long hard work to catch up. They absorbed theory and asked that teachers come to

Naneg with laboratory equipment to set up courses.

"I don't understand why Heesh physical science and engineering are more advanced than ours while biology and medicine lag behind," Allie said to a Heesh leader.

"It may be a matter of chance," answered the leader, who was a female. "We're not that far apart, for each of us can understand what the other is doing. We have concentrated on technology because it helps us do so many things that make life easier." She hesitated. "As for biology, we have been too well satisfied with the rules of inheritance, which were laid down by the Cosmic Egg, to look into the details of genetics on the cellular level. That's where your greater knowledge of biology begins."

Heesh experts in electronics and engineering did all that Marfor had hoped. "I would like to give your people something they will be happy to get and make them glad we are here," she told the president.

"Do you have any suggestions?"

"Yes. Our robots are useful because, within the directives they are given, they can show initiative. Yours have to be programmed in detail. Ours have a randomizing factor that lets them choose among alternatives and determine the optimum action, within limits."

"We can do some of that, as in traffic control."

"But they don't have the flexibility or the capacity for many different actions simultaneously that our spider robot does. We can pack more computer circuits into the same space, and we have cross-linkages that you haven't developed yet. I suggest that we show your engineers how to build spider robots. They can roam up and down assembly lines to control the work better and take over an assembly flow if necessary. All they need to know is what the finished product and its parts should be. They can do almost any task you set them." Marfor hesitated before confessing. "I have one guarding my embassy, along with the guards you have provided, and another at the Heesh hotel."

"Do they have guns?" the president asked with alarm.

"No. They are ready to grab people if they have to and hold them until one of your guards arrives."

The president thought for a moment. "You need to introduce something that a lot of people can use. Some everyday gadget. Like a lawn mower."

Heesh engineers worked out circuitry that would guide a lawn mower while it cut grass, avoided flowers, and trimmed the edges. It could distinguish among objects in its path, turning around dogs, babies, and decorative statuary while picking up pebbles or loose paper. Naturally it collected all the cuttings and took them to a trash bag. For a small additional charge it could be adapted to dig dandelions. These Heesh had something, people agreed.

"Don't forget to take out patents," Allie advised Marfor. "You'll lease them for plenty to pay your bills on Earth."

"I would rather let people use the techniques free as a gesture of goodwill."

That all was not yet well became plain one night while Lippor and Dorkin were being driven from the hotel to a movie theater. A security car preceded theirs. Lippor's sensitive eyes picked out a furtive movement ahead. "Somebody's hiding in the shadows in that alley," she told the driver.

He stopped and radioed ahead. A spotlight from the lead car flooded the alley. A man stood erect, tossed something in a high arc, and threw himself to the ground. A moment later a bomb exploded in violent sound and flames. Lippor, Dorkin, and their driver were thrown backward in their car. As the car accelerated to escape from the area, they saw that the car ahead had become a flaming tangle of metal.

"Can we get them out of the fire?" Lippor demanded.

"No chance." The driver talked on his radio. "Emergency vehicles will be here soon, but those men are gone."

She saw walls on both sides of the alley, lit by flames, that had been shattered by the explosion.

"Are you hurt?" Dorkin asked, taking her hand.

"No. Are you?"

"Shaken up is all. I guess there are still people here who want to see us out of the way."

The best that firemen could do was keep the fire from spreading. Police found the two security men who had been in the car burned beyond recognition. The man who had thrown the bomb was also dead. He carried a card identifying him as a member of Save America.

The news made front-page headlines and became the first item on broadcasts. The president denounced the attack, and pundits assured the populace that every right-thinking person should be outraged. Only Max Lannin of Save America said that, naturally, he was sorry that a man who claimed to be one of his followers had descended to violence, but, after all, it was understandable.

"It doesn't appear that Lannin ordered the bombing," a Secret Service man told Carlos. "The bomb was an amateur job. A professional bomb would have taken out half the block."

"He might as well have ordered it. He was the one who got the man worked up to do it."

A different, continuing story pleased nearly everyone. Holovision made the most of it. Nim tapped America's love of sports by trying them out himself.

"Nim hits homer," headlines said when he did it. His keen eyesight, corded muscles, speed, and coordination made him a natural at wielding a bat. Unfortunately, he couldn't catch well, even with a glove made to fit his three-fingered hand. "Nim slams dunks a basket; bruised in court collision," read another headline. Nim knew better than to risk his slender body in a football game. He couldn't get the hang of golf. But bowling! "Nim rolls 260," readers learned. Three-holed bowling balls were just right for his three-fingered hand when they were drilled deeper, and he had precise control. And he could have been born with a tennis racquet in his hand. "Nim slams 23 aces, beats Davis Cupper." He could leap high in the air and whip a racquet down to hit a serve at an angle impossible to return, and his speed and agility made him good at returns himself. His only weakness was a ball driven straight at his body.

"Slow down," Marfor ordered him. "You're not here to win trophies."

"I'm just showing Americans that we like the same games they do," he protested. She snorted, and he admitted that he was having fun. He promised to lose a rematch with the Davis Cupper.

"I have an idea," he added. "Bring teams of Heesh athletes here to compete with each other. Humans love to watch sports. They would like to see new ones. Earth could send teams to Naneg too."

"That's worth thinking about."

After several months Marfor concluded that antipathy toward the Heesh would never be eliminated but that her mission was a success. Carlos made arrangements to take her back to Naneg to report. She would leave many of the Heesh behind to continue their work.

"This may be our last trip to Naneg," Carlos told Rusty. "The president has decided to follow his original plan and appoint a woman ambassador. I will introduce her to all the Heesh wheels."

"I hope we can go often. I like the Heesh. We have to have constant personal contact between the two worlds because we haven't found a way to send messages."

"I don't want to be nothing but a messenger boy."

"How about a tour director? Tours of Naneg would be more popular than Caribbean cruises."

"Not a tour director, either," Carlos said. "I've been spoiled by the habit of responsibility."

"And you're good at it. The president could make you a special envoy, liaison between him and the ambassador."

"That's still just a messenger boy," Carlos said. "It's not for me. I'll finish my job on Naneg this trip. If we go back another time, it will be on vacation."

Before the *Ishtar* left, the presidents of several women's organizations managed to see Marfor without any males present by inviting her to a meeting of the board of the World Council of Women. Rusty accompanied her, as did Miss Ormsbee, the president's assistant, and two women from the Secret Service.

Hazel Mackintosh, the president of the council, had a scroll tied with a gold ribbon on the table in front of her. She was glad that Miss Ormsbee was present. President Parker would learn promptly what they talked about. It would be good for him.

Marfor had learned to judge the age of human women by wrinkles on their hands, lines in their faces, pouches under their eyes, and loose skin under their chins, not by the gray or white of their hair, which could be dyed. None of these women looked young, but they didn't look old, either. Their faces showed the confidence of experience in substantive affairs. She felt as if she were attending a meeting of grand matrons.

"We have been extremely interested, Your Excellency, in the fact that affairs on Naneg are managed by females," Mackintosh said. "We envy your status. You have seen differences in our society and yours. Do you think that any of these differences arise because females are in charge?"

Marfor answered cautiously. "Our societies are more alike than may appear on the surface. At a certain stage in its development, any society becomes technological to be able to do more things and do them easily. I don't think it is important that we build low buildings and you build tall ones, or that most of our transportation is public while yours is private."

"Superficial differences, I agree," Mackintosh said. "But I have heard that Naneg is much less crowded and that there are no wars. Are those things true because of domination by females?"

"You should be talking to a sociologist or a historian. We have no wars because there are no antagonistic countries or religions. All Heesh follow the teachings of the Cosmic Egg."

Rusty couldn't remain silent. "Those are taught by females, not males, aren't they?"

"True." Marfor decided to be more open. "What our females want most is the preservation of their egg lines. For that we need stability, and we oppose violence."

Mackintosh nodded. "The greatest opposition to our wars has always come from women, who think of the children who may be killed. But doesn't the preservation of your egg lines require you to have as many children as possible? That could bring overcrowding."

"No, because too many children would strain our resources to the point of widespread poverty and crime and possible starvation. Many egg lines would suffer. On that question Heesh everywhere stand united for the common good. Besides, a female controls the number of eggs she will produce. Who wants to spend all her time bearing eggs?"

"A lot of men don't think about those things," another woman said. "They think they prove their manhood by having as many children as possible and don't worry about how the children will survive. Women, and many men, are working to change that attitude."

Marfor had no comment. She had not come to change the customs and mores of Earth.

Mackintosh stared at the table. "Men always want too much."

"Ork! Females on Naneg can be just as competitive as men on Earth, but they are subtle and devious. They may lie and slander each other to gain advantage, and they form and re-form political alliances. They can be fierce, as they had to be in our days of savagery, but they do not like violence for its own sake. They prefer harmony to discord. They settle disputes, in the end, by negotiation and compromise, not violence."

"We can be subtle and devious too, but we also have to apply pressure on males, and we can't always be subtle. I hope that reports about things that are done better on Naneg will give women here more chances to show what they can do. Well! Thank you for joining us today. We have prepared a resolution of appreciation for the enlightenment you have brought to Earth."

Mackintosh handed the scroll to Marfor, who thanked her. "I know that women on Earth have slowly been approaching equality with men," she said. "That's what we both want: equality, not dominance. Men and women should be working together, not quarreling over precedence."

Supreme Matriarch Tellima walked slowly down a line of females who were taking fish from a conveyor belt, slitting them open with knives, and pulling out the innards with gloved hands. Males had extended their strike to the fish canneries, and the females hired to replace them looked sullen.

"They're slow and sloppy," the plant manager had told her. "Some of them have never worked before. And they don't like doing dirty work like cleaning fish, which is a job for males."

Tellima watched a worker toss fish guts into a trough of running water and wash out a bloody abdominal cavity. A junior matron from the Hall of Guardians who led her personal escort stayed close to her. The plant manager and the matriarch from the Hall of Sustenance accompanied them.

"How is it going?" Tellima asked a worker.

"I'll manage, but I'd like to soak a crest in this mess."

"I don't blame you. The best way to get the males back on the job is to show them we can get along without them. You're doing important work."

Tellima talked briefly to every female on the cannery line and gave a short speech before she left. Her task was to praise them for sacrificing their pride and to encourage them by telling them how valuable she considered their work. Recognition from the supreme matriarch evidently improved their morale, for they slapped their tables in applause at her speech.

"You're doing well in a difficult situation," Tellima told the matriarch from the Hall of Sustenance as they flew back to the city.

"Thank you. It will be harder if the strike spreads to crops. We can plant and harvest grains with machinery, but vegetables take stoop labor, which males do. And can you imagine females forced to stoop down and pick berries!"

"We'll get enough food. Males care for the children, and they won't let the children starve. Many males are too close to their females to let them suffer either. If we have to ration food, everyone will get a fair share."

Tellima took the commander of her escort into her office with her when she returned. The junior matron was loyal to her personally and was a reliable source of information. "I have heard rumors about Grand Matron Oomis," Tellima said. "What do you know?"

"The rumors are true," the Guardian answered. "She is organizing an intrigue to force you out of office."

"On what grounds?" Tellima asked.

"She claims that you violate doctrine by negotiating with males when you should crush them with stern measures. She quotes the Book of Precepts: 'Let females provide for their males and guide and protect them. Let males serve the females who lend them strength and wisdom.' "

Tellima knew the text. "What success is Oomis having?"

"Many of the Guardians support her because you disgraced her by censuring her publicly after she fought with the human. She has support from the Hall of Rites, of course. Some of the other halls don't like it that you won a concession from the males for your own hall, the Hall of Finance, but left their halls to struggle with the strike."

"Would they like the banks to close? Well, I understand their attitude. Thank you for informing me, and let me know what else you hear."

Can an overbearing fanatic like Oomis organize a following to oust me? Tellima wondered. Perhaps she can in these unsettled times, when many Heesh fear that the standards they value are being abandoned. Some matrons may remember their grudges, not the favors I have given them and the good I have done for Naneg. Others may envy the honor I have brought to my egg line. I will not let it be disgraced.

At a meeting of the Council of the Matriarchy that afternoon to discuss the strike, one the matriarchs muttered a curse and said, "It's those humans. Without their example, males would not be trying to rise above their station. Will the humans return?"

"Yes," Tellima said. She too wished that the humans had never arrived to make her life so difficult, but she had to deal with the situation as it was, not as she would prefer it to be. "The human example encouraged the League of Males, but the League was active before they came. I urge you all to consider what minimum concessions we could grant the males to restore our social equilibrium."

Before the *Ishtar* landed a second time on Naneg, Marfor again called Tellima, the supreme matriarch. This time she didn't have to hurdle lesser officials. "The ambassador from Earth, Carlos Lecompte, is aboard," Marfor said, "and other humans you have met, along with experts in various fields to talk to ours. The, uh, president of their Council of Churches came too, to talk about religion."

"Let them listen to his drivel at the Hall of Rites. Bring the ambassador to see me tomorrow morning. I want to see you now."

Tellima sent her personal car to take Carlos and Rusty to an embassy erected for them in their absence. With careful weighing of protocol and precedence, it had been built to match the home and office of a grand matron, with a high dome and other domes around it, but not as imposing as one for a member of the Matriarchy. Quarters for all the humans adjoined it. Marfor and Nim took a robot cab to the Grand Hall of the Matriarchy, while Lippor and Dorkin took one to the Hall of Transportation.

"Something's holding us up," Nim observed as the cab slowed to a halt in a line behind others. He got out to look ahead. "Something's happening in the Plaza of the Cosmic Egg."

Several thousand Heesh, males and females together, marched around the Grand Hall of the Egg, in which the golden statue of the Prime Mother stood. Many of them carried chimes, cymbals, and gongs, which they struck loudly, discordantly, and continuously. They chanted words hard to distinguish above the cacophony of their instruments. Moving closer, near where the marchers blocked rails for the cabs, Marfor heard them yell, "No Ishinol! Melt the gold! No Ishinol! Melt the gold!" An unbroken chain of Guardians kept the marchers away from the hall itself. Marfor saw Oomis commanding them.

Skirting the edge of the demonstration, content to wait until later to learn more about it, Marfor and Nim walked down the street that led to the Hall of the Matriarchy. Nim talked to a group of males, who deferred to him as a celebrity, while Marfor went to the supreme matriarch's office.

"Welcome home, Marfor," Tellima said. "How are you being received on Earth?"

"Quite well, Your Supremacy. It's an unpleasant world but fascinating. Their males are somewhat dominant, but they accept a female ambassador with little quibbling. The United States has female ambassadors of its own. The president has sent a female ambassador to the Heesh. General Lecompte will present her to you when you wish."

"I will make arrangements with Lecompte when I see him tomorrow. Now tell me more about Earth."

"In general, the Heesh are welcome. There is a group that hates us, but except for tossing a bomb at Lippor, which missed, they have not caused serious trouble. What's been happening here? I passed a demonstration at the Grand Hall of the Egg."

Tellima laughed. "Blame yourself. You brought the Prime Mother and her mate here. As soon as we put them on display, everybody had to see them. They have obnoxious habits. They fight over food, and they throw scraps at people watching. They deposit their waste wherever they happen to be. They pick up some of that and throw it at spectators. They mate in public. They are not the sort of creatures that the Heesh want to honor as ancestors. The Prime Mother is absolutely vicious when she claws her mate. So there is now a very loud demand that the Prime Mother be demoted in status to just another unavoidable primitive ancestor, and her golden statue be removed."

"What do they say at the Hall of Rites?"

"They will study the texts for a new interpretation. They are good at that. After all, the idea of a Prime Mother is only a couple of hundred years old."

"I saw Oomis at the demonstration," Marfor said.

"Oomis will be wherever she thinks she can find action. She wants to hold back the forces of change, which she believes are evil, single-handed. I gave her a job that should keep her out of the way, but she delegates her duties to others and charges around with her personal band of loyal bigots to root out heresy wherever she can find it. Sometimes I think grand matrons have too much freedom to exercise initiative. Oomis would rather destroy us all than abandon one shred of her beliefs."

Dorkin had left Lippor at the Hall of Transportation and slipped into the secret council chamber of the League of Males to ask what progress had been made on male rights.

"The Matriarchy has accepted the principle that males should have equal opportunity," a male on duty told him. "Not equal status but equal opportunity. It sounds good, but I don't think it means much. Tellima has agreed to add males to her commission considering male demands but she wants to appoint tame attendant males, like hers, and leave the League of Males out of it."

With his talent for languages, Carlos spoke Heesh fluently by now, although he would never master the pronunciation of coughlike gutturals. When he visited Tellima with Marfor the next morning, he described the experts he had brought with him to exchange knowledge. "They include agricultural specialists. I would like to plant a garden and build pens for cattle and sheep so that I can have familiar foods."

"You may do so if you wait until we have built protected enclosures," Tellima said. "We do not want strange organisms, including seeds, to escape into our environment and change it in ways we cannot predict."

"Very understandable," Carlos said. He tried to imagine tomatoes and onions conquering a world. They would be weeds here, and weeds were notoriously troublesome. "We will, of course, abide by your restrictions." Humans in the most important posting in history shouldn't object to losing weight because they didn't like the food. Think of it as survival rations.

"What are you doing with our space-jump technology?"

"Getting ready to use it. We know that the Heesh found no life around the nearest stars, but one more jump might have been successful. We might have better luck with a different star. There may be a thousand planets with advanced races in the galaxy, and millions in other galaxies."

"And how many on different time lines?" Tellima asked. "I believe that our two worlds should conduct a systematic search, allocating sectors for exploration."

"We have not observed any different time lines, but you are right, they may exist."

Back at the new American Embassy, Carlos reported the conversation to his original *Pegasus* team. "We may be on our way to an interstellar civilization."

"We'll need a translation computer the size of the sun," Rusty said.

"And we'll have to keep our powder dry," Carlos added. He explained the old-fashioned term for those who knew nothing about flintlock muskets. "Some races may be hostile."

"Tellima is starting the right way with us, the cautious way," Dan said. "She won't let strange forms of life come from one planet to another and louse up local ecology. That will be Rule One for an interstellar civilization."

"Rule One will be peace, enforced by everyone else against an aggressor," Rusty said.

Remembering the way nations on Earth had often formed alliances for war, Carlos felt that she was optimistic, but he didn't say so.

Oomis watched a junior matron deploy a detachment of Guardians along both sides of a path from the main entrance of the Grand Hall of the Egg. They carried whips but they wouldn't need them. The crowd of Heesh in the plaza outside the hall chattered noisily in high good humor. Pootas darted on swift brief flights from the shoulders of their owners like sparks of happiness.

They celebrate their degradation, Oomis thought. One step after another, all that I live for is being lost. My father and my brother resented the precedence granted to me for being a female. They teased me and insulted me and denied they had done it when I told my mother. My comfort came from the doctrines of the Egg, which taught me that I was superior to all males. In the Hall of Guardians I have enforced observance of those doctrines. Now hideous alien males are among us, Heesh males are rebellious, and the Guardians can do nothing about them.

A band of musicians emerged from the hall and rang ceremonial chimes harmoniously. They were all females, Oomis saw; males had not yet been given this role of honor. A grand matron from the Hall of Rites appeared at the head of an escort around a platform carried by males that held the gold statue of the Prime Mother. Yes, males had come back to work, but only to help perpetrate an abomination.

The grand matron led her procession to the center of the plaza, where Grand Matron Marfor waited to receive the statue on behalf of the Hall of Ancients. Lippor, that timid dimwit, that treacherous apostate, was the one primarily to blame for this ceremony. She had proposed that the statue of the Prime Mother be placed in the foyer of the Hall of Ancients, where visitors could see it before they looked at all the fossils. It was none of Lippor's business! She was supposed to be an expert on space and time ships. Look at what was happening when she meddled in affairs that were not her concern.

The Hall of Rites, that nest of weaklings, had hastily agreed that the symbolic importance of the Prime Mother would not be diminished by the move. They had grown soft from many years of propounding doctrine without dissent. Tellima had approved their decision. She was a weakling too. It was clear to Oomis that the Prime Mother was being relegated to a position of being nothing more than a display to introduce visitors to the far distant past.

Lippor was present too, near Marfor. Their attendant males, Dorkin and Nim, were with them. Oomis's bleak depression turned to anger. Males had no place in a ceremony, not even a base, inexcusable ceremony like this one. Humans were at one side, watching. Vermin! If they had not come here, the doctrines of the Egg would never have been challenged.

Oomis could not hear the quiet comment of Carlos to Rusty. "This is close to revolutionary. It's as if the Catholic Church announced that St. Peter was not a saint after all, but merely the first pope."

"That's still not bad," Rusty said.

"Put it this way: the Prime Mother has lost her halo."

Oomis wanted to cover the small openings to her ears as the grand matron from the Hall of Rites and Marfor exchanged short speeches, but she stood at attention. Marfor formally received the statue. Chimes rang. A group of males came forward to lift the platform, and Marfor led her delegation past the crowd, now cheering, and down the street to the Hall of Ancients.

I was right from the beginning, Oomis thought. We should have destroyed the humans when we met them. Now the Hall of Rites is changing its doctrines to suit the rabble, and males have a precedent for their demands. All because of radical ideas brought from a loathsome planet.

It will become worse. We have exchanged embassies and will grow tolerant of ways ruinous to the Heesh. If only our contacts with these abominable creatures could be wiped out! Make them avoid us, refuse all further dealings with us. I must do something that no apologies, no reparations, will persuade them to forgive.

A male working undercover for the Hall of Guardians learned about the hidden entrance to the council chamber of the League of Males under the Hall of Rites. Guardians found several males in the chamber and arrested them.

That won't do much good, Tellima thought. The Guardians didn't find any records. The males kept the names of their principal supporters in their heads. The council of the League will meet someplace else and put on more pressure.

She was right. Almost immediately the League of Males extended its strike from fisheries to the entire food industry, farms, orchards, the ranches for domesticated Hanishan, and the packinghouses, even the mushroom growers. Tellima had expected this. She had had the warehouses filled, as if for a siege, and she had prepared a food-rationing plan, which she put into effect. Nobody liked it, and everybody blamed the males. Many females who had supported the males turned against them.

The males could not be discouraged so easily. The strike continued.

One night a large grain elevator exploded with tremendous force, leveling several buildings nearby and setting fire to others. No remains of Heesh were found in the ashes of the elevator, but two females and two males were killed in the other buildings.

An unsigned message came to the Hall of Communications. "The Matriarchy has been warned. Release all males from prison."

"The League of Males has shown us what it really is, a league of dangerous criminals," the matriarch from the Hall of Guardians said next day. "They have become desperate and will stop at nothing. We have endured their strike but we will not endure arson and murder. The guilty ones will be found and punished. I urge all other males to show that they reject the tactics of terror and return to work."

Dorkin, who had become recognized as spokesman for the League of Males, answered her immediately. "The League of Males had nothing to do with the explosion of the grain elevator. We denounce it. We regret the loss of lives. Our policy is firmness and patience. We oppose sabotage or any violence. We believe that whoever caused the explosion did so to incite the Heesh against us."

Many of the Heesh did not believe him. That night more females than usual found pretexts to beat up their attendant males at home.

Marfor brought Nim to see Tellima. "As you know, I rely heavily upon the views of Nim," Marfor said. "He has an idea about the explosion that I think you should hear."

Nim does not look as diffident as a male having an audience with the supreme matriarch should be, Tellima thought. Travel to the past and two trips to Earth have given him confidence. "What is it, Nim?"

"I trust Dorkin, so I wondered who might have caused the explosion. Males had nothing to gain from it. All of the Heesh who worked at the elevator have been accounted for, including two who died nearby, so it had to be someone else. Oomis could have been responsible. She could have sent one of her personal followers to start a fire. The follower might not have known that the dust in the air in a grain elevator will explode at a spark, or she may have known but was willing to be a martyr to her cause. The fire consumed whoever did this so that you can't tell whether it was a male or female. Oomis would martyr herself, I think, and would not hesitate to sacrifice a follower."

"That is a harsh accusation, but I will consider it," said Tellima, who had already thought of the same possibility. "Since nothing is left of the arsonist, I see no way to trace the fire to Oomis or anyone else. Do you?"

"No, Your Supremacy," Nim admitted. "I hope only that you will not be too ready to blame the males."

I won't, Tellima thought, but I will take advantage of the reaction against them. Two more pieces have to be put into place.

She summoned Lippor and Dorkin. Lippor looked apprehensive, as if she was surprised at hearing from Tellima herself, and Dorkin wary.

"I have watched your career more closely than you realize, Lippor," Tellima said. "You have been moving rapidly to adapt one of our ships to cross between time tracks. I know, of course, that moving the golden statue of the Prime Mother was your idea, and it was a good one. It solved a problem. I also know that you have sometimes argued eloquently for the cause of males on my commission considering their status. Ork! Travel does indeed appear to be broadening. Dorkin, I am far from agreeing with much of what you say, but I will not deny that you are persuasive. I believe your statement that the League of Males did not cause the grain elevator to explode. Your tactics are very different."

She watched them glance at each other before she said, "I have a job for you, Dorkin. The time has come to resolve our crisis with a meeting of all parties concerned. I want you to be present along with the chairman of the League of Males."

"I will do as you say, of course," Dorkin answered. "What are you going to offer the chairman?"

"He will have to come to my meeting to find out. I will give him, like you, safe conduct."

I grow very tired these days but things are going better than they seem, Tellima thought. Now I must explore with each matriarch, individually, my ideas for a settlement.

* * *

Carlos and Rusty were surprised to be asked to be present when Heesh males met with the Council of the Matriarchy to discuss settlement of the strike. "Tellima wants you there to answer any questions about the relations between males and females on your planet," Marfor told them. "Those of us who have visited Earth will be there for the same reason."

Tellima wouldn't have us anywhere near the meeting unless she wanted to help the males, Carlos thought.

He and Rusty sat at one of two tables directly in front of a long, curving table for the matriarchs. Dorkin and the chairman of the League of Males, whose name was Harbar, sat at the other. Marfor, Nim, and Lippor sat at a table farther back, as if their testimony was unlikely to be needed.

Gold and silver medallions gleamed on the matriarchs' Necklaces of Twelves. Because of their egg lines they think of themselves as nobility, Carlos thought, like duchesses of ancient lineage, and they do not like to negotiate with scullery maids, which is the way they must think of males. No more formidable group could be assembled anywhere, and they look it, with their heavy jaws and large, hypnotic eyes. Tellima must have a job keeping them in line.

Dorkin and Harbar did not appear to be intimidated.

"We are here to settle issues that have caused grave divisions among the Heesh," Tellima began. "We must succeed. Females and males alike are weary of dissension, very weary of disruptions to our normal life. The matriarchy faces a dilemma. It is not possible to make abrupt and radical changes in our society without wrecking it. Yet we must show the males that we value them and their views. If we consider all demands negotiable, we can find a settlement. For example, males have asked that legal status be given to the position of companion male as well as that of attendant male. I believe that the Matriarchy would approve in return for an end to the strike."

"That is not nearly enough," Dorkin answered. "It merely recognizes a situation that in many cases already exists. Males want full equality."

"I cannot agree to anything contrary to the Book of Precepts," said the matriarch from the Hall of Rites. She had been battered by criticism for approving the move of the Prime Mother out of the Grand Hall of the Egg.

"Equality is the path to harmony," Harbar said.

"We had harmony here before the strike," a matriarch growled.

"Less than you thought," Dorkin answered in a tone as surly as hers.

Tellima ignored the exchange and said to Carlos, "Please review for us the extent to which males and females are equal in your nation."

She knows my answer, Carlos thought. "In principle, and legally, males and females are fully equal. In practice, because old habits die slowly, there are more high-ranking males than females. My wife and I treat each other as equals. Otherwise she would not stay with me. You might answer that I am the one who holds high rank, but we both consider her my equal. I brought a female to replace me as ambassador."

"Do you advise us to move toward equality?"

"It is not my place to advise you on domestic issues that do not affect Earth." Carlos lifted a hand in a gesture to assure attention. "I will raise a point that affects Heesh and humans together. We have a common destiny. Travel to distant planets around the sun already takes place, and all space remains to be explored. The exploration of the continents of Earth brought bloody conflicts between rival nations. It would be much better if we could explore space together. Who know what other races live among the stars, or whether they will be friendly? The fewer the disputes between our two planets, the more effectively we can deal with others."

The matriarch from the Hall of Science and Technology slapped the table in applause.

"No demonstrations," Tellima warned her. She stared at Carlos. "So we should compromise with males to explore space? Ork! That is an original idea. Well, Dorkin, are there any demands that you think it would not be hard for us to meet?"

"One would be easy," Dorkin answered. "Register the male line as well as the female line in the Hall of Records."

"What do you think?" Tellima asked the matriarch from the hall.

"I will agree to that."

She agreed before the meeting, Carlos thought. It will give her an excuse to build a larger bureaucracy. Tellima came to this meeting well prepared.

Harbar spoke again. "That will be an improvement but it doesn't give good jobs and high rank to males. What can you do about that?"

"I will establish a permanent Council of Males to advise the Matriarchy." Creating new jobs would deprive no one of an old job. "The members will be males, and the chairman will have the rank of grand patron, the equal of grand matron. Because of the leadership you have shown, Harbar, I would like to appoint you grand patron."

"You are generous to a male who has been called a criminal rebel," Harbar said, "but I feel that Dorkin should have the honor of heading the advisory council. He is much better known than I am, and, as you have seen, he is fully competent."

"I am glad to hear that your opinion of Dorkin is as high as mine." Tellima marveled at the way events were turning out as she wished. "Dorkin, will you accept?"

"Permit me to ask: what are your plans for Lippor?"

"She will be grand matron in charge of the exploration of space and time. Her first task will be to modify a ship for Marfor to travel between time tracks. As a grand patron, you will have equal rank."

Dorkin and Lippor exchanged pleased whispers before he said, "I accept gladly, Your Supremacy."

"Good. In view of our progress toward male goals today, perhaps the League of Males will call off its strike."

Dorkin glanced at Harbar, who said, "The males in prison must be released."

"Done." Tellima turned to the matriarch from the Hall of Guardians, who was frowning, and said, "Give the orders."

"One more thing," Dorkin said. "The Advisory Council of Males must be more than a token group. We will call off the strike while we wait for the council's advice to lead to further improvements in male status and job conditions."

"Understood, but do not expect changes to come so rapidly that they would be disruptive."

Tellima will have Dorkin near her, where she can keep an eye on him, Carlos thought. If you can't lick someone, reward him for joining you. Tellima is a born pickpocket.

The Matriarchy accepted Tellima's plans.

Oomis was not invited to the reception that Carlos gave to introduce the new ambassador, President Zena McClusky of Harvard, to the matriarchs before he returned to Earth. Seeing an opportunity to catch traitors and those who had incited them together, she came anyway. "I am here to check on security arrangements," she told a Guardian outside the embassy door.

"Certainly, grand matron, but you will have to leave your laser with me. That is a standing order. Even the Guardians who accompany Tellima will not have lasers. It would be an insult to the ambassador."

As if one could insult such creatures! Oomis left her laser at the door and entered, fuming. She had her whip and a knife, and she would have to do as much with those as possible. They should be enough; she had been well trained in their use. Some embassy functionary, a male, met her inside the door and conducted her to the reception room. Oomis walked slowly around the room, pretending to look behind curtains and chairs and under tables, until her escort left. A table was loaded with Heesh delicacies like pickled livka eggs. She did not sample them.

Carlos and Rusty entered to be ready to greet guests. They stopped in a doorway when they saw Oomis. "Get the others," Carlos whispered, and Rusty turned back. "I had not expected you to help welcome my successor, grand matron," he said.

"Someone must see to security," she answered. Should she take them one at a time before they all assembled? Very well, this one was the worst, the leader of the humans. He needed a whipping before he died. She took her whip from her belt.

Alert to the threat, Carlos attempted a diversion, exclaiming immediately, "Dan! You're just in time!"

Oomis turned quickly to look behind her. She did not see Dan or any other of these human abominations. Turning back, she swung the whip toward Carlos's eyes, but he had leaped close to her, and all she could do was hit him a glancing blow with the handle. He staggered but recovered his balance quickly and struck her chin with a left jab. As her head snapped backward, he followed with a right cross and knocked her to the floor.

But Oomis, as Dan and Meg had reported, was not easily beaten. Lying on her back, she was able to swing the whip flat to the floor, coil it around his legs, and jerk him off his feet. She rose quickly.

As she raised her whip again she saw Dan run toward her. The whip met him straight on, cutting through the cloth over his chest and opening a gash. He kept coming, and she dropped to the floor to kick him on the legs, sending him sprawling. Bouncing to her feet, she caught movement out of the corner of her eye and saw that Nick had appeared and was charging at her. She sidestepped and slapped him off-balance and down. Carlos was back on his feet, and she whipped one of his arms, staggering him with pain.

Let them all come, Oomis thought in the berserk frenzy of revenge. And they were coming, the human females now, led by one she didn't recognize, presumably the new ambassador. The traitor Heesh too, Marfor and Nim and Lippor and Dorkin, through the entry arch. She slashed at Nick as he rose, and decided to meet Carlos's charge, this time, with her knife.

An arm was around her neck, choking her. She found it, and gashed it with her knife. As the arm was jerked away, she saw Dorkin behind her, retreating in pain from the wound. Then two arms, Nim's arms, were around her, holding both of hers tightly against her body. Before she could use her greater strength to wrench free, Carlos struck her in the belly with a hard right hook. She collapsed to the floor, all air driven from her lungs, unable to gasp for more. Desperately, she looked up, and she saw Supreme Matriarch Tellima entering with two Guardians.

The Guardians ran to Oomis, lifted her to her feet, and held her upright. Tellima saw four females, Heesh and human, tending to wounds on males. "What happened?" she asked.

Carlos pointed at Oomis. "She attacked me, and the others when they came to my aid."

Tellima saw Oomis shake off the Guardians who held her, walk slowly to a wall, and sit on the floor against it. Lippor was tightening her Necklace of Twelves as a tourniquet around the arm of Dorkin, who sat on the floor, bleeding.

"How badly are you wounded?" Tellima asked him.

"Badly, I think. I need a bandage."

"You have been seriously injured. You need treatment and a rest. Lippor, escort him to the embassy's infirmary." Lippor helped Dorkin rise and supported him as they walked away.

Marfor and the new ambassador confirmed Carlos's report of what had happened. "What do you say to this, Oomis?" Tellima asked. Oomis stared at the floor and said nothing. "Oomis, you are under arrest. Stand up and go with the Guardians." Oomis remained silent, huddled against the wall.

"I apologize for what happened here, Your Excellency," Tellima said to Carlos. She stared appraisingly at Oomis. "Oomis was too self-righteous to accept change. I think she lost the last shreds of sanity when she came here. She blamed you humans for inciting our males, and she may have thought that she could change the world back to what it was by punishing you." She passed a hand back and forth in front of Oomis's face without getting a reaction. "Having failed in her attack, it appears to me, she has retreated into an endless circle of delusions, a world of her own that no one else can enter. Guardians, take her to a hospital."

"She's catatonic," Rusty said. The computer serving the translation robot buzzed because it did not know that word.

As the two Guardians carried Oomis out, like two ants carrying a termite, Tellima said to Carlos, "I hope this incident will not damage our relations."

"Certainly not. Oomis was crazy, and two Heesh came to my aid. Dorkin kept her from stabbing me and Nim subdued her."

Tellima looked around at the others. "Several of you are bleeding and need attention. You had better go to the infirmary too. It appears that you will have to postpone your reception, General Lecompte."

"I would rather not. The guests will arrive soon. Let them assemble. Meg can bandage my arm where the whip cut it, and I can hide the bandage under a shirt, then return to escort you and our new ambassador to meet the matriarchs. If they ask what delayed us, we can answer truthfully that we were attacked by an unbalanced Heesh, but no great harm was done, and the matter is closed."

He does everything right, Rusty thought.

A ship shaped like a thick saucer appeared beside his when Carlos brought the *Ishtar* back to Earth. At last Marfor had a ship of her own, modified so that she could travel between time tracks without hitching a ride. She couldn't resist showing off horizontal flight at low altitudes, and she circled the space center proudly twice before setting down.

Carlos reported recent events on Naneg to the president. "There will be more problems, but we've made a good start," he concluded.

"Your face will go on a postage stamp," the president said. "Too bad they wait for someone to die for that, and you won't see it. I'll think up a new medal for you. Meanwhile I have a surprise."

He pressed a buzzer, and a door to his office opened. Two spiderlike robots of the Heesh type entered the room. They stood silently awaiting orders.

"One is the Heesh robot and the other is a duplicate our engineers whipped up from their specs," the president said. "I'll bet you can't tell them apart."

"Not at first glance," Carlos agreed.

The president pointed and said, "That one is H-1, the Heesh robot. The other one is H-2. Or maybe it's the other way around. Building H-2 taught us some new tricks in computer circuitry. We are already putting those into use in factories and on construction jobs. Take both of them with you to show Marfor. They have ID plates on their backs to tell them apart, and they answer when their names are called. Robots dedicated to one task are valuable, but you can't beat versatility."

Carlos displayed the robots when he talked to Rusty, Marfor, and Nim later. "I think one of them is supposed to be my personal robot," he told Marfor. "I can use it for a guard the way you use one already. Install a metal detector in it. I don't like the idea. I don't want to look paranoid."

"I don't like the idea either," she said, "but I need one. Earth has crazies like Oomis, fanatics on religion, race superiority, and sex roles."

"And the only right way to part your hair—or brush your down—in the morning," Carlos said.

"Spider robots will become status symbols," Rusty predicted. "Everybody who is anybody will have one trailing him around."

"Status symbols aren't my style," Carlos objected. "Let what I do speak for itself. We have a lot to do. The Heesh can teach us space jockeys how to maintain level atmospheric flight in a space ship. Then I want to take a ship to the stars."

"Suppose there is more than one time track," Rusty said. "Don't we have to go looking for others?"

"I suppose so, but I don't know how to search except by trial and error. We saw nothing like a universe of stars or anything outside the solar system when we traveled between tracks, only our destination. It's as if the curve between two moving points on a plane of time lies outside that plane in a different dimension. It wasn't until we finished the trip and reached Naneg that the stars we know sprang into view. That makes me more certain that a time track applies to the entire solar system of a planet on a given track but not beyond it. Somebody in the future might go back and start a new time track, but I don't think that has happened, or we would have seen more than one alternate world when we went looking for Naneg."

Nim spoke up. "Suppose some fanatic Heesh or human gains power and decides to eliminate the other race. Go back to our nexus, wait for a ship to appear, and shoot it down."

"The theory of that is beyond me." Carlos shook his head. "Can a loop in time be disrupted? We don't travel back and forth in time on a narrow line, or a ship going one way would crash into itself coming back. There's a lot about time we don't know yet. Or space-time, for space and time are always linked. How many dimensions can we work with?"

Rusty shook her head. "Cosmologists will have fun with that one."

"I think we should be more concerned about what we will find exploring the stars. Who knows? It might even be dinosaurs. We'll be lucky if it isn't something more deadly."

THE MAGICAL *XANTH* SERIES!

PIERS ANTHONY

QUESTION QUEST
75948-9/ $4.99 US/ $5.99 Can

ISLE OF VIEW
75947-0/ $4.99 US/ $5.99 Can

VALE OF THE VOLE
75287-5/ $4.95 US/ $5.95 Can

HEAVEN CENT
75288-3/ $4.99 US/ $5.99 Can

MAN FROM MUNDANIA
75289-1/ $4.95 US/ $5.95 Can

THE COLOR OF HER PANTIES
75949-7/ $4.99 US/ $5.99 Can

AVONOVA PRESENTS
AWARD-WINNING NOVELS
FROM MASTERS OF SCIENCE FICTION

WULFSYARN
by Phillip Mann   71717-4/ $4.99 US

MIRROR TO THE SKY
by Mark S. Geston   71703-4/ $4.99 US/ $5.99 Can

THE DESTINY MAKERS
by George Turner   71887-1/ $4.99 US/ $5.99 Can

A DEEPER SEA
by Alexander Jablokov   71709-3/ $4.99 US/ $5.99 Can

BEGGARS IN SPAIN
by Nancy Kress   71877-4/ $4.99 US/ $5.99 Can

FLYING TO VALHALLA
by Charles Pellegrino   71881-2/ $4.99 US/ $5.99 Can